IN WANT
OF A
SUSPECT

A LIZZIE & DARCY MYSTERY

ALSO BY TIRZAH PRICE

IN WANT OF A SUSPECT

OF A

SUSPECT

A LIZZIE & DARCY MYSTERY

TIRZAH PRICE

HARPER

An Imprint of HarperCollinsPublishers

Library of Congress Control Number: 2023948878
ISBN 978-0-06-327802-8

Typography by Corina Lupp
24 25 26 27 28 LBC 5 4 3 2 1

First Edition

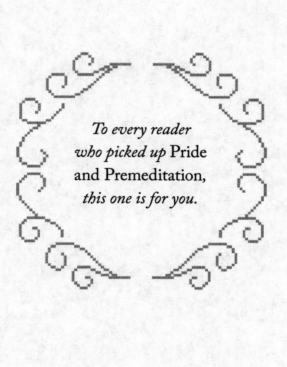

*To every reader
who picked up* Pride
and Premeditation, *
this one is for you.*

"Business, you know, may bring money,
but friendship hardly ever does."
—*Emma* by Jane Austen

"Every murderer is probably
somebody's old friend."
—*The Mysterious Affair at Styles*
by Agatha Christie

ONE

In Which Miss Elizabeth Bennet and Mr. Fitzwilliam Darcy Get Caught Out in the Rain

"IT'S TIME YOU ACKNOWLEDGE the truth."

The words reached Miss Elizabeth Bennet's ears as she was striding with determination down an unfamiliar London street, causing her to falter—but only for a moment. She squared her shoulders and kept pushing forward. "I don't know what you're talking about," she called over her shoulder, but refused to turn around.

"Lizzie."

She stopped, causing the few pedestrians around to skirt her. The neighborhood was working-class, and consisted of packed flats, shops, and storehouses. The damp spring air was crisp and carried the scent of the docks, not far off. It was, in short, not the type of neighborhood a respectable young lady might linger in. Lizzie turned and looked at her companion, Mr. Fitzwilliam Darcy, who lagged behind with mud-coated boots and his usual serious expression.

"Lizzie." He repeated her name with a small amount of exasperation. "It's all right to admit that you're lost."

"I know that," she said, making sure to keep a bright smile on her face. "But I'm not, so why would I?"

Darcy sighed. "What street are we on?"

"What does it matter?" she asked. "We're headed in the right direction."

"Yes, but do you know how to get home?"

She shot him a reproving look. "Of course I know how to get home, Darcy. Do you?"

"No," he admitted. "That's rather the point."

"Well, then, you better stick close to me."

Darcy grumbled under his breath but took her arm and allowed himself to be led on. Lizzie bit back a smile. One of the reasons she liked Darcy well enough to keep him around was that unlike most young gentlemen she was acquainted with, Darcy did not engage in the tiresome business of always acting like he was the only one who could possibly be right about something.

"We should have taken my carriage," he added.

That did not mean, however, that he held back when asserting his opinion.

"On these narrow streets?" Lizzie asked, indicating the one they were currently traversing. It was crowded with pushcarts and buckets, children playing and women lingering on stoops. "It wouldn't fit! Besides, it's a wonderful day for a good stroll."

Darcy snorted, a most ungentlemanly sound, and glanced pointedly up at the deep gray sky. Not that this was anything new—the skies were gray half the year. But—and Lizzie wasn't about to admit this to Darcy—the skies to the east had gotten particularly dark, and there was a charged sense to the air that told her on this one point, Darcy was correct.

"You would go walking in a downpour," he muttered, but there was a fondness in his voice, too.

"So would you, if you'd spent the last week indoors, bent over briefs! I swear, it was as though all the courts did this week was produce the most inscrutable paperwork imaginable for my own personal punishment."

"They're testing you," Darcy said. "They don't like the fact that your father recognizes you as a solicitor, and therefore expects the courts to do so as well."

"I know," Lizzie said, but she was unable to keep from sounding peeved. "And they can keep trying to trip me up, but I am one step ahead of them."

Despite her bravado, Lizzie didn't always feel quite so confident. She hadn't admitted to Darcy that she'd needed her father's help on two of the cases, and she'd misfiled one of her responses to a patent case that had nearly cost her client everything he owned. Only her father—and his influence—had kept the case from completely unraveling.

Even though she didn't tell Darcy these things, he seemed to understand her inner turmoil, for he squeezed her arm gently and said, "Naturally. I have no doubt that you shall show them your mettle. I do, however, have doubts as to your sense of direction."

They had come upon an intersection, and despite her confidence up until this moment in navigating their way, Lizzie had hesitated ever so slightly. Darcy, being attuned to her movement, had certainly noticed. "I'm not lost," she repeated as she looked left, then right.

"Lizzie," he said with a sigh. "If we need——"

"This way!"

She made the impulsive decision to turn left, dragging him along with her.

"Do not think I am unsupportive of your more unusual business practices," Darcy said, allowing himself to be led. "But I have to wonder, if this Mr. Mullins truly wanted to engage your services, wouldn't he come to Longbourn rather than have you wandering through unfamiliar dockside neighborhoods?"

"First of all, it's not unfamiliar—I told you, I've been there before! Second, I am hardly alone when I have you."

At that, Darcy finally cracked a small smile, and Lizzie felt a thrill of triumph rush through her. Getting Darcy to smile was akin to writing a perfectly elegant, unimpeachable sentence in a brief, one no sour solicitor at a competitor's firm could find fault with. But as he was Darcy, he was not content to let her win this argument. "My point still stands—I don't see how a permitting disagreement in the Western Exchange requires a visit to the gentleman's storehouse."

"Gentlemen," she corrected. "Mr. Mullins—Jack—and his brother, Simon, co-own the business. And besides, we have a history—the Mullins brothers were my first case."

"The one where the man died and his business partner tried to take the assets?" Darcy's forehead creased as he drew up the memory, and Lizzie smiled. Despite his grumbling, Darcy always listened, and, what's more, he remembered what she told him.

"Yes, and his sons came to Papa to get the business back," she continued. "The brothers sued the man. There was some nonsense involving paperwork and missing files, but, well, we got that all cleared up in no time!"

She smiled brightly at Darcy, but he was shaking his head. "Missing files, hmm?"

"They were recovered!"

"You are good at recovering missing or lost things," he noted. "Do you think you can recover your sense of direction?"

He indicated up ahead, where the street dead-ended into a brick wall. Lizzie stopped sharply. "Oh. That's new."

"Is it?" Darcy asked, dubious.

"Come on, we'll go around." She pulled Darcy down a nearby alley, sidestepping dank puddles. "And don't look at me that way—you were happy for an excuse to leave the office and get out, too! Besides, it's just a little alley, and I'm sure once we come out up here . . ."

Lizzie trailed off, because unfortunately for her and for Darcy's opinion of her navigational skills, when they emerged onto the street, Lizzie was completely lost. This street was full of storehouses and work yards, with laborers—mostly men— focused on their tasks or coming and going. Lizzie and Darcy stuck out like a sore thumb in their finely made clothes, and

Lizzie's dainty boots didn't stand a chance against the muddy trenches of the street. A nearby blacksmith looked up from his outdoor fire and stared at the pair of them with obvious disgust.

"Right," said Darcy, and asked more gently, "do you know where we are?"

"No," she finally admitted. It had been three years since she'd last seen Jack Mullins and visited the storehouse he and his brother had inherited from their father. London's streets had changed in that time as new buildings and businesses had sprung up, and the skies were just cloudy enough that she was no longer certain which direction she was facing.

"There's nothing more to it then," Darcy said gravely. "We must ask for directions."

"I have a feeling that if we were to approach anyone on this street, they'd tell us to walk directly into the Thames," Lizzie muttered. As much as she despised the notion that she needed a male chaperone to conduct business, she was glad she'd wheedled Darcy away from his desk now. It wasn't just in the courtroom where the presence of an unaccompanied lady drew ire and the wrong sort of interest.

"Look ahead," Darcy urged.

At the end of the block, two spots of red stood out. Officers, some of the many that had flooded the streets of London lately—even more so than usual. It seemed that Britain was always engaged in one war or another, usually with the French, for as long as Lizzie had been alive. But the latest news from the Continent of Napoleon's advance had everyone on edge, and Lizzie's youngest sister, Lydia, in a constant state of hope that she would find love with a handsome war hero.

Lizzie allowed Darcy to take the lead as they navigated through the muddy streets in the direction of the officers, who would surely be honorable enough to steer them in the right direction. One was tall and stout and stood like a man who knew he was in charge. His companion was slight and Lizzie's height, and seemed to keep one half step behind the taller officer as they strolled down the muddy streets, their backs to them.

Lizzie and Darcy picked up the pace to catch up to them and were still a good distance away when the pair halted and seemed to have an exchange with someone ahead of them. Lizzie couldn't see who they were talking to, but she saw the taller officer raise his hand and bring it down to strike something. A woman cried out in fear, and the sound jolted down Lizzie's spine, spurring her on.

"Lizzie! Wait!" Darcy called.

But Lizzie charged forward, and caught up with the officers just in time to see the taller one shove a small pushcart laden with various worn-out odds and ends. Its wheels had become mired in the muck of the streets, and a rail-thin woman strained to push it out of the officers' way. She wore a shabby brown dress with a faded blue kerchief holding back her hair, and her frantic gaze skittered between the officers and her sad-looking wares as she struggled. The shorter officer cleared his throat to say something as the taller brute growled in frustration, but Lizzie interrupted.

"Excuse me!"

The taller officer stopped his rough manhandling of the cart and looked behind him at Lizzie and Darcy.

Lizzie caught a flash of annoyance on his face as he took them in. It was tempered only slightly when he registered the state of their dress and realized he was speaking with a gentleman and lady. "You're an awfully long way from home, aren't you?" he asked.

Lizzie felt her training kick in, even if she would have liked to roll her eyes. She had found that a kind and sympathetic attitude went much further than impatience or authority, no matter how ridiculous the other party was acting. "We are indeed, but we've business to tend to, and it seems like we might have taken a wrong turn. How fortunate we were to run into you *gentlemen*." She made sure to emphasize the word, as if it might remind them to find their manners. "We were hoping you might give us directions, after you are finished assisting this *lady*."

Lizzie's not-so-subtle hints went unregistered. The poor woman looked between them all, uncomprehending. The tall officer raised his eyebrows. "What business?" he asked Darcy.

Lizzie sensed rather than saw Darcy assume the haughty, bored posture of the privileged and powerful son of one of London's most powerful barristers. "I'm afraid that's confidential. But please, don't let us interrupt your civic duty to assist this lady with her cart."

"Lady," the officer echoed disdainfully. "Dirty French, more like. They're worse than the rats."

"She is not a rat!" Lizzie shot back. "She is a human being deserving of respect."

The officer laughed as if he found Lizzie's words humorous. "You wouldn't be saying the same if they were sleeping on your doorstep."

Darcy stepped forward and Lizzie recognized the coiled energy in his stance. "Even so, I think we can agree, as gentlemen, that the ladies need not be exposed to this sort of conduct."

For a suspended moment, it was unclear how the tall officer would react. His expression was slack with shock, and Lizzie felt her stomach tighten unpleasantly. But then, so quickly that she almost missed it, the slight officer yanked the cart out of the mud, sending the woman's wares clattering.

The noise broke the moment, and the poor woman jumped forward, pushing her cart. "Merci," she murmured. "Merci."

She hurried away quickly, and Lizzie felt both a pang of regret that she couldn't offer more help to the woman and relief that she was away from the tall brute. The officer who'd freed her cart from the mud stepped aside and turned his face away from Lizzie, so she assumed he was likely as uncomfortable about the exchange as she. And yet, would he have intervened if not for Lizzie and Darcy showing up when they did?

Coward, she thought.

"Where are you headed?" the tall officer barked out, his eyes settling on Lizzie and Darcy as though they were little more than another obstacle in his path.

"The storehouse of Mullins Brothers, wool merchants," Darcy said smoothly.

"And I don't suppose you have a card, do you?" he asked. "Considering you're 'on official business'?"

Lizzie disliked the sarcasm in his tone, but she extracted her card from her reticule with a calm she didn't feel inside. She presented it to the taller man, who took it from her with a small smirk. The slight officer didn't even glance at it, she noticed, fastidiously looking down the street.

"'Miss Elizabeth Bennet, Solicitor. Longbourn and Sons,'" the incredulous officer read. "Is this a joke?"

At the sound of her name, the other officer looked in Lizzie's direction. She caught surprise on his face, but she refocused her attention at the man in front of her.

"No joke," she assured him. "And as my partner said, we are on official business—"

"I've never heard of a lady solicitor," the tall officer spat. "Seems like some sort of scam to me."

Lizzie was, unfortunately, familiar with this type of reaction. It usually preceded some kind of absurd runaround wherein she was questioned ceaselessly about the exact nature of her role, how she became a solicitor, and whether or not Longbourn was aware she carried these cards. It was all quite tiring, and no amount of patience or logic would fend off these inquiries. She'd simply have to endure them, and hope that by name-dropping the magistrate she might be able to convince them that her business was legitimate.

But before she could mount her defense, Darcy cleared his throat. "What are you suggesting?"

"I don't suppose you have a card as well?" the officer asked, sarcasm dripping from his words.

"I do," Darcy said, although he made no move to offer one. "Mr. Darcy, of Pemberley and Associates."

The soldiers straightened just the slightest. Longbourn & Sons might have been reputable, but they were small. The Pemberley name—nay, the Darcy name—carried far more weight.

"Well, then," the taller soldier sputtered. "Down this street two more blocks, and then take a left. You should be able to see it up ahead."

"Thank you," Darcy said coolly, and tipped his hat. "Good day."

Darcy took Lizzie's arm and they sidestepped the officers. As she swept past the slight officer, she caught his gaze unexpectedly. His eyes were light brown, as unremarkable as his sandy, brownish-blond hair. She had the unsettling feeling that his eyes were far older than his face, but before she could take in further details about his appearance, she and Darcy had left them behind.

Lizzie sighed with impatience, but when they were out of earshot, she whispered, "Thank you."

"For what?"

She smiled a little then, because Darcy knew exactly what she was thanking him for. It was *probably* true that Lizzie could have charmed them into giving her directions and letting her go on her way. It was also true that the tall one could have decided his afternoon's duty was to make Lizzie's life very difficult by hauling her all the way back to Longbourn and demanding to speak to her father. (That had happened once, and it had been humiliating.) And it was *also* true that she was in a hurry and Darcy using his name and social clout had hastened the process.

Lizzie didn't like any of this. But she had grown to appreciate that Darcy's presence, at least, made things easier. And unlike other gentlemen who might remind her of how useful they could be, Darcy never made her feel as though she needed him in order to do her job.

"For asking for directions, obviously," Lizzie teased. "I am sure that was a blow to your ego."

"My ego has suffered greater indignities," he assured her. "Although next time, promise me we can take my carriage."

"Maybe," Lizzie conceded, a smile lighting her face.

It was moments like this, when he was acting grave as he teased her, and when he showed more patience for her misadventures than any person ever had, even her beloved sister Jane, that Lizzie felt a swell of emotion bubble up inside of her. She let herself feel it, but not name it. Putting it into words felt risky somehow.

Lizzie could hear Jane's voice in her head. *He must feel some affection for you, Lizzie. What else do you require?*

But before Lizzie could allow her thoughts to be mired by

this question, a shout from up the street caught her attention. "Fire!" a man's rough voice called out. "Fire!"

Immediately the atmosphere of the street shifted as people began to look about frantically for signs of flame or smoke. Lizzie and Darcy did the same, and Darcy's hand tightened on her arm as people began grabbing possessions and running in the opposite direction of the cry. Fire was no trifling matter—it took very little for flames to spread from building to building, especially in a neighborhood as cramped as this, with narrow streets and even narrower alleys.

As other panicked pedestrians took up the cry of "Fire!" a sense of unease overtook Lizzie. A man ran toward them, pulling two goats, and Darcy stopped him. "Where?" he asked.

"Up that way," the man said, gesturing behind him. He couldn't be bothered to give an exact location. "One of the storehouses," he added and continued to shepherd his animals away from the danger.

Lizzie's uneasy feeling solidified into dread and she took off in the direction the man had indicated—not straight behind him but down a side street. The street the officers had instructed them to turn down.

"Lizzie!" Darcy cried, but she didn't slow, nor did she heed the advice she'd always been given by her father in the event of fire: *Get as far away as you can from the flames and anything else that may catch fire.* She rounded the corner and was horrified to find that her hunch had been correct.

The Mullins Brothers storehouse was smoking.

It had been three years since she'd last visited the unassuming two-story brick structure, and aside from the smoke billowing from the open door, it hadn't changed. A small group of brave souls was clustered around the front of the building, loudly arguing.

Darcy caught up with her and took her arm. "We need to leave," he said, low and urgent.

"It's the Mullinses!" she protested over the din of men shouting and bells clanging. "We need to help!"

"No." The steel edge of Darcy's tone made her shiver. She didn't hear it often, and never directed toward her. "It's too dangerous."

"But—"

"We don't know how quickly the fire will move. I need to get you far away, *now*."

Lizzie didn't try to get any closer, but she wasn't ready to leave just yet. She couldn't see inside the building and so she had no idea how extensive the fire inside might be, although she could smell the smoke, heavy and acrid. It was not unlike when one of her sisters singed a wool gown with a clothes iron, but much, much worse. Most of the people who had a mind to flee had streamed past them, and those who had decided to stay— likely workers and owners of the surrounding buildings—were frantically hauling buckets of water from a nearby well. Next to the storehouse was a smithy, and the blacksmith and his assistant rolled an entire barrel toward the entrance of the burning building.

"Do you think Jack and Simon are inside?" she asked, trying to peer through the crowd of men.

"Let's pray they're not."

From her vantage point, Lizzie watched as men tied wet handkerchiefs over their faces and took turns running to the building with buckets. They must not have been able to go far, for it seemed that they'd no sooner disappeared inside than they'd stumble back out again, coughing and swiping at their burning eyes.

Lizzie saw no sign of either Mullins brother.

"Need I remind you that it only takes a small fire to burn down the entire city?" Darcy asked. "Do not put me in the position of having to inform your mother of your untimely death!"

He was right, but it was a rather low blow, bringing her mother into it. "Fine," she said. "But you won't be telling her a thing about us coming here unchaperoned—"

Lizzie was just about ready to turn her back on the scene when two figures came bursting out of the front doors. They were coughing so hard that their bodies shook. One was an older man, hair and beard graying, and the other was a young, slim man with tears running down his face.

"That's Jack!" Lizzie cried.

Jack Mullins kept trying to turn to face the wreckage of his family business. To see the destruction of everything his father had worked for, that he and his brother worked for, going up in literal flames . . . Lizzie's heart broke for him.

But then he pulled his jacket up to cover the bottom of his

15

face and ran toward the door. Three men peeled away from the firefighting efforts to hold him back and Lizzie realized with slick horror that he was screaming. "Simon! You have to get Simon!"

"Oh no," Lizzie whispered.

Even Darcy stopped pulling at her. "God help him," he whispered.

The older man conferred with one of the men holding back Jack, and he shook his head gravely. They nodded and tried to pull Jack away from the burning building, but he was still screaming for his brother.

No one was going back inside to save him.

Which, in all probability, meant he was already dead.

"Lizzie," Darcy said again, and his voice sounded desperate. "Please, come. There's little you can do for Mr. Mullins now."

She knew he was right, but that still didn't lessen the heavy weight of despair in her chest. Poor, poor Jack. And Simon . . . She shuddered to think at how horrifying it must be to be swallowed up by smoke and flame. She was so lost in her dark imaginings that it didn't register until Darcy murmured, "Thank God," that fat drops of rain had started falling. "This will help keep it from spreading, at least," he offered.

Lizzie nodded, but it was a small grace.

The men kept running inside with their buckets, but a stupendous crash from inside the building seemed to rattle the entire street and sent them all back out into the street once more, coughing and shaking their heads. Lizzie wondered what the source of the crash had been—the second floor falling in? Some essential building support? Whatever it was, it didn't deter the men. Lizzie and Darcy watched until they were thoroughly soaked and the men's movements grew less frantic. Heavy smoke hung in the air despite the downpour, but the fire appeared contained, much to everyone's relief.

"We should go," Darcy said. "There's nothing more to be gained here today."

Lizzie nodded in agreement, knowing that Jack Mullins wouldn't be thinking about his permitting issues now that his business was ruined and his brother dead. But she couldn't just walk away, either.

"I just need to . . . Wait for me a moment?" she asked.

Darcy released her arm, and nodded his understanding. Lizzie sloshed through the mud and puddles to where Jack sat on an overturned crate, the rain making the soot run down his face in gray rivulets. He held his wet jacket around his shoulders, but his face was blank as he watched the men go in and out of the smoking building.

"Mr. Mullins?" Lizzie asked. "Jack?"

He looked up at her slowly, and no recognition lit his face. Lizzie felt half-drowned and she knew her bonnet would never recover. She pushed the brim back and said, "Jack, it's me. Lizzie Bennet."

"Oh." Jack didn't appear to register her words. He stared blankly at her.

"Jack, I am so sorry," Lizzie said, realizing now that some

17

urge to comfort him had propelled her to approach, but the same urge hadn't given her the words to express her condolences. "If you need anything, please don't hesitate to write to me. Or come call. If I can help in any way . . ."

She trailed off, uncertain how to continue. She felt helpless in the face of such a tragedy. She could argue a case in court, scour documentation, brainstorm a legal loophole, but in the face of such a terrible disaster, she could do nothing.

Jack didn't acknowledge her words, and didn't show any sign of saying anything in return, so she offered him a weak smile. "I'll go now. But remember—I'm here if you need me."

She had gone only three paces when she felt a cold, clammy hand grab her wrist. She turned in surprise and found Jack staring down at her, his forehead creased with urgency. He gripped her wrist so tightly it hurt.

"Jack?"

"You can help," he whispered. "You have to find the woman who set the fire."

"A woman?" Lizzie asked. She hadn't yet pondered how the fire had started, let alone whether someone had set it.

"Yes," Jack insisted. "You have to find the woman who killed my brother."

TWO

In Which Lizzie Receives an Early Morning Caller, and a Rather Unconventional Case

A REASONABLE PERSON MIGHT have written off Jack Mullins's plea as the grief-stricken reaction of a man still in shock, and while Lizzie did consider herself quite reasonable, she couldn't help the sharp intake of breath that followed his request.

"Jack," she said, but then took a moment to sort through her thoughts. Why did he think a *woman* had set the fire? Had he seen her do it?

But before she could decide which of these questions to ask first, one of the men approached. "Jack! We need you!"

Jack turned and nodded at the man. Then, to Lizzie, he said, "I'll call on you soon."

And with that, he was gone.

Lizzie trudged back toward Darcy, noticing the squelch in her boots. Her stockings were soaked, and the thought of walking the long way home was suddenly incredibly tiresome.

"What happened?" Darcy asked in concern tinged with suspicion.

"He told me that someone set the fire," Lizzie said. "A woman."

"A woman?" Darcy parroted. "Why?"

"He didn't say."

Darcy didn't prod her, which Lizzie appreciated. She didn't volunteer the information that Jack Mullins wanted her to find the person, but Darcy was no fool. He simply shook his head and said, "Let's see if I can hail a hackney." But the rain seemed to have driven everyone indoors, for he was unsuccessful, even the closer they got to Cheapside. And so they trudged in the rain, silent, until they finally arrived at the top of Gracechurch Street, and Lizzie paused to say goodbye. Darcy was normally quite the gentleman and would insist on seeing her to her door, if not inside, but ever since her mother had taken note of Darcy's and Lizzie's unconventional business partnership, she'd not let up about when Darcy was going to start formally courting her. Try as Lizzie might to persuade Mrs. Bennet that there was a difference between courtship and a working relationship, her mother failed to see it. And so they'd taken to parting up the street, out of view of the Bennets' front window.

"You won't do anything rash, will you?" Darcy asked.

"Me? Never." But she couldn't stop thinking about Jack's words—*you have to find the woman who killed my brother.* They stirred up questions inside of Lizzie that wouldn't be silenced easily.

Darcy's smile was more of a grimace. "Well, if you should

change your mind, then you know where to find me."

She was too tired to even protest, but she did impulsively grab his hand and pull him close to her. She brushed her lips on his cheek in a chaste peck. "Thank you for today," she said.

Darcy's eyebrows rose in surprise, but a small smile appeared on his lips. "Next time, we'll take my carriage."

"So you admit there will be a next time."

"With you? There's always a next time." And before Lizzie could say anything more to that, he tipped his hat and said, "Good evening, Miss Bennet."

"Good evening, Mr. Darcy," she said with a chuckle, and turned to make the short walk to her front door.

As she let herself in and fended off her mother's cries of dismay at her bedraggled state, Lizzie thought about Jack's peculiar request. She considered every angle as she bathed and attempted to scrub the scent of smoke from her hair. She ruminated on how one might connect arson with murder charges as she tossed and turned that night in bed. She thought about it so much that even the ever-patient Jane rolled over after the clock struck four and said, "Honestly, Lizzie!"

The following morning, she was weary and still brooding over the question of arson and Jack Mullins while mindlessly buttering some toast when a knock came at the front door. Lizzie, her younger sisters, and her father all looked up in surprise.

"Who could that be?" Lydia demanded.

"Maybe it's Dar-cy!" Kitty sang, widening her eyes comically in Lizzie's direction.

Lizzie threw down her napkin. "Not this again."

"Ooh, is it Darcy?" Lydia asked. "Has he finally come to ask Papa—"

"It's not Darcy," Mary announced, leaning back in her chair to look out the window. "This fellow is shorter."

"Is he handsome?" Lydia jumped up from her seat and was followed by Kitty to the window, where they both peeked shamelessly through the curtains. "Lizzie, have you thrown over Darcy because he refuses to propose?"

"I haven't thrown him over!" Lizzie glared at her youngest sister as she stood. "And who says I want Darcy to propose?"

"Why wouldn't you?"

"Girls, come away from that window," Mr. Bennet said, also standing. "How about I put us all out of our misery and go answer the door?"

"I've got it, Papa," Lizzie assured him, and rushed out into the hall. She beat even the housemaid to the door, and threw it open to reveal Jack Mullins.

He was dressed in fresh clothes that fit him poorly, and his skin had a gray pallor that suggested he'd not gotten much sleep since she last saw him. Despite her request that he call on her, she hardly expected that he'd call so quickly—and at her home, not at Longbourn.

"Mr. Mullins!" she exclaimed, then stepped aside. "Please, do come in."

"You called me Jack yesterday," he said quietly as he entered the home and removed his hat.

"Yes, well . . . yesterday was an unusually terrible day." They'd called each other by their Christian names when they were following his father's business partner around London, trying to discover his plot. It had felt natural to call him Jack in the chaos of yesterday; but in the cool, pale light of morning, standing in her own foyer with her sisters and father in the next room, Lizzie fell back on formalities.

"Lizzie, who is this?" her father asked, attempting to sound gruff and not quite managing as he entered the hall and firmly closed the dining room door on the eager and curious faces of Mary, Kitty, and Lydia.

"Papa, you remember Mr. Mullins?" she asked, cringing at how high her voice sounded.

"Of course, of course," her father said, clapping the younger man on the shoulder. "To what do we owe this pleasure?"

"Less than pleasurable circumstances, I'm afraid," he said. "May we speak?"

Mr. Bennet nodded and ushered him into the drawing room rather than his study, and Lizzie followed. When the door had been closed behind them and Lizzie rang for tea, Mr. Bennet looked between Jack and Lizzie and said, "Why do I have a feeling my daughter is already in the middle of these less than pleasurable circumstances?"

"Mr. Mullins wrote to me three days ago," Lizzie said, deciding to start at the beginning. "He wanted a consult on some permitting issues—is that correct?"

Jack nodded.

"And I decided to visit the storehouse yesterday, but when I got there, it had caught fire. And . . . Mr. Simon Mullins perished in the fire."

Jack sat stoically in a stuffed chair, head bent. Mr. Bennet closed his eyes briefly. "My God, I am sorry."

"Thank you," Jack said quietly, but offered no more.

As much as Lizzie wanted to leap directly to Jack's peculiar request the night before, social tact—and her own instincts—told her to wait for Jack to bring it up. "Is the building a total loss?" she asked gently.

"Most of our wares were destroyed or damaged," Jack said, seeming to come alive a little more at the change of subject. "The brick seems to be solid enough, although the second floor is unstable."

"You and Simon were still living above the storehouse?" Mr. Bennet asked.

"Yes. We were still saving to buy a place of our own. Now all that money will have to go into rebuilding."

"I'm sorry," Lizzie murmured. "Have you anyplace to stay?"

"I'm letting a room here in Cheapside until repairs can be made," he told her. "Hopefully not for long. Thank God for the rain yesterday, and the quick thinking of my foreman."

"Thank God," Mr. Bennet echoed. "I imagine permitting issues are the least of your worries now, so you'll be here about insurance?"

"No," Jack said. "Or rather, yes. I'll need copies of the

insurance documents, seeing as mine burned. But I also would like to hire Miss Bennet."

"That is no problem," Mr. Bennet said, glancing at Lizzie. "Lizzie has been my protégée for the last year. She's more than capable of handling your case."

"I want Miss Bennet to find the person who set the fire."

Lizzie knew why Jack had come, but it still made her heart race to hear the words. Her father seemed to sink back into his chair, but he didn't look particularly surprised. His hand came up to rub his temple, and he said, "I think you ought to explain, Mr. Mullins."

"The fire was no accident—a young lady set it. She was in the storehouse minutes before the fire broke out. My brother, our foreman, and I were discussing shipments for the upcoming week when we spotted her. Parry and I went after her but she took off at a run—suspicious! Simon tried to cut her off near the entrance. The next thing we knew, we heard a crash and something breaking, and as we investigated we saw that a fire had broken out. Parry and I tried to put it out before it could spread, but when it became apparent that it was out of control, I searched for my brother—"

Here, Jack's voice broke and he buried his head in his hands as if he were ashamed to show emotion. Lizzie looked about and found one of the handkerchiefs that Jane had just finished embroidering—it was filled in with roses. She plucked a stray thread from it and offered it to Jack, who accepted with a nod.

"He had collapsed behind a stack of shipping crates and wasn't moving," he said finally. "I tried to get to him. The flames . . . and Parry . . ."

Lizzie recalled how she had seen the man, presumably Parry, pull a struggling Jack out of the burning building. It was a small comfort, but she rested her hand on Jack's arm. "You did all you could. It sounds as though Parry saved your life."

Jack wiped at his eyes, but didn't respond directly to Lizzie. "I want you to find that lady, Miss Bennet."

Before Lizzie could respond, Mr. Bennet leaned forward. "My daughter is a solicitor, not an investigator."

"Papa," Lizzie said, but her father held up a hand.

"Perhaps you need a referral to an investigator. We have a few to recommend. And if it comes to it, and you identify this woman, we can be of assistance with bringing charges against her."

"I read about the case you solved last year," Jack said, addressing Lizzie. "You were able to clear Mr. Bingley's name and implicate the true murderer."

"That was an unusual case," Mr. Bennet protested.

On this, Lizzie was inclined to agree with her father. For one, she was trying to clear someone's name, not find a mysterious lady who might or might not be responsible for arson. But both cases had involved untimely deaths, after all. "It was a unique case, but that's not to say that I am not capable of helping Mr. Mullins, Papa."

"You're certain that none of you accidentally knocked over a lantern or a candle? I am not trying to be difficult, but these are questions anyone will ask. It is unusual and confusing to find a strange woman in your storehouse, but who's to say that she didn't wander in by accident, and then flee when she saw you? Any one of you could have started the fire."

"No!" Jack was adamant. "No one had any business just wandering in when our doors were closed. And we wouldn't be so careless as to leave a lit candle where it could easily be knocked over. She was up to something, and she's the cause of the fire, I am sure of it!"

"And if I find her," Lizzie said, attempting to cut to the chase before her father could distract Jack, "and it was just an accident?"

"Then it was an accident," he conceded. "But I'll still have questions for her."

Lizzie wasn't sure she was comfortable with his dark tone, but she couldn't find fault with his words. If one of her sisters were dead as a result of a tragic accident, Lizzie would do everything she could to ensure that answers were found and those responsible were brought to justice. Unfortunately, even if the woman's intentions were innocent, if she had caused the fire, then she could be liable in a court of law for Simon Mullins's death.

Lizzie didn't relish the thought of attempting to bring a vindictive case before a court, but she wanted to do more than draft briefs for her father and present wills before magistrates. She wanted cases that interested her, and she wanted clients who wanted *her* expertise.

"I'll do it," she told Jack.

"Wait one moment," her father protested. "You have a rather full caseload, if I recall correctly, and my faculties haven't deserted me yet."

"Papa, Mr. Mullins has lost everything—surely this case takes priority!"

"I will not argue that," Mr. Bennet said, more to Jack than to Lizzie. "But I am not certain that Lizzie is best equipped for the investigative role."

"You cannot claim that as a solicitor I don't act as an investigator at times," Lizzie argued. "Not only must we find this lady, but a legal expert must confirm that there is enough evidence of a crime to bring before the magistrate."

Mr. Bennet's gaze narrowed, and Lizzie knew he was crafting a counterargument, but before he had a chance, Jack stood up. "I want Lizzie! No one else!"

Before Lizzie could respond to that, the door to the drawing room burst open. "Is it finally happening?" a loud voice cried.

"Oh no," Lizzie murmured.

It was Mrs. Bennet.

Mrs. Bennet appeared to have dressed in haste—her skirts were uncharacteristically rumpled, and she was quick to tuck strands of hair under her cap. Her cheeks were pink, and she was as giddy as a child as she looked from Lizzie to Mr. Bennet to Mr. Mullins with unconstrained excitement. "Well?" she demanded.

Lydia and Kitty stood behind her, the traitors, trying and failing to suppress giggles.

"Mother, this is a business meeting, not a social call!" Lizzie sprang forward in an attempt to shut the door in her mother's face, but Mrs. Bennet anticipated her move and stepped past her.

"Marriage is business," she said before turning to her husband. "Well?"

Mr. Bennet merely sighed. "You mistake the situation, my dear. Mr. Mullins wants to hire our Lizzie, not marry her."

Lizzie could have happily melted into the carpet as Lydia and Kitty burst into a peal of giggles behind their stricken-looking mother. "*Oh.*"

"Yes," Lizzie agreed. "So now, if you don't mind . . ."

And then she pushed her mother out of the room, despite her protests. "My apologies," she said, turning to face her new client once more. She was certain her own cheeks were flaming but decided to carry on as if this were an entirely natural interruption. "I don't often receive business calls at home, and my mother is easily confused!"

"I am not, Elizabeth!" Mrs. Bennet shouted through the door.

"It's quite all right," Jack said, although it was clear by his stunned expression that he hadn't expected his words to be mistaken for a marriage proposal. "I suppose I was speaking rather . . . passionately."

"Are you sure you won't reconsider?" Mr. Bennet asked once more, much to Lizzie's annoyance.

"Lizzie is dogged, and she thinks outside of the box. I know it's been three years since we last worked together, but without her I wouldn't have the business I do. Or, rather, did." He had to clear his throat a few times before continuing. "I want someone who is willing to investigate—and litigate."

Mr. Bennet didn't appear to take offense. It was no secret that he preferred studying and writing in his comfortable office to tracking down witnesses and taking statements.

In the end, he simply sighed and said, "And I trust you're prepared to take on the financial burden of a potentially costly investigation?"

"I'll do whatever it takes," he promised. "Just find that lady."

Lizzie asked a series of follow-up questions about Jack's and Simon's whereabouts the day before, their routine, and anyone who might have had access to the storehouse. Then she took a detailed description of the lady Jack claimed to have seen, but unfortunately for her, Jack didn't give her much to go on—the lady was tall, in a gray dress, with brown hair. Lizzie tried not to feel a bit discouraged that he was describing hundreds of ladies in London. You always had to start somewhere.

Jack gave her the address of his temporary lodgings and took his leave soon after, and Lizzie watched him make his way down the street before closing the door behind him. She felt infused with purpose, and excited for the day ahead. Her fingers itched to make a list of tasks. She needed to change clothes. She needed to take a proper look at the scene of the crime. She'd have to report back to the office, tell Charlotte to reschedule her appointments for the next few days, and then go to Pemberley. . . .

"So you were at the scene of the fire last night," Mr. Bennet said. It was not a question.

"Er . . . yes?"

"What a coincidence," he remarked.

"It was! He wrote me with questions about permits, and I could have responded, but then it might have delayed the matter another day or two. I had the time, so . . ."

"Indeed," Mr. Bennet said. "And I trust you didn't walk all the way to the Mullinses' storehouse alone?"

Lizzie winced. "Well, not exactly . . ."

Mr. Bennet fixed her with a pointed look. "Tell Mr. Darcy that if he's going to accompany you on cases and get your mother's hopes up, he ought to have the decency to at least walk you to the door afterward."

And with that, Mr. Bennet returned to the dining room and his cold breakfast.

THREE

In Which Darcy Encounters Trouble at Pemberley

DARCY WAS SEATED AT his desk, poring over a lengthy contract, when a stack of folders fell onto his desk with a thwack!

He startled, a half-formed protest rising to his lips when he looked up and saw Mr. Tomlinson, his superior, smirking down at him. "More briefs," he said. "For the Cooper case."

Darcy didn't express frustration in the way that one might expect—there would be no sighs or grimaces, no muttered complaints. Instead, Darcy merely blinked, then neatly picked up the files that had been unceremoniously dumped upon his desk, straightened them, and set them aside.

"Thank you, sir," he said, then flicked his gaze back to his work.

There was a small scoff from Tomlinson, but he didn't move. He continued to stare down at Darcy with a mocking grin while Darcy seethed.

Privately, of course.

"Composure," his father always told him, "makes the gentleman. If you cannot control yourself, then you're no better than the common man."

Darcy was good at composure. Some—all right, Bingley—would say *too* good. There was that whole matter of Lizzie thinking him prideful and cold at the beginning of their acquaintance. And well . . . he had a reputation among the ton as being unfeeling and coldly logical. He wasn't exactly proud of this, but his strong, silent composure had come in handy too many times to count.

Darcy was especially glad now, for it allowed him to take Mr. Tomlinson's abuses with a straight face. His supervisor would like nothing more than to find fault with Darcy's work—any reason to file a bad report to his father, who was currently traveling the Continent.

"Was there something else I can help you with?" Darcy asked Mr. Tomlinson.

"The motion for the Crawley case," Mr. Tomlinson said. "I need it now."

Darcy did his very best not to look in the direction of Mr. Tomlinson's office. The motion should be on his supervisor's desk, exactly where Darcy had left it when he first arrived—*before* Tomlinson, not that anyone was keeping score on that matter. "I delivered it to your office when I arrived. Sir."

The slight pause before the *sir* rankled on Tomlinson—Darcy could tell by the way he scrunched his large nose just slightly. "It's not there now. If I don't have it in my hands in the next ten minutes, then you'll be explaining your incompetence before our client *and* the magistrate!"

Darcy clenched his jaw. "Understood. Sir."

Tomlinson stared at him a beat longer before striding away once more. Darcy waited until he rounded the corner out of sight before peeking into the leather satchel tucked beneath his desk. Inside was a packet of documents, and Darcy double-checked to ensure . . . yes.

The copy of the motion he'd delivered to Tomlinson was still there.

Once upon a time, Darcy would have said his ideal working environment was "ordered disarray" even if Lizzie claimed that there was no such thing. She didn't like clutter, but Darcy had never had any trouble keeping track of any stray paper or document on his desk, and he resisted all attempts by anyone, including Lizzie, to organize his desk. It might look messy, but he knew where everything was. And when his father was around, no one had any issue with this.

But then the first missing contract had cost Pemberley their case in court.

As soon as Tomlinson returned from court, he'd marched over to Darcy's desk and taken him to task before sweeping every file off his desk. "Clean this mess up!" he'd shouted. "You are a disgrace to the Pemberley name!"

If anyone was going to call him a disgrace to the Pemberley name, Darcy would have preferred it had been his father, not some newly appointed barrister who barked orders like a sergeant. However, he'd been racked with miserable guilt at the prospect of facing their client. So rather than argue, he'd done what he was told.

And he had found the missing contract in the mess.

But the thing was, he was positive that the contract *hadn't* been on his desk at all. He knew what was on his desk, and what wasn't. Which meant either Darcy couldn't trust himself and his memory, or someone had planted the contract on his messy desk to discredit him.

He said nothing, of course. But he did clean up his desk, spent more time organizing and filing, and bided his time. And then a week and a half later, a report on a client's business holdings had gone missing. Darcy hurriedly rewrote it while Tomlinson seethed and raged at him, and just as he'd nearly finished while Tomlinson loomed impatiently over him, a hopeful clerk approached, the original document in hand.

"It was on the floor, sirs," he'd said. "Under the liquor cabinet in Mr. Tomlinson's office."

"Good God, man," Tomlinson had shouted at him, almost as if on cue. "You've got to be more careful. Keep an eye on where you place things. And, Darcy . . . steer clear of the liquor during the workday."

Tomlinson had pretended to whisper, but his voice had carried through the bullpen of desks to the other solicitors and clerks nonetheless. Then he clapped a hand on Darcy's shoulder before striding off, and Darcy was left sitting in the middle of the firm that his father had built, so very angry that he might have nearly challenged Tomlinson to a duel, except the last time he'd done that things hadn't quite worked out for him, and he was trying to be better.

After that, Darcy kept copies of all the paperwork he submitted to Tomlinson. He didn't let on, though, preferring to let Tomlinson think he was getting one over on him. Darcy didn't care if they thought him a little disorganized. But he wasn't about to let Tomlinson throw a case and hurt a client because he enjoyed humiliating *his* superior's son.

Darcy slid the copy of the Crawley motion out of his satchel and placed it on his desk. He'd stayed up half the night writing out the copy, but he was glad of it.

Now he just had to wait an appropriate amount of time before he told Tomlinson that he'd "discovered" the missing document.

One thing that bothered Darcy was that he hadn't figured out what he'd done to bring Tomlinson's ire down upon him. Before his father's absence, he'd hardly noted Tomlinson's presence beyond acknowledging him as one of the many more senior members of the firm. It could be that Tomlinson simply despised Darcy's privilege and connection, but he couldn't help but feel as if there were simply more to it than his name. . . .

As he waited, Darcy became aware of a clerk walking in his direction, wearing a pinched expression. The man's name was Perkins, and he stopped at Darcy's desk. "Sir, I think you might want to come out front."

"Perkins, no need to call me sir," Darcy said. The man was

older than he by five years, but Darcy was the heir apparent of the firm and that commanded a bit of respect still . . . at least in some people's eyes. "What's the matter?"

"That lady is here again," Perkins said with an apologetic grimace. "And you know how Mr. Tomlinson gets . . ."

Now Darcy was the one grimacing. He stood, grabbing the copy of the Crawley motion—it wouldn't do for this one to go "missing" as well. "Thank you, Perkins."

Darcy could hear Lizzie's voice before he could see her, and that brought a small smile to his lips before he could properly contain it. She was chatting with the clerk who sat at the front desk, inquiring about the health of his wife, saying, "I do hope she hasn't caught the nasty cough that seems to be going around." Her gaze snagged on the sight of him but she kept her attention on the desk clerk.

"Thankfully not, Miss Bennet," Mr. Reeves said. "She's feeling much better these days."

"I am so pleased to hear that," Lizzie said. "Please give her my regards."

To Darcy's knowledge, Lizzie had never even laid eyes on Mrs. Reeves . . . although it wouldn't surprise him to hear they regularly took tea together. Lizzie had a way of connecting with people that Darcy often found utterly confounding.

"Good day," he greeted her, allowing her a nod. What he really wanted to do was kiss her hand and get close enough to inhale her intoxicating scent, but the last thing he needed was to draw Mr. Tomlinson's attention to her presence.

"Darcy!" Lizzie exclaimed, rather loudly. Inwardly, he winced. "I'm afraid that I come bearing absolutely dreadful news."

Her tone indicated otherwise—she sounded downright giddy. "Oh?"

She dropped her voice to whisper. "Yesterday's excursion has produced a case."

He tried very hard not to shiver at the memory of yesterday. That fire had been downright terrifying, and when he did finally get to sleep that night, he'd dreamt that he and Lizzie were lost in a maze of confusing London back alleys while the scent of smoke and roar of flames got ever closer. "Congratulations?"

Lizzie wasn't bothered by his lack of enthusiasm. Heaven help him, she had enough for the both of them. "Thank you. Now I came to inquire as to whether or not you— Yes? Can I help you?"

Darcy turned and was startled to find Mr. Tomlinson standing a mere three paces behind him, wearing an irked expression. "Now, Miss Bennet, I believe that is a question I should be asking you."

Lizzie smiled sweetly, and only someone who knew her well could tell that her manner wasn't genuine in the least. "Oh, no thank you, Mr. Tomlinson. Mr. Darcy is assisting me."

"Is he?" The man's sour tone grated on Darcy. "Why, if you have the time to receive visitors in the lobby during the workday, I think I ought to assign you a few more cases, Darcy."

Darcy saw Lizzie's shoulders square up for a fight, and he rushed to stop her. He arranged his features into a bored, distant expression. "I beg your pardon, sir. I was merely stepping out for a moment."

Mr. Tomlinson's falsely genial expression turned into glee. "In the middle of the workday? Your last name might be Darcy, but that doesn't mean you get to leave whenever your . . ." He trailed off suggestively.

"Colleague," Darcy supplied, the word coming out harder than he intended.

"Colleague," Tomlinson repeated, the word dripping with disdain. "Yes, well, unless there is a legitimate reason you need to consult with your colleague, it's back to your desk."

Darcy could practically feel Lizzie bristle beside him. "We are consulting," he said, before she could jump to his defense. "Mr. Bennet recently took on and won a case very similar to Mr. Crawley's suit last year. I was consulting with him yesterday evening on the finer points of the motion, and I must have left the paperwork with him. Miss Bennet was kind enough to deliver it to me."

Darcy held the copy of the motion aloft, and kept his gaze fixed on Mr. Tomlinson. Surely the man wouldn't accuse him of lying in front of a lady and at least three other Pemberley employees?

Tomlinson seemed to realize that he was indeed backed into a corner. "How kind of Miss Bennet. Your father must find your secretarial services a great help in his business."

"I beg your pardon—" Lizzie started to say, but Darcy cut her off.

39

"Now, I'm afraid because of my oversight in misplacing these documents, I will have to rush this over to the courts myself. You won't object if I escort Miss Bennet back to her offices along the way?"

Tomlinson's lips disappeared into a thin line. "I suppose not."

Darcy nodded and turned to go. That had gone better than he'd hoped. But just as he offered Lizzie his arm, he heard Tomlinson say, "But I will have to write your father and tell him about this habit of forgetfulness."

Darcy paused, but only for a moment. "Of course," he said over his shoulder, not quite looking at Tomlinson. He couldn't bear facing what he knew he'd see: smug satisfaction on the odious man's face. Instead, he nodded at Mr. Reeves, and swept Lizzie out the front door.

"*What* was that about?" Lizzie asked the moment they were out on the busy street. She leaned in conspiratorially, and Darcy felt his eyes flutter shut just for a moment. She smelled of something sweet, and of ink and tea. "You never forget a thing, and you aren't consulting with my father on anything . . . unless. Are you?" She sounded suspicious, but there was a note of something frantic in her question.

"Would you object if I did?"

"No, but I would be awfully cross if you went behind my back to do so."

"Noted," Darcy said. "Don't worry—Tomlinson was just being difficult. He lost the first copy of this motion, and well . . . you know how men like him are."

"Oh," she said. "Is he giving you problems?"

"Oh, not really." The lie came easily, before he could really consider his words. "He's just a stickler for protocol. But he is right—most junior solicitors don't get to just walk out in the middle of the day."

Lizzie bit her bottom lip just briefly. "I'm sorry. I didn't mean to come drag you from your work."

He raised one eyebrow. "Didn't you?"

"All right, fine. I sort of did. Goodness, but Mr. Tomlinson is annoying. You had much more autonomy to consult with me on cases before your father left. Any chance he'll be back soon? Tomorrow, perhaps?"

Darcy allowed a tiny smile to crack through his opaque exterior. "I'm afraid not."

"Oh well," she said good-naturedly. "One can hope."

Darcy wasn't certain why he felt the need to lie to her about Tomlinson. Perhaps it was nothing. Perhaps he enjoyed being in charge a bit too much. Either way, things weren't likely to change any time soon. Five months ago, his father had called him and Georgiana into his study and informed them he'd be leaving in two days' time to see to business on the Continent. Georgiana was sent to their country estate with a small battalion of servants, much to her strenuous objections, and Darcy was expected to stay in London and apply himself at the firm. He continued to live in the family town house; but at the firm, Mr. Tomlinson would be his direct supervisor, sending his father regular reports on his progress.

But even if the elder Mr. Darcy had been in London, it likely wouldn't have helped things. Darcy knew that his father disapproved of his work with Lizzie. In his eyes, she was a troublesome young lady who had no business meddling in various legal affairs and cases. At one time, Darcy had thought the same thing. But Lizzie Bennet had as sharp a mind as any man employed at Pemberley, and Darcy regularly benefitted from her insights and unconventional modes of thinking; and if he was being honest, he was glad that she included him on her more interesting cases, for it gave them an excuse to spend time together. His father and Mr. Tomlinson hadn't gone so far as to forbid him from fraternizing with her . . . yet.

"In the meantime, it's best not to draw his attention," Darcy said now, hailing a carriage. He was glad to see that Lizzie didn't insist on walking again. "What exactly, though, is your case? An insurance investigation? Something about that woman he mentioned?"

Lizzie looked up at him, smugly pleased. "A bit more than that."

Two bay mares pulling a small cab stopped in front of them, and the driver had to say, "Are you getting in or not?" before Darcy broke out of his surprised trance. He opened the door and helped Lizzie in, then gave the address for the courts before climbing in after her.

"What do you mean, a bit more than that?" he asked as soon as the carriage jumped forward with a lurch. "Don't tell me—"

"Arson," Lizzie confirmed. She looked far too delighted to

be speaking of such a serious subject, but there were few young ladies as fascinated by crime and its legal implications as Lizzie Bennet. "Yesterday he said he thought a woman set the fire, and he was on my doorstep this morning telling me that this young lady most certainly entered the storehouse and set it on purpose. And since his brother died as a result, he's bent on seeing that justice is done."

Darcy was already shaking his head. "I don't know, Lizzie. It sounds like a case for detectives, not for solicitors."

"That's precisely what my father said," she told him, almost disapprovingly. "But Jack Mullins wants me. He read about Bingley's case in the papers, and he said that since I solved a murder—"

"Don't you mean *we* solved a murder?"

"Exactly." She grinned. "Why else do you think I've come to fetch you in the middle of the day? I want you on the case with me."

Darcy found that the concept of composure went out the window when Lizzie was nearby, for he grinned like a fool. "And what does your client have to say about that?"

"I hardly need to disclose every person I consult with to him," she said.

But Darcy couldn't help but wonder if this Jack wouldn't object to Darcy's involvement. "And your father?"

"What do you think?"

"He'd rather you be safe indoors doing paperwork?"

"Precisely," she said. "Now, are you in or not? Or are you

going to ask me what my sisters, my mother, and all the society papers will think?"

Darcy laughed then. He didn't mean to be a wet blanket. Who was he to question her judgment or abilities when he'd seen firsthand what she was capable of? "All right," he said. "But what will they say about all of this unchaperoned time spent together?"

He was joking, of course—it wasn't as though seeing to business was the same thing as sneaking off to an empty room at a society ball, and Lizzie had made it perfectly clear that she cared more about closing a case than what the ton might say about who she was seen with. But a small shadow seemed to flit across Lizzie's face.

Then she smiled and rolled her eyes. "What my mother doesn't know has never hurt her."

It was this Lizzie—coy and clever—that he found absolutely irresistible. When she was sitting across from him, in the close quarters of the carriage, consequences like Tomlinson and their reputations seemed to matter very little.

"All right. But I'm not walking all the way across town again."

FOUR

In Which Lizzie's Investigation
Encounters a (Rather Flimsy) Wall

DARCY WAS RIGHT: TAKING the cab was much faster.
And less muddy.

Not that Lizzie was going to admit it. He'd be insufferable!

She was glad for his presence, though. The last few months
had been so busy; she'd hardly seen him except for little snatches
of time here and there, and even then they were always surrounded by people or not very far from her mother's watchful
eye. And lately the merest mention of Darcy brought up not-so-
subtle-hints that Lizzie ought to be married soon.

But if Lizzie was being honest, the idea of Darcy proposing made her feel vaguely queasy. It wasn't that she didn't like
him—she liked him a great deal. And she enjoyed their stolen
kisses (five in total since the first time he kissed her outside the
courthouse, but who was counting?) and the way he looked at her
like he both knew what she would say next and was delightfully
surprised by her every action. But *marriage?* Lizzie liked her life.

She enjoyed working for her father, boring tasks aside, and she wasn't sure if she was ready to change her life, her address, and her name for Darcy.

Besides, she'd only recently gotten the courthouse clerks to remember her name. If she changed it now, they'd never take her seriously!

Lizzie sighed.

"What the matter?" Darcy asked.

"Nothing!" Lizzie smiled reassuringly. The last thing she wanted was to say any of this to Darcy and to have him think that she was indifferent to him. Far from it.

Luckily for her, the carriage slowed as it arrived at their destination. The driver deposited them at the end of the street and Darcy slipped him extra coin to wait. It was just as muddy here as it had been the day before—so much for avoiding soiling her hems—and a patchy fog had settled over the neighborhood, even though it was nearly noon. The faint scent of smoke still hung about, and for an unsettling moment Lizzie felt as though her mind was playing tricks on her and the fog that encased the street was actually smoke.

"Well, someone worked quickly," Darcy remarked, just as Lizzie registered a hastily erected barrier that stood before the storehouse. It was made of what appeared to be scaffolding, scrap wood, and canvas, completely blocking the view of the lower level of the storehouse.

"It looks flimsy enough," Lizzie observed. "I daresay you or I could knock it all over with a good shove."

"So they aren't worried about securing the place as much as they want to keep out prying eyes," Darcy mused. "Tell me everything that Mr. Mullins said."

Lizzie recited all the details that Jack had shared, and she was glad for it. Going over the information solidified it in her mind . . . but it also brought up more questions. When she'd finished, Darcy asked, "How did this mysterious woman get in? Presumably the doors were locked if it was only the Mullins brothers and their foreman?"

"I am less curious about how she got in and more interested in *why*," Lizzie murmured. "Why would a woman wander into a strange building, especially one that seemed closed? Do you recall, were the shutters open when we arrived yesterday?"

Darcy thought about this a moment. "You know, I don't believe they were. At least, I only remember smoke coming out of the front door, but nowhere else."

"Indeed," Lizzie murmured in agreement. They could see over the hastily erected wall to the second story, where the inner shutters were closed. To passersby, the storehouse was closed up tight and secretive. Which made sense, Lizzie supposed, after yesterday's events, but . . . "Why do you think that the three of them were inside in the middle of the day, windows and shutters closed?"

Darcy looked at her sidelong. "Usually people close their shutters when they don't want anyone looking in."

She knew that, of course. But that begged the question: What exactly was so secretive about discussing the day's shipments?

Unless Jack wasn't telling the whole truth.

Lizzie was not prepared to go down that path quite yet. "All right, Jack said they were inside talking business. They would have needed a lamp."

"Did he say where exactly they were when they first noticed this intruder?"

"No," Lizzie said, suddenly wishing she'd asked Jack to meet them there and walk them through it exactly. "But there is an office in the back, if I recall correctly. And Jack talked about chasing the woman, so it's likely that's where they were. Lizzie closed her eyes and tried to picture it. A quiet day, no shipments in or out, discussing business when suddenly they hear a sound— someone is in the storehouse.

She opened her eyes. "There is one thing . . ."

"What is it?"

"Jack said that he saw her, and all three men immediately 'went after her.'"

Darcy understood immediately. "They went after her, rather than ask her what she was doing there?"

"I suppose they could have assumed she was a thief. But why assume the lady is a thief and not someone who was lost?"

"Guilty minds often leap to guilty assumptions," Darcy pointed out. "But wait—did he actually see this lady start the fire?"

"No." Lizzie knew what he was thinking: Any solicitor worth their salt would argue that if no one witnessed this woman start the fire, then no one could know with any certainty that she was responsible. Lizzie would deal with that detail later—first, they had to find her.

Darcy let out a hmph. "And if we can presume that they have a lamp or lantern, and they're chasing after a young woman, then it could have just as easily been any one of them who set the fire."

"I can't disagree with your logic, but I think before we can come to any definitive conclusions, we need to see inside." *And find that young lady*, she thought.

Lizzie and Darcy approached the front of the building, where there was a makeshift gate nailed together out of broken-down shipping crates. A stout man with a dark beard and distrustful eyes watched them approach, and Lizzie recognized him from the day before as one of the men who'd held Jack back from running into the building.

"Good day, sir," Lizzie said smoothly. "I'm Miss Bennet of Longbourn and Sons, and Mr. Mullins has hired me."

"Longbourn and Sons?" the man repeated. "What are you, then? Accountants?"

"Solicitors," Lizzie clarified. "Our condolences for yesterday's tragedy, Mr. . . . ?"

The man eyed her suspiciously, but reluctantly said, "Parry."

"Mr. Parry," Lizzie repeated. So this was the foreman. "I'm so sorry. I'm certain you're still shaken. But as you may know, Mr. Mullins hired me to try to get to the bottom of who, or what, caused the fire. May we ask you a few questions?"

"What's there to get to the bottom of? There was a fire. Simon died."

Lizzie and Darcy exchanged confused looks. Lizzie proceeded carefully. "Jack told me that a lady entered the storehouse yesterday, and he believed that she started the fire. Did you see anything?"

"I didn't see a woman, but Jack-o said something about her."

"You didn't see her? Not at all?"

"No." The one-word response was sullen.

"Can you describe what happened right before the fire?" Lizzie asked.

Mr. Parry looked at Darcy, which made Lizzie want to roll her eyes, but she held herself in check.

"We aren't questioning what you saw or didn't, Mr. Parry," Darcy assured him. "We are simply seeking information."

"Jack-o didn't say anything about hiring solicitors," Parry grumbled, but seemed to relent. "We were goin' over the invoices and bills of lading in the office. We thought we heard some creakin' like footsteps, but there wasn't supposed to be anyone there."

"Were the doors locked?" Lizzie asked.

Parry shook his head. "Can't rightly say. Should have been, but Jack-o was always careless about lockin' a door behind him. Anyway, Simon, he was skittish and thought someone was inside. Both he and Jack stepped out of the office to look around. That's when I heard them shoutin', and by the time I ran out, both were nowhere to be found. I went lookin' for them, but the next thing I knew, the building was on fire. I found Jack-o, but we couldn't get to Simon. I hauled Jack-o out, and if I hadn't, all three of us would have been dead—understand?"

"I'm sure you did what you had to," Lizzie assured him. "How did the fire start, do you think?"

"Simon probably knocked over a lamp. Bloody stupid, if you ask me." Parry spat on the ground, and upon noting Darcy's glare, mumbled, "Beggin' your pardon, miss."

But Lizzie didn't mind—her thoughts were tumbling through this information. "But you don't doubt there *was* a woman?"

A strange look came over Parry's face. "Could have been. Likely one of those bloo—er, I mean one of those French womenfolk. There's a bunch of them down the street, always tryin' to sell rubbish and jabberin' away in their language."

Lizzie bristled at his choice of words, but tried to hide her reaction. "Are there many émigrés in this area?"

"Too many," was Parry's blunt response. "They're goin' to stir up trouble."

"Any in particular that stand out?" Darcy asked. "Perhaps one that had a disagreement with any of your laborers or the Mullinses themselves?"

Parry paused before answering, and for a moment Lizzie was certain that he'd give them the lead they were hoping for. But then he shook his head. "I keep away from them. And I tell my men to do the same."

That very well might have been the truth, but Lizzie didn't believe for a moment that there wasn't more to it than that . . . and that Parry didn't at least have suspicions. "Jack mentioned that he thought he'd seen this lady before. Has anyone been hanging about lately? Anyone that would have no business being around?"

"I already told you, I don't know anythin' about any woman!" He seemed to draw himself up taller. "And I think you should leave. Jack-o never said he'd hired any solicitor, and how am I supposed to know you're not here to cause trouble?"

What an absolutely inane thing to say! Lizzie barely stopped herself from huffing in exasperation. "Mr. Mullins hired me this morning. I had hoped to take a look around inside."

She stepped forward as if her entering the premises was a foregone conclusion. More polite people than Mr. Parry might have stepped aside so as to avoid colliding with her, but the man didn't budge, and Lizzie found herself uncomfortably close to him. He was several inches taller than she, and he glanced down at her, unimpressed. "No one is to go inside, miss. Not until repairs can be made and a surveyor conducts an inspection. City orders."

She stiffened, not wanting to be the one to step back. He smelled of sweat and smoke, and something else underneath it all, tangy and sour.

Spirits.

Lizzie turned to face Darcy, and he was eyeing the man. "It looks like we'll have to report this to Mr. Mullins, doesn't it, Miss Bennet?"

"Do what you will. Jack-o is responsible for repairs, and we've got to follow the law, don't we?" His sarcasm was not lost on Lizzie.

"Well, then, I suppose I shall wait until Mr. Mullins returns and can vouch for us. It would be a horrid waste of my time and his money, but since you insist . . ."

"Not sure when he'll be back. Told me not to expect him all day."

If it hadn't been unladylike, Lizzie might have grunted in frustration. Instead, she took a step back and looked up and down the street. "Well, then, we'll take a look around. Outside."

"Suits me," Parry said.

Lizzie marched down the street, Darcy on her heels. "He's hiding something," Lizzie muttered as they came to a halt outside of earshot.

"I think that is abundantly apparent," Darcy agreed. "Why place a guard at a burned-out building unless you wanted to hide evidence?"

"What? No, I meant Parry."

"Oh. Well, he's hiding something, too. But I don't think *Jack-o* is exactly as forthcoming as he ought to be."

Lizzie disliked the sarcastic tone in Darcy's voice when he voiced Jack's nickname. "Jack hasn't given me any reason to doubt his honesty."

"And when has that ever stopped you?"

"What is that supposed to mean?"

"Isn't this why you dragged me along—to ask questions?"

"I dragged you along to help," Lizzie corrected. "Not cast aspersions on my client!"

"Casting aspersions is one of my specialties," Darcy countered.

"But come, Lizzie. You have questions about this case, and you know there's something odd here. Besides, you cannot stand here and tell me that you aren't curious as to why, less than a day after the fire, this monstrosity has been erected?"

He pointed at the wall, and Lizzie relented. "I'll ask Jack when we see him next. In the meantime, I'm not ready to entertain the idea that Jack has had anything to do with his own brother's death. You saw him yesterday."

This reminder seemed to chasten Darcy. "All right. I'll give you that he appeared genuine."

"Thank you."

"Either that, or he belongs on the stage."

"You! You are just so . . ."

"Charming?" Darcy deadpanned.

"I am going to go over there," Lizzie said, pointing toward the corner of the building. "And I am going to look for clues or anyone who might have seen anything. Please go do the same, but over there."

"Aye, aye," Darcy said, softening the teasing tone with a wink that made Lizzie go weak in the knees.

She hated when he was aggravating and attractive at the same time.

She took three deep breaths, and then forced herself to study the barrier more closely. It was only the height of the average man, which meant that it was difficult to see around but didn't completely obstruct the brick building behind. She took a few steps back and then crossed the street to take in the storehouse from a wider angle while Darcy ambled toward a group of men loading a wagon.

From her vantage point, the building looked surprisingly intact. The roof showed no signs of damage from the outside, and though the second-story windows were darkened by inner shutters, the window glass appeared intact. She couldn't get a good view of the damage below, so she crossed the street once more and peered down the alley that separated the storehouse from the smithy next door. It had a small yard for outdoor fires and a water pump, and a single skinny scraggly tree stood in the yard. It looked dead, and the lower branches had been hacked away, but the upper branches—if one was able to reach them—could be climbed and would provide a nice view into the storehouse's upper windows.

Hmm.

Lizzie followed the barrier down the alley and confirmed her suspicions—it encircled the entire building. At first there didn't seem to be anything of interest this way, but as she looked down to pick her way through the mud, something glinted in the weak sunlight.

She crouched low to the ground and removed her glove to carefully pick up the shining object. Broken glass, smeared with mud. And not a small shard, but a large piece.

Intriguing. Lizzie made a mental note to write Elinor Dashwood and ask her what happened to window glass when a building caught fire. The elder Dashwood sister studied the sciences, and Lizzie had found that her insight was incredibly helpful at times. Were the shards of glass the result of the fire, or had someone broken a window deliberately? Someone wanting to escape the fire, perhaps? Lizzie had seen Jack and Mr. Parry come out the front door yesterday, but perhaps this was evidence that there was a young lady—or someone, anyway—who might have escaped the fire by another route.

Farther down the alley, she heard a small scuffing noise. Lizzie looked up, steeling herself for the sight of rats.

Nothing.

"Hello?" she called out.

She waited, and the scuffing sound came again from a large stack of wood and various construction materials haphazardly piled on the edge of the smithy's yard. A piece of wood shifted and fell from the stack.

That was either a very large rat, or not a rat at all.

"Hello?" Lizzie tried again. "I'm sorry to bother you. I'm just looking . . . for clues. You know there was a fire here yesterday?"

Another piece fell, revealing a child.

He was small and skinny, like most of the street children tended to be. He wore tattered trousers, which had been patched many times, and a green jacket, which had likely once been fine but was now faded and worn. An overlarge gray cap fell down his face, but when he pushed it back as he scrambled to his feet, Lizzie could see the whites of his widened eyes on his grimy face.

"Hello," Lizzie said, softer.

The boy ran.

Lizzie hesitated only a moment, but then followed. Not at a

run, of course—it was never good when a lady like herself was seen running after a boy who clearly lived on the streets. People tended to get the wrong idea. But she followed him through the alley, calling out, "Wait! I just want to talk!" and came out on the next street over.

She looked up and down the street, but saw nothing but storehouses and work yards, very much like the street she'd just left. One difference, however, was a small throng of women who were gathered just a stone's throw to her left. She approached them. "Pardon me," she said. "I am so sorry to interrupt, but did any of you happen to see a boy run this way just a moment ago?"

She was met with blank—and fearful—looks. The women appeared to be peddlers of some kind, for they carried baskets and were standing next to carts stacked with wares, not unlike the woman she'd seen the day before. And when Lizzie looked from face to face, she saw her—the woman with the blue kerchief the officers had been harassing before Lizzie and Darcy had stepped in.

These had to be the Frenchwomen that Parry had referred to. Their clothes were worn and their wares weren't much better, but before Lizzie had approached they'd been chatting. Now they looked at her with wariness. Lizzie mustered up her rudimentary French, which Mrs. Bennet had insisted that all five Bennet sisters learn—with varying degrees of success.

"Un garçon," she repeated, looking from face to face. "Avez-vous vu un garçon?"

The women murmured among themselves, but nothing that Lizzie could make out. Finally, the woman that Lizzie had seen the day before stepped forward. "Non."

She regarded Lizzie with curiosity, recognition lighting up her face. One of the other women hissed something to her, but she shook her head and responded in rapid-fire French, too quick for Lizzie to translate, although she caught the word *soldat*. Soldier.

"Je cherche une femme," Lizzie tried. If they didn't see the boy, maybe they knew something about this mysterious woman that had apparently been inside the storehouse. "Grande, brunette . . . une dame?"

Her description was not much to go on. Tall, brown hair, likely a lady given her dress. But the woman from yesterday shook her head rapidly. "Il n'y a pas des dames ici, mademoiselle."

"Please. S'il vouz plait. It's important." But the woman continued to shake her head. No ladies here. Lizzie wasn't certain whether they didn't understand her, or didn't wish to help her. "I want to help," she added truthfully. "Aider?"

Her words brought out a flurry of whispers, and finally one of the women produced a name. "Josette," she said, looking between Lizzie and her friends. The other women nodded in agreement.

"Josette?" Lizzie asked. "Does she have a surname? Um, nom de famille?"

At this question, there seemed to be a bit of a disagreement. After some whispering and rapid-fire discussions, the blue-kerchiefed woman said, "Beaufort. Josette Beaufort."

The women nodded, repeating the name among themselves. Lizzie felt uncertain—she had no way of knowing if the woman she was looking for was Josette Beaufort, but the women all seemed confident that the description she gave matched, so she said nothing more. Lizzie wished she could ask them more about this Josette Beaufort, but she didn't know how to ask her questions in French, and she didn't wish to press her luck. At least she had a name. "Merci. Merci beaucoup."

And with that, there was nothing more for Lizzie to do but to turn around and head back toward the Mullinses' storehouse and find Darcy. The Frenchwomen waved, but they closed ranks into a tight knot once Lizzie turned away.

As she passed the pile of wood where the boy had been hiding, Lizzie paused. The pile concealed bits of newspaper and a few old rags fashioned into a sort of nest, ringed by small rocks and sticks. The sight pulled at her heartstrings. She sometimes wished she could sweep up all the poor children of the streets and give them homes, but judging by the way the boy had run, he likely wouldn't allow it. Still, some impulse to help propelled her to draw two coins from her reticule and drop them in the boy's nest. Maybe he would find them, maybe he wouldn't. . . .

After a moment's hesitation, she added her calling card as well. In all likelihood, he wouldn't be able to read it, but perhaps someone he knew would know how, and he'd find his way back to her. She knew it was unlikely, but she weighed it down with one of the bricks so it wouldn't blow away, and straightened up, brushing the dirt from her gloves. There. Nothing ventured, nothing gained.

She found Darcy in front of the storehouse and waved to get his attention. "Any luck?" she called out.

He shook her head and strode over to her. "I've asked every man on this street who will talk to me if they'd seen a lady matching the description, and I got no responses that are fit for your ears," he said with a bit of disgust. "Shockingly, not many ladies patronize the establishments here."

"Shocking," Lizzie echoed.

She was about to tell him what she'd discovered when a voice called, "Oy! You two!"

They turned to find Mr. Parry waving at them. He gestured for them to approach, and Lizzie and Darcy hurried over, Lizzie's heart pounding with hope. Perhaps he'd changed his mind and would be willing to talk. . . .

"Here," the man said, handing Darcy the end of a rope. Lizzie traced it down to a very small, very dirty dog. The poor animal came reluctantly. His body was long, with very short legs, and he had a mess of fur on the top of his head that looked like a lady's bouffant. He was dark cream in color, but his fur was streaked with soot.

"Mr. Mullins's dog," Mr. Parry explained. "That is, the late Mr. Mullins. Guy's the name. He's been whining all day. Wants his master."

"Oh, poor thing!" Lizzie crouched down to say hello to the small dog, who sat without command and looked up at her with sad brown eyes. "But why are you giving him to us?"

"Simon is dead, and Jack-o doesn't want him. Always made him sneeze, Guy did, so he stayed downstairs. Now it's no place for him, and it's on to the streets if I don't find him a new home."

"But I don't understand," she said, looking at Darcy. "What makes you think we want him?"

Mr. Parry shrugged. "Suit yourself. I'll turn him loose otherwise. Don't have patience for a dog myself."

And then he dropped the leash and resumed his post.

Lizzie looked up at Darcy, who was regarding the small dog with horror. "We can't just take another man's dog," he said.

"We can't leave him! You heard Mr. Parry—he'll be homeless unless someone takes him in. And take a look around—who's likely to take home a stray dog?"

"He's filthy," Darcy protested.

"He'll wash! Won't you, Guy?" Lizzie patted the dog's head. The creature leaned into her touch and whined. "Oh, Darcy. You can't say no to him."

"So you'll be taking him home, then?"

"Oh. Well . . . er, I mean. My mother . . ."

"Ha. Exactly what I thought! You don't want him either."

Lizzie looked down at the poor dog. He was trembling and cold, likely missing his master and confused at the loss of his home. Her mother would have an absolute fit, but maybe Lizzie could sneak him into the kitchen, bribe the scullery maid to give him a bath . . . and then find him a home? Yes, that was what she'd do.

"Yes, I do. I'll take him home, and then we'll figure things out from there."

"You can't help yourself, can you?" Darcy asked.

"I'm sure I don't know what you're talking about."

Darcy did her the kindness of not pressing the matter. "All right, then. Now, did you find anything?"

"Not a lot," she admitted, standing and coaxing the dog along on his makeshift leash. "Although I did manage to talk to some of the Frenchwomen on the next street over. I'm not sure how well I made myself understood, but they did give me a name that we can try to chase down. Josette Beaufort."

Darcy stopped suddenly, causing Lizzie to nearly stumble. "Darcy?" she asked. "What is it?"

He stared straight ahead, seemingly at nothing. "Josette Beaufort," he repeated. "Now that is a name I have not heard in a while."

FIVE

*In Which Darcy Reckons with His Past, and
Faces a Rather Inconvenient Rejection*

"WHO IS JOSETTE BEAUFORT?" Lizzie asked.

Memory came to Darcy in flashes—a gentle smile, hands clasped in a candlelit ballroom, the whispers of half a dozen society young ladies. Her downcast eyes, the tightness in his chest that last day, the slick heat of shame . . .

What on earth did *Josette Beaufort* have to do with a burned-out storehouse near the docks?

Lizzie's voice reached him through a fog. "Darcy. What is the matter? Who is Josette Beaufort?"

"Um . . . she, well, you see, she's a lady."

"A lady," Lizzie repeated. "How descriptive. Care to elaborate?"

Something about the way Lizzie teased him shook him out of his stunned reverie. "She's a young lady. Her grandfather and my father are business acquaintances. Were. Her grandfather has since passed."

63

"So you've met," Lizzie stated.

Oh heaven help him, he'd have to tell her the whole story. "We've more than met. There was a time—a few years ago, mind you—that we, uh, briefly . . . courted?"

"I see," Lizzie said, and Darcy wasn't sure whether he should be relieved or concerned that she appeared to be unmoved by this revelation.

"It wasn't even for an entire season," he rushed to assure her. Then added, "It's complicated."

"How so?"

"In the way that everything with my father is complicated," Darcy said with a sigh. "Look, can we go back to the carriage? It feels rather untoward having this conversation out in the open."

He expected Lizzie to make a sharp quip, but she simply nodded and tugged gently on Guy's leash. The little dog trotted after her, and Darcy resigned himself both to the fact that the dog was theirs and to the unpleasantness of the conversation that awaited him.

They returned to the carriage, took their seats, and were on their way before Darcy said in an awkward burst, "It's not that I was *never* going to tell you about her. It's just that we never have gotten around to talking about it."

"Do go on, or I shall start to imagine the most scandalous of things."

His eyes widened and his pulse sped up. "Nothing scandalous, I assure you! You already know all my most scandalous secrets."

"Good," she said. "Then this should be quite easy to explain."

Oh, Lizzie. Darcy couldn't help but smile at the way she'd neatly backed him into that corner. "Miss Josette Beaufort is an heiress. She's half French, but she was brought up here in London by her grandmother Mrs. Cavendish."

"Half French? What a thing to be in London society."

"You know what the ton is like. They love their French brandy and silks. But an actual French lady . . ."

"The poor girl," Lizzie said, and there was real sympathy in her voice. "I can't imagine many proper society mamas wanting her as a match for their darling sons."

Was it his imagination, or was Lizzie watching him extra closely? "Quite the contrary—she had many suitors. Her dowry was . . . not insignificant."

"Oh, so you courted her long enough to learn the exact amount of her dowry?"

"No! I mean . . . it wasn't like that. My father's firm represented her grandfather, so my father had an . . . idea. It was likely just much more accurate than anyone else's guesses."

Luckily, Lizzie seemed more amused than upset to hear the details of him courting another woman. "All right, then. She has beauty, money, connections . . ."

"It was just . . . awful timing. Her dance card was always full, but . . . it seemed as though she never had any serious offers. She was brought up by her grandmother, but little was known about her father. And then there was the scandal of her mother. She was quite the diamond of the first water, but she ran off with a Frenchman."

"I loathe that term," Lizzie complained. "Women are human beings, not jewels for men to buy."

"I know, I know," Darcy said. "Sorry."

"No, go on. So, really, it was just a small matter of a long-ago scandal that kept her from receiving serious marriage proposals. Is that what prevented you from proposing marriage?"

"I— What, no! I genuinely enjoyed her company. I thought her a very accomplished young lady. She has a poise to her . . ." Darcy fumbled for the words to explain his opinion of Josette Beaufort that would not give Lizzie reason to think he still had feelings for her. "Truth be told, I felt sorry for her. It's not her fault she was born in France or grew up during a time of social upheaval, but she doesn't indulge in self-pity."

He'd hoped that would be satisfactory to Lizzie, but then she asked, "What is she like?"

Darcy shifted uncomfortably, and looked down at the dog, who was also staring at him. "Lizzie, if this is too uncomfortable for you . . ."

Now, she revealed a small ironic smile. "It's not, although it does seem to be making you rather restless."

Damn this lady and her ability to make him so unsure of himself! "I just don't want you to get any false impressions!"

"So tell me what happened," she implored him. "Darcy, we've known each other a year, but we both have friends and acquaintances from before then. You're the Pemberley heir. I am not so naive to think that you haven't had interest from other young ladies before." Her cheeks seemed to pink at the word *interest*, but she rushed to add, "That doesn't hurt my feelings."

Relief washed over him. "Really?"

"The only way I'll be cross is if you keep things from me," she told him with a playful smile. "I promise I shall not dislike Miss Beaufort unless I have valid reason to do so."

"I did like her," Darcy allowed. "But as we got to know each other, I began to suspect that we'd never be well suited to each other. First of all, she hoped to marry quickly and be settled away from London. She doesn't like the prying eyes and gossip that come with being on the marriage mart."

"And you'd never settle away from London," Lizzie concluded.

"Maybe one day. But not now, and not while I am establishing my career." Lizzie seemed surprised by that, but now was not the time to talk about Darcy's far-off future dreams. "And I certainly was not seriously interested in marrying two years ago. I believe she wanted a husband who would be more of a society gentleman than my work allows me to be."

"What happened?"

"Why do you think anything happened?"

"Because you keep looking out the window or down at your hands rather than at me. Something happened."

Darcy shook his head and forced himself to look at her. Arguing with a fellow solicitor was rather difficult. "I proposed."

"You *what*?"

"Proposed," Darcy repeated, fighting the urge to once again

look away from Lizzie. "Clearly, she turned me down. And I am grateful she did, really. But it was all so long ago—"

"Two years is not *that* long ago!"

He supposed she was right. He'd known Lizzie nearly a year and he'd yet to tell her this. "It's not that I didn't want to tell you, you know. I wasn't trying to hide it. It's just . . . we never discuss this sort of thing."

He waited for what she'd say next, hoping that she wouldn't be angry. Honestly, he might have told her sooner if it wasn't for the fact that whenever he even made mention of attachments or intentions, she seemed to vigorously change the subject.

Like now. "What does she look like?"

For a moment, Darcy thought she was asking because she was jealous. But then, understanding slid into place. "Lizzie, you can't actually think that Josette—"

"Why not? I asked the Frenchwomen back there for help finding this woman, and I described a lady who was tall and brunette and the only name they gave me was Josette Beaufort. How else might they have come across her, if she hadn't been present in the area?"

"That's quite a leap!" Darcy wasn't sure why he felt so defensive, except that Lizzie didn't know Josette. "If she had been skulking about the Mullins Brothers storehouse, someone would have noticed. And besides, it doesn't make any sense that she would want to set it on fire!"

"But Jack did say he thought he'd seen her before. Is she tall and brunette?"

Darcy sighed. "Yes."

"Well, then. Let's go ask her where she was yesterday afternoon!"

"I can't simply call on her after not seeing her for two years and say, 'Good day, are you well, and, by the way, have you set fire to any storehouses near the docks lately?' "

"I agree," Lizzie said. "That would be a terrible interrogation strategy."

"Lizzie, be serious!"

"I am! Josette is a lead."

"You must trust me when I say that it is not in Josette's nature to do something like this," Darcy said.

"I do trust you. But I also must follow leads. Don't think of her as a suspect but as a person of interest. Perhaps there's a simple explanation."

"Perhaps," Darcy allowed.

"Now that's settled, what is her address?"

Darcy merely gaped at her in astonishment. "We aren't going to call on her *now*."

"No time like the present!"

"Lizzie. Look at your hems."

Lizzie looked down. Guy sat on the floor of the carriage, tucked into Lizzie's skirts, brushing soot and muck on the pale gray linen. He looked up at her rather balefully, but Lizzie didn't seem to mind.

"Oh," was all she said.

"I don't know how well Josette will receive me," Darcy

admitted. "We parted on . . . not exactly unfriendly terms, but awkward ones. And she is a proper lady. We must be careful about how we approach her. And we'll need a chaperone, or her grandmother will think it awfully improper that we are calling on her together."

"Fine," Lizzie relented. "I'll clean up, and I'll find us a proper chaperone. Can we go tomorrow, though?"

Old Tomlinson would just love that. But Darcy couldn't think of a good reason to tell her no, so he nodded. He'd deal with work tomorrow.

"Now, there is still the matter of getting inside that building," Lizzie continued. "If there is any evidence that's been overlooked, I want to get in there before work crews start making repairs and trample all over everything."

"I suppose I could petition the magistrate for a special search permit," Darcy said.

Lizzie's eyes went wide with excitement. "Is that something we can do?"

"It is a good alternative to breaking and entering," Darcy told her dryly.

"Can you take care of that? And if you drop me off at Longbourn, I'll see what I can find about who owns the buildings around the Mullinses' storehouse. Perhaps there was a jealous or angry neighbor who wanted to destroy the business."

"Thank you," Darcy said, gladdened by her willingness to consider other options. If they were lucky, they'd find this villain without having to bother with Josette Beaufort.

Lizzie smiled as if she could read his thoughts. "Half the trouble of finding a good suspect is eliminating the bad ones."

After seeing Lizzie and Guy off at Longbourn & Sons, Darcy ordered the carriage to take him to the courthouse straight-away.

As it turned out, the paperwork for a search permit took far longer to fill out than he'd anticipated, and then when he finally handed it off to a serious-looking clerk with heavy lines around his eyes from squinting at too many documents, it was past midafternoon. Knowing that it would take a while for his application to work its slow way through the cogs of bureaucracy, Darcy ducked out to a nearby pub, popular with other solicitors, for a late midday meal. By the time he got back, the clerk still had no answer for him, so Darcy paced about for three-quarters of an hour. He'd pay for it later at work, but he couldn't help it—he was invested in the case now, too. And it was all because of Josette Beaufort.

It had been such an awkward time in his life. He'd barely been out of school and was struggling under the weight of his father's expectations and his own ambitions. Wickham had been around, making a muck of things, and Darcy had felt stretched in too many different directions. Courting Josette had felt . . . nice. She hadn't expected very much of him except for his atten-tion and respect. Proposing had felt expected, even if his heart hadn't stirred when he looked at her.

Well, to be fair, no lady had ever stirred his heart until he met Lizzie. And even then, he mostly felt exasperation at first.

For Josette to reappear in his life now, after so much time, felt disorienting. He could hardly imagine Lizzie and Josette in the same room, so different they were. And now with Lizzie in his life, it seemed laughable that he'd ever considered marrying Josette. There was nothing wrong with her, of course, and he'd truly never minded her French parentage. But Josette was reserved, proper, and careful to speak. She was rarely animated, although she wasn't without passion. She bore the injustices that society dealt her with a stoicism that Darcy had admired at the time.

Lizzie, on the other hand, spoke her mind loudly and frequently. Darcy preferred to think of her as unconventional rather than improper because, as it turned out, Lizzie had impeccable manners . . . just very little patience for foolishness or injustice. Lizzie was like a bubbling brook whose passions burst forth in great spurts; and while he suspected that she didn't complain nearly half as much as she could about the injustice of being a female in society, she made no secret of how she felt about said injustices.

Lizzie was also incredibly persuasive, which is why he was wearing a rut in the courthouse floor instead of sitting at his desk back at Pemberley. Yet strangely, Darcy found that he didn't mind very much. She had a knack for picking up interesting cases, that was for certain.

"Mr. Darcy?" a clerk called out, and all heads swiveled in his direction. He turned and stalked up to the desk.

"Yes?"

The clerk slid across his application for a search permit. "Denied," he reported in a bored tone.

"What!" Darcy snatched up the paper and inspected the bottom of the document, where the six-letter word was clearly spelled out, along with the magistrate's signature. "Why?"

The clerk seemed used to such questions, for he didn't show any emotion or interest. "Not for me to know."

Darcy had expected the paperwork to take some time, but he hadn't expected the application to be *denied*. He scoured the bottom of the page for some reason. Had he missed something, some technicality that he'd overlooked in his rush?

But there was no explanation.

"Where's Lord Templeton?" he demanded.

The clerk gave him a tired look. "No appeals."

"But . . ." Darcy looked down at the paper again. "I made no mistakes in this form. This should not have been denied."

"No appeals," the clerk repeated, then pointedly looked beyond Darcy. "Next."

Darcy was forced to step aside, but he wasn't about to give up. He'd never had a request denied outright without a legitimate reason. Had he inadvertently done something to put himself on Lord Templeton's blacklist? No, Tomlinson had kept him far too busy rewriting memos and chasing down paperwork lately to get in trouble with any of the magistrates. He could hardly remember the last time he'd stepped foot in a courtroom, and it had been months since he'd appeared before Templeton.

There had to be an explanation.

Darcy pulled out his pocket watch to check the time. He'd already disappeared for nearly five hours on an errand that should have taken one, two at the most. And the workday was nearly over, which meant it made no sense to return to Pemberley's offices. He could just as easily be lambasted for his disappearance tomorrow morning, although not returning tonight meant he would pay for it.

Darcy snapped the watch shut with a decisive click and thought of Lizzie, of the case, and how much it mattered to her. So be it.

It took him two hours, three bribes, and one very humiliating conversation with Lord Templeton's butler before he finally tracked the magistrate down at his gentleman's club. Luckily for Darcy, his name carried enough weight that he was granted entry and shown to a shadowy room with a handful of men quietly engaged in conversation or reading the papers. The magistrate sat before a roaring fire, smoking a cigar while reading the *Sun*. He looked up with heavily lidded eyes to regard Darcy, slightly out of breath and not at all dressed for an evening out. "Mr. Darcy," the magistrate said, not sounding surprised in the least. "I expected you, although not until tomorrow at the earliest."

This caught Darcy off guard. "I beg your pardon, sir?"

"Sit," the magistrate said, setting down his paper. "You look as though you've run all the way here."

Darcy sat, and did not share that he had, in fact, run at least part of the way. "I'm sorry to disturb your evening," he began, trying to hide the fact that he was still panting a bit. "But in regard to my application for a search permit this afternoon—"

The man waved a hand. "Yes, yes. Tell me, Mr. Darcy—why exactly do you want to search that storehouse?"

Darcy paused. "Sir, my application clearly stated—"

"Yes, I read it. But I am asking you. Why do you want to search that storehouse?"

He felt as though the magistrate were asking him a trick question, and Darcy did not like tricks. He wished that Lizzie were here. She was charming and clever, and she'd likely understand what the man was asking before him and give him some sort of subtle indication.

But Lizzie wouldn't be permitted past the doors of the club, and so it was up to him.

"I believe my client is hiding something that could be of value to this case," he said.

"Your client," the magistrate repeated. His gray, bushy eyebrows rose just a little.

"Yes . . ."

"And who else are you consulting with on this case?"

Ah. Darcy was beginning to understand. It wasn't he who'd crossed Lord Templeton lately—it was Lizzie. He couldn't help but feel a slight twinge of fond exasperation toward her and her tendency to ruffle feathers. "Longbourn and Sons, sir."

"Mm-hmm." The magistrate was no fool. "And in particular, Longbourn's newest solicitor?"

"Yes, sir." Darcy kept his chin up. He would not be ashamed for his professional—or personal—association with Lizzie, no matter what this man thought.

But even as his pride took over, a quiet voice in the back of Darcy's mind wondered: *How does he know about Lizzie's new case already?*

"A bit of advice, Mr. Darcy. These early days practicing law will determine the course of your career. Think of it as setting sail into unknown waters. Your father has provided you with a good ship and a strong crew in Pemberley and Associates. But it seems to me that you'd sooner cast yourself out in a raft with this Miss Bennet and tackle waves that neither of you is prepared to navigate. Now, your father's ship is never far, and is ready to pluck you out of dangerous waters, but the farther you drift out to sea with Miss Bennet, the less likely you are to be whisked back to safety." He paused heavily and said, "Make sure you don't chart an unsound course."

Only years of training kept Darcy's fury under control. How dare this man presume that he knew Darcy, that he knew what Darcy wanted or where he was headed? And how dare he speak so ill of Lizzie? What he wanted to do was stand and raise his voice and tell this smug old man that Lizzie showed more promise in her left pinkie than most men twice her age, and that he'd follow her to the ends of the map any day rather than stay the same, tired old course with his father's firm.

But, Darcy realized, that was exactly what Lord Templeton *wanted*.

He was trying to throw Darcy off his true purpose for coming here.

"Thank you for your wisdom, sir," Darcy managed to say. His words were above reproach, but his tone was frosty. "However, I am afraid I am not here for career advice, no matter how much I appreciate your generosity in offering it. I am here to understand why my request was denied when, as far as I can tell, I filed all the paperwork correctly."

Lord Templeton didn't react, except to signal for some unseen staff member. "You did file the paperwork correctly."

"Then why—" Darcy was cut off by the appearance of a black-clad man who firmly took his elbow, signaling the end of his welcome.

"This conversation is over," said the magistrate, picking up his paper once more.

"I will appeal," Darcy said, twisting about to look at the magistrate. "First thing in the morning. I'll take it above your head."

His words got the attention of every other gentleman in the room. Darcy could feel the prickle of their judgmental gazes as they looked at him behind pipes and newspapers, but kept his own eyes locked on Lord Templeton.

"Then you'll have very far to go indeed," said the magistrate, face already hidden once more by his paper. "Because that storehouse is protected under official Crown business."

SIX

In Which the Bennet Women
Consider Numerous Proposals

"AND THEN HE ADMITTED to actually proposing to her! My suspect!" Lizzie's voice tipped perilously toward a wail.

"Oh my," Jane said rather mildly, considering Lizzie's distress.

"Is that all you have to say? Darcy has actually proposed to someone before, and I find out about it during the course of an investigation! What if she's the criminal? What if Darcy almost married a criminal?"

"Well, he's not married now," Jane pointed out. "That's what matters."

"Ugh!"

Lizzie threw herself down upon the bed, burying her face in her pillow. The sisters were taking advantage of the first bit of peace they'd managed to finagle since Lizzie had returned home the previous evening with a scruffy dog in tow. As Lizzie had predicted, Guy's arrival had upset the delicate balance of her mother's moods and her sisters' whims. There had been much crying and shouting, and Lizzie had greatly embellished Guy's sorry predicament to convince her mother to let him stay the night in the shed. By breakfast, Lydia and Kitty had declared him the most precious creature they'd ever laid eyes on and took it upon themselves to give him a bath. Lizzie was not one to waste the opportunity and pulled Jane upstairs.

"Lizzie, you're being dramatic," Jane said, stroking her hair. "Miss Beaufort is in his past. You said he seemed utterly surprised to hear her name. For as large as London is, it really can feel like a small town, especially among society members."

"I suppose." Lizzie knew her sister was right about connections, but it still irked her. "But why didn't he tell me?"

"Have you told him about every young man you've ever flirted with?" Jane countered. "Did he hear about Mr. Mullins for the first time two days ago?"

"Jack never courted me! We worked together."

"But you call him Jack, and he calls you Lizzie," Jane pointed out. "And Darcy has said that he and Josette were ill-suited."

"I suppose," Lizzie said.

"So then, what's the matter?" Jane tugged at Lizzie's shoulder until she was sitting up, albeit with a grumpy expression. "You're being more dramatic than Lydia and Kitty put together."

Lizzie scowled, but then Jane nudged her with a sly smile and Lizzie felt herself relent. It was impossible to be angry at Jane— she was too perfect. "It's not that he courted another young lady once. And I suppose it's not even the marriage proposal that upset me. It was what he said about them not being well suited. He said that she wanted to settle down and leave London behind. And he said he didn't want those things."

Jane's head was tilted to the side. "All right . . ."

"And I didn't know any of that."

"Ah," Jane said, sounding as if she understood. If she did, Lizzie was desperate for her older sister to share, because the tumult of feelings inside of her was making her nauseous.

"You and Bingley talk about the future, don't you?"

"Of course," Jane said, and a small, sweet smile graced her face, as it always did when her beau was brought up. "But, Lizzie—"

"And even though he hasn't asked for your hand yet, you know you'll marry and you've talked about where you'll live and how many children you want and if you'll spend summers in the country and—"

"Lizzie, slow down!" Jane was laughing, but she also looked a bit concerned. "Yes, we've discussed all that. Although don't tell Mama—she's already got it in her head that he needs nudging along."

"But if Bingley were to ask for your hand tomorrow, you'd say yes?"

"Of course," Jane said.

"Ughhh!" Lizzie flopped back so she was lying across the bed.

"Lizzie, are you saying that you and Darcy haven't . . . discussed the future?"

"Oh no, we've discussed it plenty," Lizzie assured her, staring up at the ceiling. "I'm going to keep working with Longbourn, and eventually make partner, once Papa figures out a legal loophole to ensure that no idiot man can take it away from me once he's gone. And Darcy is going to rise up through the ranks at Pemberley and prove to his father that he's a worthy successor. When we've both achieved the career recognition we deserve . . ." Lizzie faltered.

"I see," said Jane. "Have you both discussed what you want your lives to look like, *together*? Nothing to do with Longbourn or Pemberley?"

Lizzie didn't answer her, because they hadn't. For nearly a year, she had merely enjoyed Darcy's company as she got to know him as a colleague and a friend . . . a friend that she on occasion kissed in between debates about the law and working cases. But lately she'd realized just how much she'd come to count on him, and now . . . well, she didn't want to imagine a future *without* him. But she also couldn't imagine a future without her work and doing what brought her joy. Learning that Darcy had actually proposed to someone else, even if it was in the past, sent Lizzie into a sudden maelstrom of nerves and uncertainty. Did Darcy want a wife? Someone to keep house, and stay home and raise children?

And what if Lizzie didn't want those things? Would Darcy still want her?

"Why don't you talk with him about it?" Jane suggested, as if it were that simple.

"Because how can I ever get married, Jane?" Lizzie surprised herself with the forcefulness of her words. "The moment I say 'I do,' everything I have becomes Darcy's!"

"Oh," Jane said, as if she finally understood. "But Darcy is—"

"Wonderful and smart and wouldn't take advantage, I know," Lizzie interrupted crossly. "But still. What I have would no longer be *mine*. And if he wanted me to quit working, he could demand it."

"Darcy wouldn't do that," Jane said with confidence that Lizzie wished she felt. "And he would respect that you want to inherit Papa's firm and not stand in your way."

"Maybe." More than maybe, likely. Darcy was honorable. He would defer to her in all matters concerning Longbourn. But Lizzie would always know, in the back of her mind, that he could take it all away from her in an instant. And even if he never did, Lizzie wasn't certain she wanted to live with that knowledge. "How can we ever be married if I know that in order to be a wife, I'd have to give up everything I'd worked for, even in name only?"

Jane had no answers for her. Her lips were turned into a tiny frown and her forehead was creased. "Lizzie, I had no idea you were so worried about this. Why don't you just talk to him about it?"

Lizzie wanted to cover her eyes and hide from Jane's reproachful gaze. Why didn't she just ask him? Because doing so would be admitting that she had entertained the idea of marriage, despite how impossible it felt. And what if Darcy hadn't considered it? What then? "Jane, you don't understand—it's not as simple with me and Darcy."

"Well, you won't know for certain until you talk with him about it," Jane said, sounding brisk and no-nonsense. "Wouldn't you rather weather an uncomfortable conversation now than worry about it all your waking hours?"

"No," Lizzie replied stubbornly.

Jane laughed then. "I don't mean to make light of your troubles, my dear, but I don't think they're as dire as you're making them out to be. Darcy has withstood a great deal, including our mama, and he hasn't gone anywhere yet. Maybe he hasn't proposed, but I think his behavior otherwise says a great deal about his character."

Lizzie knew Jane was right. Darcy's behavior was always honorable. He didn't mind that she was a delightfully eccentric young lady trained in the law. It did not win her many friends, but she was not interested in balls and tea parties. However, how long before the gossip turned nasty or her reputation suffered a blow? What if something happened that would lead Darcy to feel *obliged* to marry her?

The last thing she wanted to be was an obligation.

"Lizzie, do you want to marry Darcy?"

The question caught her off guard. She looked at Jane and felt afraid to answer. Afraid, even though it was just her beloved sister! "Yes?" she said. "But also . . ."

"Not right now?" Jane suggested.

"Yes!" Lizzie felt as if a great stone had been lifted off her chest. "Exactly. I like things as they are. Or, as they were before—"

The door to their bedroom opened and Mary swept in, looking harried. "There you are! Lizzie, I don't think Mama is very happy about what Kitty and Lydia are doing with your dog. Jane, are you going to the high street soon?"

"He's not my dog," Lizzie said.

"Yes," Jane said. "I'm running errands for Mama."

"Oh, thank heavens," Mary said, rolling her eyes dramatically. "I need to get out of this house and away from Kitty and Lydia."

"What have they done to Guy?" Lizzie asked, now growing concerned for the poor creature.

But Mary didn't respond, for there was the sound of small paws on the carpet and then Guy himself came bounding through the open bedroom door as if looking for escape. The two eldest Bennet sisters gasped while Mary just tsked and shook her head.

Guy's bath had revealed a much lighter coat than Lizzie had first realized. His fur was the color of cream around his face and legs, but his back was a light golden color. He had been carefully combed and Lizzie recognized Kitty's second-best blue hair ribbon tied neatly around his neck in a bow. Tiny pink ribbons held back the floof that had previously covered his eyes, and his excess fur had been trimmed on his legs and around his paws.

Jane let out a strangled laugh. "Is his hair . . . *curled*?"

"Yes," Mary confirmed.

Before Lizzie could react, Lydia and Kitty burst into the room, falling over themselves giggling. "Chouchou!" Lydia cried.

"I beg your pardon?" Lizzie asked as the poor dog jumped

on the bed and tried to press himself into Lizzie's arms. His eyes pleaded with her to save him. "You are not allowed up here, sir!"

"Doesn't he look divine?" Lydia asked.

"I prefer cats," Mary said, edging away from the dog.

Kitty held out her arms for Guy. "Here, Chouchou!"

"His name is Guy," Lizzie protested. The dog looked up at the sound of his true name. "See? He knows it."

"Guy sounds gauche," Lydia informed her. "We've renamed him."

"He's not yours to rename!" Lizzie hadn't been overly thrilled to have the dog thrust into her care, but this was too much. "He was entrusted to me and Darcy, and his name is Guy."

"Chouchou," Lydia repeated stubbornly. *"Mama!"*

The remaining Bennet sisters cringed, and a moment later Mrs. Bennet swept into the room. "Elizabeth Bennet! Get that nasty ratcatcher off the bed this instant!"

Guy trembled, sensing he was in trouble. "Come on," Lizzie cajoled, picking up the dog. "Dogs stay off the furniture."

"Dirty creatures stay out on the streets where they belong!" Mrs. Bennet huffed. "What on earth were you thinking, bringing him back here? He could have fleas!"

"He doesn't," Kitty protested. "We checked. And he's not dirty any longer, Mama—doesn't he look precious? Sarah Lawrenson will be so jealous when she sees him!"

Mrs. Bennet paid Guy no mind. "I don't understand why Mr. Darcy dumped him on our doorstep! He ought to know better."

Lizzie and Jane exchanged pained looks. Darcy was not

Mrs. Bennet's favorite person at the moment, least of all because of the dog. Mrs. Bennet took his lack of a proposal to Lizzie as a personal affront. Given the conversation that Lizzie had just had with her sister, she really did not want to go down that path with her mother. "Darcy didn't dump Guy on me, Mama."

"Chouchou," Lydia corrected.

"In fact, Darcy very gallantly offered to take him home," Lizzie continued. "He said that he wouldn't dream of burdening us with his care, but I insisted. I . . . fell in love with Guy. Isn't he just the sweetest?"

Looking down at the dog, Lizzie felt a twinge of affection. Now that he was cleaned up, he looked much more respectable, and Lizzie couldn't help but smile at the way he gazed up at her. He was clearly intelligent, and as long as she kept Lydia and Kitty from spoiling him, Lizzie found that she didn't terribly mind the thought of keeping him around.

Mrs. Bennet crossed her arms and looked skeptically at the dog. "Is that your second-best hair ribbon, Kitty?"

"And besides, he's practically an orphan," Lizzie continued. "He lost his owner in a tragic, tragic fire and he needs love and attention, and a happy home. And couldn't we provide that for him, much better than Darcy can? You know he works such long hours and lives all alone in his town house. Guy would be absolutely depressed to lose the only family he's ever known, and then be left alone all day."

"Mr. Darcy would hardly be alone if he had a wife." Mrs. Bennet sniffed, and Lizzie could have kicked herself for opening that line of argument. But, if there was one rhetorical strategy that was always effective with her mother, it was pathos. And while Mrs. Bennet might not have been moved by the plight of an abandoned dog, she was motivated by pride. If she believed that Darcy wanted the dog but could not take care of him as he ought, then she wouldn't turn down the opportunity to appear to be the bigger person. "All right," she relented. "But if he soils the carpet or sleeps on the furniture or—"

"He won't!" Lydia promised.

"I'll see to it," Lizzie said. Guy looked up at her, and she couldn't help but smile a little at his soulful brown eyes.

"Now that you're all here, I think it's a perfect time to discuss expectations for the dinner," Mrs. Bennet announced.

Mary sighed, and Lydia and Kitty began to make kissing sounds. "Jane's getting married, Jane's getting married!"

"No one has proposed to me, thank you!" Jane protested.

"Not yet!" Mrs. Bennet's eyes gleamed with delight. "But after our little dinner party, it will be a certain thing!"

Lizzie and Jane exchanged worried looks. Mrs. Bennet had been pleased when Jane and Mr. Bingley had formally met after Lizzie and Darcy cleared his name the previous year, and then overjoyed to see a genuine affection grow between them. Lizzie had been pleased, too. Although Jane was not particularly outgoing when it came to expressing her feelings, Lizzie knew when her sister was smitten—and the best part was, Bingley seemed equally besotted.

However, this wasn't enough for Mrs. Bennet. It had been

nearly a year and no proposal. Jane didn't seem worried, but Mrs. Bennet was fearful that Bingley would move on to other young ladies unless Jane managed to secure his hand; and so she had decided to try to force matters with a carefully plotted dinner party at which she intended to make it abundantly clear to Mr. Bingley that he *must* propose to Jane. No amount of pleading with her to let things take their natural course would sway her.

"Mama, it's just a dinner party," Lizzie said now. "I'm sure we don't need instructions on how to behave. We aren't children. Well, at least some of us aren't."

She said this with a pointed look at Lydia and Kitty, who were very much children, and playing with Guy.

"And what do you know of dinner parties and proposals, Lizzie? You've consorted with Mr. Darcy for nearly a year, and with no hint of a proposal or attachment. Speaking of which—I expect Mr. Darcy to be present."

"Is that so Darcy will feel influenced to propose to Lizzie as well?" Lydia asked.

"Darcy isn't proposing," Lizzie told her quickly.

"Why not?"

"Because he isn't, and that's that!"

"Not with that attitude, he won't," Mrs. Bennet reprimanded her. "No matter, we'll work on Mr. Darcy later. But we need a well-rounded party, of course—Mr. Bingley's sisters were invited, although they've not bothered to respond. But I invited Charlotte just in case. We cannot have any guests that might detract from Jane's loveliness, but we also don't want

Mr. Bingley to feel pressured."

"God forbid," Lizzie muttered to Jane, who'd had no say thus far on the dinner that was supposedly going to alter the course of her life.

"We shall keep the conversation light and cheerful!" Mrs. Bennet seemed to direct this instruction at Lizzie in particular. "No talk of sad things, or business! Kitty, you may bring up Miss Hartford's recent engagement, and Lydia, you may give your opinions on spring weddings."

"They'll be as subtle as sledgehammers," Lizzie whispered.

"And then we shall retire to the drawing room, but Lizzie, you'll need to find a way to entice Mr. Darcy to come with us and leave your father and Bingley alone so that he can inquire as to Bingley's intentions. With any luck, we'll have a proposal within the hour!"

Lydia, Kitty, and Mrs. Bennet dissolved into squeals and descended upon Jane like a swarm of hungry hens. Lizzie shared a rare look of solidarity with Mary, who appeared bored with the conversation.

"He'll have to propose then," Kitty said. "Won't he, Jane?"

"I don't know," she said mildly. "I suppose we'll just have to wait and see."

Lydia tsked dismissively. "Of course he will! He'll come bearing exotic flowers and chocolates, and after dinner he shall recite a poem he's composed about Jane's breathtaking beauty! He'll prostrate himself before her, declaring his love, and when she consents to be his wife, he shall present her with jewels—no!

One of those charming necklaces that looks like a pendant but is a secret locket—Felicity Carlton received one from her fiancé with an opal and it's divine! It contains a lock of his hair, and—"

"I'm sorry, have you met Mr. Bingley?" Lizzie demanded. She had nothing against the man and would be very glad to see him become her brother-in-law, but she doubted he'd even read a poem in his life, much less composed one. "Is this how you think he ought to propose, or how you'd want someone to propose to you?"

"What's wrong with chocolates and flowers and poetry?"

"I think it's a fine way to propose," Kitty said.

"Now, girls. Remember that this is about Jane! Jane is the one who shall be married!"

"Hopefully," Jane managed to say, inciting a round of objections from all her sisters and her mother.

"He shall propose," Lizzie promised her. "I'm not sure we need to go quite to these extreme lengths to force the matter."

"Hush," her mother told her. "You may be a professional lady now, but there are things a mother knows! Just as I know that you're still sneaking off to see Mr. Darcy while you're at work."

Lizzie hadn't anticipated this but tried to brush off the accusation. "I don't know what you mean, Mama. Mr. Darcy comes to Longbourn, and occasionally I'll see him at Pemberley but—"

"You were seen together! Stepping out of a carriage yesterday! Mrs. Kittredge saw you!"

"We were consulting on a case, and he wished to escort me to the courthouse; that's all!"

Mrs. Bennet studied her, and Lizzie felt only a little bad about lying to her mother. All right, more than a little bad. Lizzie generally considered herself honest. She didn't lie for the fun of it, and when she did lie, well . . . it was the useful kind of lies. The types to reassure or spare feelings, not liable to hurt anyone. But this . . . this was a bald-faced lie.

"And are you seeing Mr. Darcy today?" her mother asked.

Guilt overcame her. She couldn't lie. "Er, well . . . yes. We must question a . . . witness."

"Chaperoned?"

Lizzie panicked. She glanced at Jane, who was shaking her head ever so slightly. "Of course!"

"Who is your chaperone? If you are leaving the Longbourn offices, I insist on knowing who your companion is."

"It's Jane!"

Mrs. Bennet turned on Jane. "Is this true?"

"Yes, Mama," Jane said, like a saint. "We're calling on a Miss Beaufort today. Darcy will take care of the introductions."

"Beaufort," her mother muttered, trying to mentally place the family. "I don't know any Beauforts, Lizzie."

"Her mother was a Cavendish," Lizzie said.

Mrs. Bennet's eyes went as round as saucers. "Lizzie! She's not related to the *Duke of Devonshire*?"

"I don't believe so," Lizzie said, because surely Darcy might have mentioned that. "Maybe very distantly."

"Unless—are you referring to the Essex Cavendishes?"

"Perhaps?"

"Now that's a good family," Mrs. Bennet said, snapping her fingers. "But they had a scandal, if I recall correctly."

"Oh?" Lizzie asked. Mrs. Bennet had two chief tasks in life. One was securing matches for her five daughters, and the other was obtaining gossip. Her encyclopedic knowledge of the ton was, Lizzie had to admit, at times quite useful.

"It was an age ago. I haven't heard anyone speak of it in a very long time. And now I can't quite remember, but there was definitely a rushed marriage? Oh, something to that effect."

"Do you remember the circumstances?" Lizzie asked, torn between wanting to question her mother further and hoping that this long-ago scandal wouldn't foil her plans.

"Oh, Lizzie! I don't know. I'm a very busy person, you know. Do you think it is easy, seeing to a household and being the mother of five daughters? There is no end to my troubles." She paused, and Lizzie waited with bated breath. "You and Jane may go anyway. But, Lizzie? Make sure that Mr. Darcy comes to dinner!"

Lizzie and Jane made quite the spectacle when they arrived at the offices of Pemberley & Associates with Guy in tow. It had not been easy to wrestle control of Guy from Lydia and Kitty, and Lizzie had insisted they stop at the market and purchase a more dignified leash for him so she didn't have to pull the poor dog around by the fraying rope.

Guy's nails clicked on the shining marble of the Pemberley

foyer and Jane whispered, "I should have stayed outside with him."

"Nonsense. He's being the perfect gentleman." This was perhaps wishful thinking on her part as Guy began to strain at his leash, sniffing about the lobby with the urgency of a hunting hound on a scent. "Guy, no!"

Lizzie recognized the clerk behind the front desk—Mr. Reeves. His eyes widened at the sight of Guy. "Miss, I don't think dogs are allowed in here," he whispered.

"We won't be staying long," she promised. "Mr. Darcy, please."

"I'll fetch him," Mr. Reeves said, casting a nervous glance over his shoulder.

"I know where his office—"

"No, really, miss. It's best if you wait." The clerk winced in what seemed an apologetic manner and scurried off.

Jane gave her a quizzical look, and Lizzie shrugged. But a vague sense of unease took over, and Lizzie tried to peer after the clerk, down the hall that led to the desks and offices. The hall was stately and subdued, with only the weak murmur of voices in the distance. There were no other clients waiting to be seen, but there was a peculiar tension in the building that Lizzie couldn't put her finger on.

They didn't have to wait long before the clerk slinked back in sight, looking extremely nervous. "A moment, miss," he said, retaking his seat. He cast another glance at Guy, whom Lizzie had managed to coax into a sitting position.

"Is everything all right?" Lizzie asked.

"Of course," he replied, but he didn't meet her eye. She frowned. This wasn't at all like him—usually she asked about his wife, and he told her about the antics of their small daughter, Julia.

Something strange was afoot, but before Lizzie could dwell on it any further, Mr. Tomlinson appeared. Lizzie sighed but plastered on a polite smile as the man approached. He matched her expression with an overly courteous look of his own that Lizzie didn't trust one bit.

"Miss Bennet," he said, inclining his head slightly to her. He glanced at Jane but didn't acknowledge her. "To what do we owe the pleasure?"

"I'm here to see Mr. Darcy," Lizzie said.

Mr. Tomlinson still wore that fake, overly solicitous smile. "I'm afraid you've called in the middle of the workday, Miss Bennet. This is a place of business."

Ah, so it would be like that then? "I am here on business."

"Pemberley business?" Mr. Tomlinson inquired.

"Legal business. Now, if you don't mind, Mr. Darcy is expecting me—"

Beside Lizzie, she felt rather than heard a low grumble. She paid it no mind.

Mr. Tomlinson held firm. "I'm afraid you and your companion must go now, Miss Bennet."

He stepped around the front desk as if to personally escort Lizzie to the door, and a furious barking exploded out of Guy. He stood to attention and placed himself between Lizzie and Jane and Mr. Tomlinson, releasing a surprisingly high-pitched yap.

Mr. Tomlinson seemed as shocked as Lizzie at the sudden outburst. "What is that animal doing inside my office?" he thundered.

Lizzie was annoyed at Mr. Tomlinson but mortified by Guy's display. "Guy! Hush! Quiet! Stop that right now!"

Poor Jane had her mouth covered in horror, but she was no help. Guy was undeterred by Lizzie's admonishments and stood his ground. Mr. Tomlinson took a step closer, and the dog added a few growls. "Honestly!" Lizzie declared and leaned down to pick up the dog.

He stopped barking then, twisting in Lizzie's arms as if to reassure himself that she was all right. "I'm so sorry, I don't know what's gotten into him."

"Leave!" the man ordered.

But behind him, she saw Darcy's tall figure emerge into the hall. He was walking briskly in her direction and she could tell by the set of his shoulders and the stony expression he wore that he was not pleased. "Miss Bennet," he said, acknowledging Jane first, then, "Miss Elizabeth."

"Darcy, get back to work," Tomlinson growled.

Darcy flicked his gaze to his supervisor but didn't move. "I beg your pardon, sir, but Miss Elizabeth is consulting on a case."

Lizzie had the satisfaction of seeing the man's eyes widen in shock. "A Pemberley case? Which one?"

"One that doesn't concern you," Darcy said.

"I demand that you answer me!"

"I'm afraid I cannot," Darcy said, pausing slightly. "It's confidential."

This seemed to infuriate Mr. Tomlinson. His cheeks reddened and he hissed. "You are digging yourself into a hole that you will not be able to get out of!"

But Darcy did not react beyond saying, "Miss Bennet, Miss Elizabeth, allow me to fetch my jacket and hat, and I will meet you outside."

Darcy could be curt, but Lizzie sensed something else brewing beneath the surface, something she didn't understand. Mr. Tomlinson had murder in his gaze. "I demand an explanation!"

"You will be receiving a letter from my father explaining the situation," was all Darcy said, and then he turned to go.

Lizzie herded Jane and Guy outside, not willing to risk drawing Mr. Tomlinson's ire. "Lizzie, are you sure that it was all right for us to come here?" Jane asked, worry creasing her pretty face.

"Don't worry, Darcy never stays cross for long," she assured her sister, although she knew that was hardly an answer to her question. The truth was, Lizzie was shocked by Tomlinson's reaction. She knew he disapproved of her, but Darcy was the Pemberley heir! How dare Tomlinson speak to Darcy in such a manner!

"Now, I expected better from you, sir," Lizzie admonished Guy. The dog looked up at her, the picture of innocence. "We do not bark at others in such a way, no matter how unpleasant they might be!"

"It seems as though it was warranted," Jane murmured, making Lizzie laugh.

Guy looked away from the sisters and observed the busy street before them. When Lizzie looked back down at the dog, his gaze was on something behind her, and he was focusing with an unusual intensity. Lizzie felt a strange prickling at the back of her neck, and turned to see what had captured the dog's attention.

She didn't get a good look—all she saw was a figure turning abruptly to disappear around the corner.

SEVEN

*In Which Darcy Comes Face-to-Face
with His Uncomfortable Past*

DARCY HATED THAT HE'D sent Lizzie to wait for him outside as if she were someone he was ashamed of. She deserved better than that. He ought to have explained about Mr. Tomlinson before now. If anyone would understand, it was she.

Why hadn't he just told her?

He took a steadying breath as he stepped outside and reminded himself that it wasn't Lizzie's fault that Tomlinson had decided to make his life miserable. However, it was his fault that he'd soon be caught in a lie about Lizzie consulting on a Pemberley case. Who would discover it first—Tomlinson, who seemed out to get him, or his father, who would surely use this as an excuse to forbid him from seeing Lizzie?

He added this to his long list of things to worry about later.

Lizzie's back had been to him when he stepped out, but she turned around now and smiled weakly when she spotted him. "Hello. Is this a bad time?"

"Of course not." Darcy rushed to reassure her, even as his conscience whispered, *Liar.* "Good day, Jane."

"We are awfully sorry for making things difficult for you," Jane added.

"Tomlinson would not be happy for me to leave at any time," Darcy said. He worked to put a smile on his face. "He would chain me to my desk from dawn to dusk if he could."

His attempt at humor pacified Jane, but Lizzie was watching him with a keen eye, and he knew that she wasn't fooled. He looked down at Guy and exclaimed, "What on earth have you done to that poor dog?"

"It wasn't me!" Lizzie protested. "That was all Lydia and Kitty. If they have their way, he'll end up a spoiled lapdog. I had to tell Mama a rather too convincing lie in order to keep her from turning him out into the streets, and now I fear she thinks you hate him."

Darcy had long given up trying to understand the convolutions of Mrs. Bennet's thoughts, and merely bent down and offered Guy his hand. The dog sniffed at his fingers and then allowed Darcy to pet his head. "I don't hate him. I've never had a dog before."

"Me neither," Lizzie said. "And I think that Lydia and Kitty might start a riot if I found him a new home now, so I suppose we're stuck with him."

We, she'd said. That simple word warmed Darcy, drawing him out of the gray mood his encounter with Mr. Tomlinson had put him in. "My apologies," he said to Jane. "I suppose the last thing your household needed was a pet."

"Don't mind Mama," Jane assured him. "She objects to everything that is not her idea at first, but she comes around more often than not."

"Speaking of my mother's objections," Lizzie said. "I asked Jane to accompany us to call on Miss Beaufort. I would have asked Charlotte, but it seems that my dear mama caught wind that we've a case and believes that the amount of time we are spending together is dangerously close to improper," she said, huffing a bit on the last word.

"I hope you don't mind," Jane said with an apologetic wince. "I promise that Mama shall get the tamest of reports."

"I don't mind in the slightest, and besides, we wouldn't want to displease your mother."

"Did you get the search permit?" Lizzie demanded.

Darcy raised a hand to hail a carriage and grimaced. "About that . . ."

Once they were all tucked into a carriage and it was rattling down the busy streets toward Cavendish House, he told Lizzie the bad news. The moment he uttered the words "official Crown business" her eyes went wide.

"How on earth is a wool merchant's storehouse official Crown business?"

"That was my question, but as you can imagine, it went unanswered."

"Why didn't Jack disclose this? In fact, why hire me if the Crown is already involved?"

Darcy waited for her to come to the conclusion herself. "Oh," she said after a moment. "You think he's hiding something."

"Either that, or he doesn't know," Darcy acknowledged. "But I think it's clear that we won't be granted entry into that storehouse anytime soon."

Lizzie sighed heavily at the setback and looked out the window as the streets of London slid by. "Let's not say anything to him just yet. Although I've already written and said we were pursuing a lead with a Miss Beaufort. Let's hope our visit proves enlightening."

Darcy had a theory that he'd been mulling over since the afternoon before, and he ventured to share it now. "We may not have a clear suspect yet, but there are a few details that aren't sitting well with me."

"What details?"

"This fire . . . it happens where French émigrés happen to be living and working. And they give you the name of a wealthy young lady with French parentage. Then, the British officers the other day, and now hearing that the storehouse has something to do with Crown business . . ."

"You think this has something to do with the war?"

Darcy sighed. "Perhaps. It just seems as though there an awful lot of connections to French factions, and then to hear the Crown is involved somehow . . ."

Lizzie's eyebrows furrowed together, and for the first time all morning, she looked unsettled. Darcy didn't blame her. It was one thing to get caught up in legal strife and various miscarriages of justice here at home, but neither of them was particularly interested in involving themselves in the war between England and France.

"What does that mean?" Jane asked, sounding worried.

"I don't know quite yet," Darcy admitted. "And we have no idea if it's true, but . . ."

"What connection could a wool merchant have with the war?" Lizzie muttered.

"Are the Mullins brothers radicals?"

"Not that I know of. But, Darcy, you can't think that perhaps the storehouse was burned down by French sympathizers?" Lizzie asked. "Just because Miss Beaufort is French?"

"I don't know," he said. "But you'll see—Miss Beaufort is quite English, despite her name and parentage."

It wasn't very long before they pulled up in front of a town house, and Darcy noticed the surprise on both Bennet sisters' faces. The home was grand, and in a very respectable neighborhood. Darcy knew what Lizzie was thinking—not likely the sort of place a sympathizer of Napoleon might live.

"Let me do the talking," Darcy instructed. "She might not be overly pleased to see me, but at one point in time she did trust me. Perhaps we can get to the bottom of this and clear her name before the gossip spreads."

Lizzie, to his surprise, didn't argue. She nodded, then looked down at Guy and said, "Guy, sit." The dog sat. "Now, stay." To Darcy, she said, "Don't worry, we shall follow your example."

Darcy wondered how long that would last.

They knocked on the door and were received by an elegantly dressed butler in his early forties who was far too well trained to reveal his surprise at seeing Mr. Fitzwilliam Darcy at his doorstep after two long years, but Darcy noted the flick of a glance between himself and the Bennet sisters. Darcy turned on his little-used charm and smiled. "Dupont," he said. "How wonderful to see you again. Is Miss Beaufort receiving today?"

"That depends," the man said with a trace of a French accent. "Is this a business or social call?"

Darcy felt Lizzie stiffen in surprise at the butler's frank question, but he merely smiled. "We promise not to take up too much of her time."

Mr. Dupont sniffed in a way that seemed to say, *We'll see about that.* But he took Darcy's, Lizzie's, and Jane's cards and bid them wait. As soon as he was out of earshot, Lizzie whispered, "You seem familiar."

"Mr. Dupont is utterly devoted to Josette," he whispered back. "He brought her to England after the death of her parents, and Mrs. Cavendish gave him a position. No one sees her without his approval."

"Well, he doesn't seem overly fond of you."

Darcy wouldn't have been surprised if Josette had revealed the whole embarrassing story of their last conversation to her beloved butler, in which case . . . he couldn't blame the man.

Mr. Dupont reappeared. "This way, please," he said, indicating the door to the drawing room.

Darcy's pulse stuttered as they followed the butler down

familiar halls and into the drawing room. It had changed very little since that last day he'd called at Cavendish House. Now the drapes were drawn, and a harp sat in the corner. Books were stacked artfully about the room, and a few of the heavier portraits that Darcy remembered had been replaced with more fashionable landscapes and scenes of everyday life. It felt lighter somehow, and less stifling than Darcy recalled, as though it were a room a young lady often entertained in.

At the center of the room stood Miss Josette Beaufort, as beautiful as ever.

Her dark hair shone in the early afternoon light, but her cheeks were thinner than they had been two years earlier. She wore a lavender bombazine dress, and she regarded them with barely concealed surprise. "Mr. Darcy," she said in a smooth voice. "To what do I owe the pleasure?"

Darcy had intended to walk into the drawing room and pretend that it wasn't familiar, and get straight to the matter of the case. He planned on being polite yet cool, and he hoped that Josette would show him the same courtesy, despite the unpleasant reason for their visit.

He hadn't expected to find her in half mourning.

A quick glance at Dupont as the butler left the room revealed that he was wearing a subtle black armband. Darcy cursed himself for missing it, and then mustered up an appropriately polite yet reserved smile. "Miss Beaufort. My apologies for dropping in unannounced. I had not realized the household was in mourning. My condolences."

An awkward silence stretched between them a beat too long as Josette looked at him with an indecipherable expression. Finally, she said, "No apology necessary. We've been receiving guests, and you are very welcome."

At the mention of "we," Darcy noted that there was another young lady in the room, tucked in the corner at a writing desk. She stood now to greet their guests, and Darcy could see that she was slightly taller than Josette but shared the same dark hair and medium complexion. But whereas Josette's eyes were a lovely brown, this young woman's were a striking blue. She was also dressed in a mourning color, her dress a dark gray, and she played with a pendant that hung at her collarbone. The necklace was quite opulent against the subdued dress. The gold pendant had a pink topaz at the center, encircled by finely worked gold filigree studded with smaller pink gems. But it wasn't how the girl was dressed or adorned that made Darcy do a double take—she and Josette looked eerily alike, even more than Jane and Lizzie resembled each other.

But Josette, to his knowledge, didn't have a sister.

Behind him, Lizzie cleared her throat ever so slightly.

Darcy gave a small bow to Josette and her lookalike, and said, "Allow me to introduce my companions, Miss Jane Bennet and Miss Elizabeth Bennet."

The Bennet sisters made the appropriate curtseys while Josette peered at them in curiosity. "Welcome, Miss Bennet and Miss Elizabeth. This is my cousin, Miss Leticia Cavendish."

Miss Cavendish stepped forward. "So this is the infamous

Mr. Darcy?" she asked. "A pleasure."

Darcy wasn't certain what was more disarming—hearing her French accent despite her English surname, or hearing her pronounce his name. "Miss Cavendish," he greeted. "How . . . lovely to meet you."

"And unexpected, no?" she asked, throwing him a coy wink.

Darcy looked to Josette, uncertain what to say. "Yes, well . . . I, um, that is, I wasn't aware that you had a cousin, Miss Beaufort."

Josette's smile was strained. "Leticia is my mother's brother's daughter. We spent our childhood together, but circumstances separated us. She has only recently joined us here in London."

Darcy deciphered her polite explanation quickly—Josette and Leticia had been born in France. *Circumstances* was a euphemism for war. But how was it that she had found her way to England? And what of her parents? He hadn't even known that old Mrs. Cavendish had a son.

"What a happy turn of events," Darcy managed.

"It is, isn't it?" Leticia asked.

But Josette looked less than overjoyed. "Please, won't you sit?"

Darcy and the Bennet sisters arranged themselves on the furniture, and Darcy couldn't help but sneak a glance at Leticia. He hadn't expected to find Josette with a companion, and in mourning; and now he felt his carefully rehearsed speech slip away so quickly, he couldn't cling to a single word of it.

"It was our grandmother, if you were wondering," Leticia said, taking a seat next to her cousin.

"I beg your pardon?" Darcy asked.

"Our grandmother passed five months ago," Josette clarified. "The reason we are in mourning."

"I'm sorry," Darcy said, and felt how inadequate those words really were. "I'm . . . oh, I'm just so sorry. I hadn't heard."

Lizzie and Jane both murmured their condolences as well, but Darcy barely heard their words. He was trying to figure out how he'd missed the death of Mrs. Cavendish. While it was true that their families were not particularly close, she had been a client. He would have sent his condolences and called out of respect for Josette and their shared history.

"Thank you," Josette said stiffly. She seemed surprised at Darcy's admission and confused. "Now, I am afraid Dupont was unclear as to whether or not this was a business or social call."

Instinct in Darcy made him want to put her at ease. "Social," he said.

"Business, I'm afraid," Lizzie said at the same time.

"Oh my," Leticia said, leaning forward. "This is shaping up to be the most interesting call we've had all week."

Josette didn't seem to share in her cousin's amusement. "Leticia," she murmured disapprovingly.

Lizzie nudged Darcy expectantly. He had asked that he allow her to lead, but he knew she was impatient. "Miss Elizabeth and I are solicitors, and I'm afraid your name came up in a recent case."

"My name?" Josette asked, genuinely surprised. She raised one elegant brow. "Whatever for?"

This was the delicate part. "No one has accused you of any-thing—but a storehouse near the docks on Burr Street caught fire, and over the course of the investigation, your name was mentioned."

"My name was mentioned?" Josette repeated. "In what con-text? I can assure you, Mr. Darcy, I do not visit any storehouses near the docks!"

As Darcy struggled to find a response to Josette's indigna-tion, he couldn't help but notice Leticia. Her pleasant expression didn't shift as Darcy spoke, but she tilted her head slightly as she took in the news. It felt too calculated, too rehearsed. Suspicion unfurled in Darcy's chest.

"You have no business connected to that area? You don't know anyone who might have any business being there?"

Josette seemed to actually consider it. To his surprise, she turned to her cousin and said, "But surely that's not where Rich-ard's storehouses were located? He would have said if there had been a fire!"

Leticia's face did not betray her thoughts. "I cannot say, cousin."

"If I may," Lizzie cut in. "Who is Richard?"

"My fiancé," Josette said, casting a nervous glance toward Darcy as she spoke the words. "Mr. Richard Hughes."

If she expected Darcy to be shocked, she was destined to be disappointed, but Darcy was a little surprised that she seemed so skittish about revealing a fiancé. He smiled and said, "Congrat-ulations, Miss Beaufort. I had not heard the happy news."

His well wishes seemed to mollify her slightly, and she smiled her thanks. Leticia, however, said, "There seems to be a great deal Mr. Darcy is unaware of!"

Next to him, Lizzie nudged his foot. Whether it was to be a show of solidarity or a reminder to keep his cool, he wasn't certain. "It seems you are correct, Miss Cavendish," he said. "I am woefully ignorant, and you must forgive my questions."

"I still don't understand how my name came up in connection to a storehouse fire," Josette said. "I have nothing to do with my fiancé's business."

"And what is his business, if I may be so impolite as to inquire?" Lizzie asked.

Josette pursed her lips, clearly uncertain as to whether or not Lizzie's rudeness was warranted.

"He owns mines, doesn't he?" Leticia responded, looking to her cousin for confirmation.

"Yes, but I'm sure I don't know the details. You'd have to ask him." Josette's tone hinted at an unwillingness to discuss the matter, and Darcy had to wonder if it was because she didn't know the details of what her fiancé did, or if she didn't care for Darcy to know them.

"How fascinating," Lizzie exclaimed. "Is he acquainted with the Mullins brothers?"

"I cannot say who my fiancé is and isn't acquainted with," Josette said. "Perhaps you ought to ask him."

"We shall," Lizzie promised.

"And what does this have to do with my cousin?" Leticia

asked. Unlike Josette, she was poised, but Darcy found her curiously hard to read. "Please, you've asked so many questions and I believe that our hospitality warrants at least an answer on this matter."

Leticia Cavendish was no fool, clearly. And she was protective of Josette.

"My apologies, Miss Cavendish," he said. "But it was the Mullins Brothers storehouse that burned. Simon Mullins did not survive the fire."

Josette gasped, and her hand flew to her mouth. "How awful."

"Jack Mullins has hired Lizzie to find the person responsible for setting the fire," he added.

"The person responsible? It was not an accident?" Leticia asked.

"Mr. Mullins doesn't believe so," Lizzie responded. "He claims that a woman—a lady—was present in the storehouse that afternoon. She was trespassing and she was the one who started the fire. I've asked around, and the only name of any lady seen in the vicinity was yours, Miss Beaufort."

Darcy held in a sigh. He hadn't wanted Josette to learn of this quite so bluntly, but Lizzie did have a talent for cutting to the chase.

"What is the meaning of this, Darcy?" Josette demanded. "Have you come here to arrest me?"

He raised his hands in an attempt to reassure her. "I don't

have the power to arrest anyone. And we have told no one that your name has been connected to the case."

"I am not connected! How dare you—" Josette got to her feet, and Darcy scrambled to stand after her. She was likely moments from summoning Dupont to throw them out.

"Wait, Miss Beaufort!" Lizzie interrupted. "Please don't be angry at Darcy—if anything, you must redirect your anger to me. We are doing our due diligence, but any impertinent questions are my fault alone. Mr. Darcy did not even want to bother you. He insisted you are above reproach."

Josette stilled, considering Lizzie and her words.

"I would like nothing more than to clear your name from this whole mess," Darcy agreed. He paused a moment, then took a gamble by adding, "This case has whiffs of Francophobia that I find most distasteful."

This finally seemed to convince Josette. She sat once again, and Darcy followed suit. Leticia fiddled with the necklace she wore, the only sign that Darcy could see that she appeared anxious. "Can you tell us who, exactly, connected my cousin to your case?" she asked.

"We were questioning bystanders," Lizzie said carefully. "And I happened to speak with a group of Frenchwomen. I asked them if they knew of a lady who might have been seen in the vicinity, and they named you, Miss Beaufort."

"A group of Frenchwomen," Josette repeated. "The refugee women?"

"You know of them?" Darcy asked.

"Yes, of course—I am the organizer of the Ladies' Helping Hands Relief Society. Our mission is to aid refugees displaced by war."

"I see," Darcy said. "And how many members do you have?"

"Well . . . two. We used to have three. My grandmother." Josette looked sideling at her cousin. "As you can imagine, helping French émigrés acclimate to their new home is not a popular charitable endeavor among society ladies."

"Indeed," Darcy said, for he did not need an imagination to picture it. "But you have not visited them in the vicinity of the storehouse?"

"Heavens, no! We meet them in a parish hall, nowhere near the docks!"

"Well, that explains it," Lizzie said pleasantly. "My French is rather mediocre, I'm afraid. When I attempted to communicate with them, I must have misspoken and they likely misunderstood my question."

Josette's furrowed expression slowly relaxed. "Oh."

"What a coincidence, though," Lizzie added brightly.

Beside Josette, Leticia was still. Too still, Darcy thought, for someone being questioned regarding their possible connection to a crime. Josette's fear was understandable—even if she and her cousin had nothing to do with the case, the merest whisper of rumor that she was connected could have serious consequences for her socially. But Leticia gave very few clues to her true feelings.

112

"Well, if that's all," Josette said slowly. "I hope that you find your mysterious lady."

Darcy forced himself to pull his gaze away from Leticia. "Me too. Thank you. We won't take up any more—"

But before he could finish his sentence, Dupont entered. "Mr. Hughes, mademoiselle."

Darcy turned in surprise, not having expected to catch a glimpse of Josette's fiancé during this visit. A tall, sandy-haired gentlemen strode into the room. His appeared to be in his midtwenties, with thick sideburns and pale blue eyes that crinkled at the corners when he smiled at Josette. But that smile quickly turned into confusion as he registered the unfamiliar guests.

"Darling," Josette said. "Allow me to introduce you to Mr. Fitzwilliam Darcy, and his . . . companions, Miss Bennet and Miss Elizabeth Bennet."

"Darcy," Mr. Hughes said, bowing stiffly toward him. He gave Lizzie and Jane a small bow. "What a surprise. What brings you to my fiancée's home this afternoon?"

"Darcy is working a case he thought we might want to know about," Leticia explained before Josette could even open her mouth.

"Oh?" Mr. Hughes looked at Darcy and the Bennet sisters in confusion. "What is your business, sir?"

Darcy didn't believe for one minute that Mr. Hughes hadn't heard of him and his business before this moment. "I'm a solicitor, with Pemberley and Associates."

"And I am a solicitor with Longbourn and Sons," Lizzie added.

"Indeed?" Hughes looked to Jane. "And you, Miss Bennet?"

"I'm afraid I have no trade, except to keep my sister company," she said with a patient smile.

"Did you send for a solicitor, darling?" Mr. Hughes asked. "I hope you haven't had any trouble."

"Oh no, nothing like that," Josette rushed to say.

"They're investigating a fire," Leticia explained. "On . . . what was it? Burr Street?"

"That's right," Darcy said slowly. "The Mullins brothers own a storehouse that burned—they're wool merchants."

"Isn't that awfully near your office, Mr. Hughes?" Leticia asked, her voice ringing with false innocence.

There was a pause, and then Mr. Hughes responded, "My former office."

"What is your business, sir?" Darcy asked. Something wasn't sitting right about this conversation. Josette looked confused and uneasy, and Leticia was needling Mr. Hughes.

"Graphite mining," Mr. Hughes said. "Or rather, it was. I own land in the Lake District, and about ten years ago we discovered veins of wad. But I'm afraid that's all in the past now. The veins dried up last year, and so I am back to being a man of leisure."

"How unfortunate," Lizzie said.

"Hardly, Miss Elizabeth. It allows me ample time to spend with my fiancée."

114

Josette smiled warmly then, and Darcy recognized it for her true smile. She was happy with Mr. Hughes.

"How lovely," Lizzie said. "May I ask, when is the happy union to take place?"

"A few weeks' time," Josette said.

"Eleven days," Mr. Hughes said at the same time. "We're waiting until Josette and Leticia are out of mourning."

"Of course."

"Well, I hope you find whoever set that fire," Mr. Hughes said. "Terrible business. It's a miracle that nothing else burned down."

"Indeed it is," Lizzie agreed. She smiled at him, and the silence stretched a beat longer. It seemed that neither Leticia nor Josette had anything more to add to the conversation, and Darcy was too busy adding up all the new information to formulate a response.

Fortunately, it was Jane who saved them all from terrible awkwardness. "It is lovely to meet you, Mr. Hughes. I am only sorry we cannot stay any longer, but we've taken up quite enough of Miss Beaufort's and Miss Cavendish's time."

It seemed as though the entire room breathed a sigh of relief as they all stood and made their appropriate goodbyes. Josette reached out a hand to ring the bell to summon the butler, but Leticia stayed her hand. "I am happy to see our guests out," she said, and led them to the foyer.

As soon as they were out of earshot of the drawing room, Leticia placed a hand on Darcy's arm, stopping him. "Do you ride, Mr. Darcy?"

"Do I— I'm sorry?"

"Ride," she said again. "I often go to Rotten Row in the early afternoons. I shall be there tomorrow. I don't suppose there is any chance I might run into you? Or Miss Bennet, Miss Elizabeth?"

"I don't—"

"We don't normally ride," Lizzie rushed to say, "but we are always open to new experiences."

Leticia smiled lightly. "My cousin, unfortunately, has a prior engagement, and she doesn't care to ride as much as I do. It is my favorite pastime in London. Don't you find it refreshing, Miss Elizabeth, to ride in the open air?" She paused slightly, as if expecting Lizzie to respond, then added, "It is the perfect place to meet and be seen, and yet one can have all manner of conversations not appropriate for drawing rooms."

Darcy found himself curious. Who was this strange cousin? "I am certain tomorrow will be a lovely day for a ride. Thank you for the suggestion, Miss Cavendish."

They departed then, and Darcy helped Jane and Elizabeth into the waiting carriage, where Guy barked with excitement at the sight of them. Before Darcy stepped in, he cast a glance up and down the street. He didn't know why, but he had the strangest sense that someone was watching him. Someone just outside of the corner of his vision. He shook his head, chalking up his unease to the strange encounter inside, and followed the ladies into the carriage. The door had barely closed before Lizzie said, "Well, that was *interesting*."

"Goodness, I had no idea that questioning suspects would be

so similar to an extremely awkward social call," Jane observed. "Are they always like that?"

"Usually not so civilized, nor as peculiar," Lizzie told her. She turned her gaze on Darcy. "You agree, don't you, that it was peculiar?"

"I had no idea she had a cousin," Darcy said.

"Yes!" Lizzie leaned forward. "She's an odd one. And did you hear the way she made a point of telling us about Mr. Hughes's office—twice!"

"Yes, that was strange. It's almost as if she was trying to implicate him."

"She knows something," Lizzie agreed. "But . . . she's also a tall, dark-haired young lady. Is she to be trusted?"

Jane gasped. "You mean to say that you think it's Miss Cavendish and not Miss Beaufort who set fire to the storehouse?"

"Perhaps," Lizzie said, but from the look on her face, Darcy knew that she thought it was more than likely.

"I suppose Miss Cavendish intends to shed some light on the subject tomorrow," he said.

Suddenly, Lizzie looked stricken. "But riding? I hate riding. And I have no horse."

"You can ride Georgiana's," Darcy said. "Father never sent her to the estate, so she's been stabled here in London. The groom has been exercising her daily so she'll be perfectly docile."

"But we cannot simply ride down Rotten Row, just the two of us, without drawing all sorts of attention, and then it's guaranteed to get back to my mother."

"Oh." Darcy hadn't considered that. "But you could tell your father you're meeting a witness?"

"Lizzie, I think—" Jane started to say.

"It won't make a difference! Papa isn't pleased I took this case, and I know what he'll say—Why don't you just conduct business in the office, where no one will ask questions?"

"Leticia Cavendish likely won't consent to meet at Long-bourn," Darcy said. "At best, it would be ruinous for her reputation. At worst, it could scare her off, and she's currently our only lead."

"I know that! It's bad enough that I have to climb atop a horse to get answers, now we have to find some sort of excuse so my mother doesn't get *ideas*."

The ominous way Lizzie uttered the word made Darcy go still for a moment, and he glanced at Jane, who appeared uncharacteristically flustered.

"Excuse me!" Jane burst out. "If I may, I have an idea."

Both Darcy and Lizzie started in surprise. Darcy didn't think he'd ever heard the oldest Bennet sister raise her voice.

"You do?" Lizzie asked.

"Yes. But I don't think you'll like it very much."

EIGHT

In Which Lizzie and Darcy Discover
Something Rotten on Rotten Row

JANE HAD BEEN CORRECT. Lizzie did not like her idea at all.

Unfortunately, it was the only one that made any sense, if Lizzie was to find a reasonable excuse for being on Rotten Row with Darcy that wouldn't stress her mother's nerves.

Which was why she found herself atop Georgiana's gentle bay mare, inexplicably named Violet, the following day. It was a damp afternoon in Rotten Row, the sandy track that ran all the way from Kensington to Whitehall, but a good number of ladies and gentlemen on horseback and in open carriages were taking advantage of the weak sunlight breaking through the cloud cover.

This was not Lizzie's idea of a good time, and even less so because she was currently in a riding party comprised of Darcy, Jane, Bingley, and, most distressingly, his sisters.

"Mr. Darcy, how wonderful of you to join us today!" Caroline

Bingley exclaimed. Unlike Lizzie, she looked beautifully at ease on the back of a horse. Lizzie didn't know much about the creatures, but this one was very tall and his shiny black coat gleamed in the midday sun. Caroline wore a handsome sapphire-blue riding habit and a smug expression as she expertly guided her mount to fall into step next to Darcy's, ignoring Lizzie. "Whatever is the occasion?"

"I wasn't aware I needed an occasion to exercise my horse," Darcy replied stiffly, and with far less bite than Lizzie would have minded.

"You never come out and join us anymore," Caroline said with a small pout. She didn't even spare a glance at Lizzie, who was awkwardly holding her reins and trying to keep her seat a stride behind them. "You're always so very busy."

"Yes, well that is the nature of jobs," Lizzie cut in. "They do require work."

Caroline sniffed and continued to address Darcy. "I don't know why you bother. It isn't as though you need one."

Lizzie noticed Darcy's jaw tighten at that. He was awfully sensitive about his job lately. She couldn't tell if Caroline's words irked him because they were true, or if something else was bothering him—something to do with his never-ending workload and why Tomlinson was so very cross when she'd visited the day before.

"Caroline, leave the man alone!" Bingley said. "So what if he works a job? *I* work a job. And need I remind you that without Mr. Darcy and Miss Elizabeth, I might not be here!"

Lizzie had to smile at that, because it soured Caroline's expression and because Mr. Bingley was never one to fail to give credit where credit was due, especially in regard to how Lizzie and Darcy had cleared his name of murder.

"I don't know why you'd bring up such horrid memories, Charles," Louisa Hurst said with a sniff. Although it hadn't been quite a year since the murder of her husband, she was out of mourning and was surveying the nearby riders with a sharp eye. "Someone might hear."

"My apologies," her brother said. "But let this be a pleasant outing, please! It's not often that I am joined by my sisters and dear friends on such a lovely spring day!"

Quietly, so no one else would hear, Lizzie leaned in her saddle toward Jane and whispered, "You are lucky that he is so charming as to make up for his sisters' lack."

Jane shot Lizzie a reproving look but could not argue with her.

Despite her displeasure at spending time with Caroline Bingley and Louisa Hurst, Lizzie had to admit that Jane's idea was a clever one. She and Darcy had been warmly welcomed to join the party by Bingley, and Mrs. Bennet had deemed it perfectly suitable that Lizzie should take the afternoon off work to spend time seeing to her sister's social life.

But Lizzie was beginning to wonder just how on earth they were supposed to find Leticia Cavendish in a park humming with society members, riding and driving their rigs, seeing and being seen. There were people everywhere she looked. Besides finding her, how were they supposed to have an open conversation with Leticia among all these witnesses?

With dexterity that Lizzie lacked, Darcy guided his horse to fall back in pace with Lizzie's borrowed mare. "Watch your reins," he advised. "Give her some slack."

Lizzie's body immediately tensed at the idea of letting this great creature have full control, but she forced herself to relax her grip. The mare took the opportunity to shake her head, making the bit and bridle jangle, but her stride seemed to loosen into something less choppy.

"See? Much better." Darcy's smile turned mischievous. "We ought to do this more often."

"Not on your life," Lizzie shot back. "I'm satisfied with where my own two legs can carry me, thank you."

"Being comfortable astride a horse has numerous advantages," Darcy said, and if Lizzie didn't know him better she'd think he was lecturing her. "Not only are you in a position to travel quickly if need be, but it's a good form of exercise and it allows one to socialize in a less structured setting."

"Well, if I were actually riding astride, maybe I'd feel the same way," Lizzie said, trying not to wriggle around too much in her sideseat saddle. "As it is I can't help but feel as if I'll slide off at a moment's notice."

Darcy had the good grace to look apologetic. "Ah. Well, yes . . . I can imagine that is awkward."

Lizzie smiled at the acknowledgment, then changed the subject. "I am certain there are no fewer than eight of Mama's acquaintances who will be calling on her to mention that two of her daughters were seen riding with *the* Mr. Darcy and Mr. Bingley."

"Do you suppose it will do anything to help your mother's opinion of me?"

It would indeed—and that was what Lizzie was afraid of. She might be able to put her mother off with excuses that they were merely consulting on each other's cases, but if the rest of society thought they were courting . . . well, nothing would invite their mother into their business quicker.

"Relax your shoulders," Darcy instructed. "She can sense your tension."

"Of course I'm tense—I feel as though I may topple off at any second!"

"Violet won't let you fall. She's far too well-mannered for that."

"That makes one of us," Lizzie grumbled. "If I do perish, I want you to promise to see to all my cases and ensure that Guy doesn't fall into Lydia's clutches."

Darcy laughed at that. "You cannot fool me, Lizzie. I know that you likely already have a will in writing. Save your dramatic proclamations and let me know if you spot Miss Cavendish."

"It's impossible," Lizzie grumbled, looking about. "What was she thinking?"

"I don't know, but I look forward to asking her that when we spot her."

Movement snagged her attention near the trees to her right.

Lizzie didn't turn her head, but she kept her eye on the bushes as Violet and Darcy's Strider kept ambling along, smiling to herself.

"What is it?" Darcy asked.

"I haven't wanted to alarm you," Lizzie said, knowing that saying those words would put him on alert nonetheless, "but I believe we've acquired a tail. Or rather, I think I have."

"What?" Darcy turned to look at her, most definitely alarmed.

"Try not to overreact—he's watching us now," Lizzie said. "And try to relax. I don't think we're in any danger."

"Lizzie," he said, his voice a warning.

"Over by the bench, between those two trees. Look to the left—there's a bush that is a little taller than the rest."

Darcy subtly tilted his head in the direction she indicated, scanning the scene. Lizzie kept her gaze forward and waited.

"Oh," Darcy said finally. "Is that . . ."

"I believe so."

She looked suddenly in the direction. There was no doubt about it now—their shadow was the boy from the storehouse. He wore a gray cap and the same green jacket from the other day. He immediately stiffened when he noticed their attention and vanished from sight.

"Oh dear," Lizzie said. "I hope we haven't scared him off."

Darcy sighed. "I was afraid someone dangerous had taken to tailing you. Yesterday, outside of Cavendish House . . ."

Lizzie looked at him in surprise. "You saw him there? I only thought I saw him at Pemberley."

"No, but it was more like I had a strange sense that we were

124

being watched. When we came out of the house . . . well, I must have been mistaken. How long has he been following you?"

"I think since yesterday. I wasn't certain as to his identity until just now."

Darcy looked uneasy. "You should have said something. Just because he's small and half-fed doesn't mean he can't be dangerous, Lizzie. Does he know where you live?"

"I wouldn't be surprised," she said. "But I think I can handle one small, half-fed boy."

He groaned. "Yes, by feeding him and trying to get information out of him."

"Why not? He seems awfully resourceful if he could make his way to Longbourn and tail me."

"He could already have an employer, you know," Darcy pointed out. "One that has ordered him to tail us."

"He could," she allowed. "But maybe not. Maybe he just needs a bit of help."

"Homeless dogs and stray children. Promise me you'll be careful."

"Don't fret. Their bark is usually worse than their bite."

"Lizzie."

"I promise."

"Oh, am I interrupting?"

Caroline had fallen back to ride abreast of them, allowing Jane, Louisa, and Bingley to move a good ten strides ahead. "Not at all," Lizzie lied, putting on a fake smile. "It's uncommonly pleasant for early spring—don't you agree, Mr. Darcy?"

"Indeed," he said with a cough. "We ought to go riding more often."

Lizzie tried not to feel delight at Caroline's obvious suspicion. For someone whose brother had been cleared of murder because of Lizzie's efforts, Caroline didn't like her very much.

Then again, that likely had something to do with Lizzie investigating Caroline for said murder first.

"It is nice to see you both," Caroline said, sounding so genuine that Lizzie didn't trust her for a moment. "And I am sorry that we won't be able to join you tomorrow evening."

"What's tomorrow evening?" Darcy asked.

"Oh, have I put my foot in it? I assumed you received an invitation. Dinner tomorrow, at the Bennets'. Louisa and I have a previous engagement, and I just hope Charles won't have to cancel at the last minute."

Lizzie winced. She'd forgotten to pass along the dinner invitation, of course. But how could she be expected to remember trivial things such as dinner invitations when she was on a case as important as this? "I—"

"Of course," Darcy said suddenly. "Is that tomorrow night? You'll have to forgive me, Lizzie—I had completely lost track of the days."

"It is understandable, and there's nothing to forgive," Lizzie said, not glancing at Caroline. "We have been very busy of late."

"It is regrettable that you cannot join us, Caroline," Darcy added. "It seems as though we are always missing each other these days."

"Hmm," was all Caroline had to say to that. Lizzie bit her lip so she wouldn't grin, but as it turned out she was too quick to celebrate, for the next thing out of Caroline's mouth was, "I hope your mother wasn't planning on going to too much trouble on our accounts, Lizzie. It was kind of her to extend an invitation when we are all barely acquainted."

"I assure you, my mother takes great pains in all the dinners she hosts," Lizzie told Caroline. "No matter the guests."

"Oh, she is too much! But she must not overtax herself, the poor dear. I am sure she will make such a charming mother-in-law one day. She's quite attentive. And always *so involved*."

Lizzie would happily have throttled Caroline, if she could have reached her without unseating herself from Violet.

Darcy merely blinked. "I'm sure I don't understand your meaning, Caroline."

Before Caroline could further insult Lizzie's family, a horrible shriek rent the air, causing Violet to pause midstep and flick her ears. A shocking silence echoed throughout the park, but only for a moment as another cry split the air and then, it seemed, everyone began to whisper or shout or call out at once.

At first, Lizzie couldn't pinpoint the exact location from which the shriek had originated, and she looked about, trying to spot the source of commotion. When a third scream permeated the air, Lizzie's head swiveled to the left. A footpath and hedges lined Rotten Row, and beyond that stood clusters of bushes, their leaves brown and dead, and copses of thick trees that almost—but not fully—obscured the view of the Serpentine in the distance. The screams were coming from beyond the riding track, where a woman stood at the edge of a very large bush.

Lizzie urged Violet in her direction.

"Lizzie, wait!" Darcy called out; and in no time at all he was alongside her, and then he'd pulled past her. Violet needed little encouragement to follow his horse and Lizzie held on as best she could. A few other concerned riders followed, but Darcy was the first to reach the screaming woman, a maid, judging by her uniform. Her mouth was wide open in horror, and her skirts were streaked with mud. As Darcy reached her, he gracefully leapt from his horse, and the maid clung to his arm, pointing behind her and babbling something incoherent.

Lizzie pulled back on the reins and followed the woman's pointing finger.

Partially obscured by a ring of shrubbery, a woman lay upon the cold ground.

Lizzie couldn't see her face, but she could tell something was very wrong with her. She was too still, and she looked crumpled, as though she'd fainted. But Lizzie guessed that by the maid's screams, this was no faint.

"Stay back," Darcy warned her as she clumsily dismounted, but Lizzie paid him no heed. Getting off Violet was far easier than getting on, and as soon as she had feet on solid ground, she ran past the sobbing maid and followed Darcy to where he crouched beside the woman. She heard him swear under his breath and then he turned and stood, trying to block her view.

"Is she . . . ?" Lizzie asked, trying to look beyond him.

"Yes." The word came out ragged, and Lizzie looked up in surprise.

Darcy's face was stricken and pale, and he looked . . . hopeless. Fear thundered through Lizzie's heart and she ducked under his arm and looked at the lifeless woman's face and gasped.

It was Leticia Cavendish.

At first, all Lizzie could see was her eyes—blue as the summer sky, wide open and unseeing. Other details emerged slowly—her hat, knocked off her head. Her hair, lightly mussed. The gray riding habit streaked with mud on the skirts.

"But how . . . why . . . ?" She turned and looked back at Darcy, who seemed fixed in place. "Darcy!"

"There's nothing we can do," he said, drawing her away. Lizzie let him, and closed her eyes against the horrid image of Leticia's eyes open and unseeing, her awkward slump on the cold, dead grass.

More bystanders were approaching now, and the screaming maid was being consoled by another lady. A few men came up to Darcy, demanding to know what was going on.

"Send for the Runners," was all Darcy said, refusing to let anyone else approach. "No one shall touch her until the Runners arrive."

Shock and horror roiled through Lizzie as she stood next to Darcy, facing the growing crowd. A few distraught wails rose up among the gathering and at least two ladies swooned, but Lizzie guessed that had less to do with genuine shock and more with the number of handsome young men willing to catch them.

Lizzie set her face grimly, not wanting to show any emotion, but as she stared at the passersby, questions began to boil up inside her. What had happened to Leticia? Who had waylaid her? And how had they managed to kill her in a park full of people?

She assessed the scenery around them. They were tucked into a pocket of the park that boasted plenty of trees and shrubbery, obscuring their position from the track of Rotten Row. Not completely hidden by any means, but hidden enough from the flow of riders that as long as someone wasn't looking directly at them . . .

Lizzie turned and forced herself to look at Leticia.

She'd seen a dead body before, of course. While working to clear Bingley's name, she'd befriended a maid named Abigail, who'd worked in the home of the slain Mr. Hurst; and Lizzie had arrived minutes after Abigail had been pulled from the Thames, drowned because she'd helped Lizzie. And she'd seen the life fade from Wickham's face after he'd been shot by Lady Catherine de Bourgh. This was somehow both the same, and completely different. It was never *not* shocking to see the human form completely empty of life. Leticia was pale, as Abigail had been, although she wasn't soaking wet, but her face was twisted into a horrible expression—shock, and anger, and . . . terror?

Perhaps Lizzie had too vivid an imagination.

"What are you doing?" Darcy hissed as Lizzie took a step closer to Leticia, but Lizzie didn't respond. In the distance, she could hear the shrill of the Runners' whistles and she knew she didn't have much time.

Lizzie avoided looking into Leticia's eyes, which had been so full of fire the day before, as she removed her gloves, reached out a trembling hand, and touched Leticia's cheek. It was cool, but even her own cheeks were cold in the early spring air.

"Lizzie!" Darcy hissed, appalled.

She didn't respond. Her hand dropped to Leticia's neck, searching for a pulse. Nothing, but . . . she was still slightly warm. It was then that Lizzie noticed the redness around Leticia's neck, which had been partially obscured by the way her riding jacket's collar had ridden up.

Leticia Cavendish had been strangled.

"She was murdered," Lizzie said in a whisper to Darcy, her eyes already searching the crowd. "And not very long ago."

She surveyed the scene once more, trying to envision how this sad fate might have befallen Leticia Cavendish. She was wearing a riding habit—where was her horse? Lizzie looked about the ground, trying to discern if any hoof marks could be seen, but she saw nothing that would indicate a heavy creature. Had Leticia been lured away from her horse to a hidden grove on foot?

In the grass, a mere five paces away, she saw something glint in the weak spring sunshine.

She strode over to inspect the object, which was gold and clearly very fine. She picked it up and wasn't entirely surprised to see it was Leticia's necklace with its pink topaz pendant hanging from a heavy chain, the clasp broken. It appeared to be unblemished and the gems were intact. Lizzie turned it over, wondering if it was too much to hope for that it would bear an inscription of some sort, some hint at who had been important enough to her to gift her such a fine piece. But there was nothing.

Had this been a robbery, then? But if someone was so bold as to kill a woman in a busy park in the middle of the day, then why drop a valuable piece of jewelry? Unless they'd been in such a hurry to get away . . .

"Let us pass! Move along!"

The imperious tone of the Runners startled Lizzie, and she pocketed the necklace before she thought it through. Instinct told her the necklace was important, and she didn't trust the Runners not to "lose" it.

Normally, whenever Lizzie and Darcy had to deal with authority figures, they were in grudging agreement that it was best for Darcy to step up and do the talking, and, once they were lulled into a false sense of security, Lizzie would dart in with her questions. But when the Runner looked between them and Leticia's still form and barked, "What happened here?" Darcy didn't say a single word.

Uneasiness grew as murmuring from the crowd heightened, and Lizzie realized that Darcy was incapable of assuming his normal role. She stepped forward and said, "She's dead, sir. We heard a scream and my companion and I came riding over to see if we could assist. The maid over there found the body. We tried to see if we could offer any assistance, but . . ."

She felt herself falter. It wasn't the heavy stare of the Runner that overwhelmed her as much as it was the futility of the situation. Leticia Cavendish was dead. Someone had killed her before she'd had a chance to meet with Lizzie and Darcy.

The Runner nodded sharply, seeming to take her reaction for shock. In short order, two Runners stood guard over Leticia's body and two more began to try to disperse the crowd. Another sidled up to the man in charge and whispered, "Undertaker or doctor?"

The head Runner made a pained face. "She's one of this lot"—nodding at the members of the ton watching on in horror. "Call a doctor."

"Her name is Leticia Cavendish," Darcy said suddenly. "Her family ought to be notified."

The Runner in charge gave him a sidelong look. "And will you be willing to do that, sir? On account of you knowing her and all?"

Lizzie peered up at Darcy. His trademark stern expression was in place, but Lizzie could tell that this was not Darcy just being aloof. He swallowed hard and nodded.

Lizzie and Darcy were ushered off to the side, and someone gave up their coat to cover Leticia's lifeless face while they waited. "Darcy," Lizzie whispered, unsure of what she was going to say next: *Are you all right? What should we do now? What does it mean for this case?*

But Darcy just shook his head.

All right then, Lizzie thought. *Time to step up.*

"Sir," she said to the head Runner, tightening her fist around the necklace. "That young lady was killed."

He gave her a passing glance. "I know, I know, right upsetting, it is."

Lizzie might have rolled her eyes, if the situation hadn't been so serious. "Her murderer might still be in the park," she hissed.

Now the man did look at her, and he seemed to take stock of her. He smiled in a condescending way that made Lizzie's scalp prickle. "Now, don't worry, miss. You're safe enough. No one will try anything untoward in this crowd."

Never mind that Leticia Cavendish had likely thought the same thing. "I am less concerned about my welfare than I am about a murderer on the loose. Don't you think your men ought to canvas the park for witnesses?"

It was what Lizzie would do if she were in charge. She'd order that this section of the park be cordoned off, and that reinforcements be brought in. Then she'd have every single person questioned—who knew what someone might have seen!

The man looked affronted. "Whoever did that poor girl in is long gone. The sad truth is that it was likely some ruffian who saw her alone and took his chance to rob her. She might have struggled or attempted to fight back, and . . ." He shrugged, as if Lizzie could finish the story.

Except, there were about five things wrong with that theory. First of all, Leticia was wearing a riding habit, suggesting that she had a horse somewhere that had yet to be recovered and that someone would have had to lure her off of her mount. Second, no young lady willingly went behind a copse of trees with someone she didn't know, and certainly not with any strange men that could be rightly classified as ruffians. Third, the park was crowded, and if Leticia had feared for her safety, all she would have had to do was call out or scream for help. Fourth, strangling was an intimate, personal way to kill a person—you had to get close enough to lay hands on them, and it took considerable force and time to kill them. If someone had managed to get close enough to her in order to strangle her without Leticia drawing any attention, that suggested it had been someone she trusted.

And fifth, the person had dropped the necklace. The same necklace that Lizzie was now glad she'd kept from this imperceptive man.

Lizzie turned to Darcy. "Tell them they need to search for evidence," she demanded.

Darcy still wore that strange, wooden look. He shook his head. "I have to reach Josette. She cannot hear about this from one of these Runners."

"But . . ." Lizzie trailed off when she realized Darcy wasn't listening. He was looking around for his horse, and she realized that he meant to go *now*.

Behind the line of Runners stood Bingley, holding each of their horses. Darcy strode toward him and Lizzie scrambled to follow. "Darcy!" she hissed.

"There's nothing more we can do here," he said. "The Runners wouldn't dare detain this many members of the ton. Most of them are probably halfway home, anyway."

Lizzie looked about and had to admit that he was right. Many of the riders had already cleared out, and the ones that remained were looking on in a most obvious fashion. She caught a glimpse of a man walking purposefully in the opposite direction, and her heart skipped a beat—perhaps it was someone who'd seen something? But then a horse obscured her view and by the time it had passed, he was gone.

She turned back to Darcy. "What are we supposed to do? She was our only lead!"

"I need to tell Josette, and ensure she isn't in danger," Darcy whispered. "If someone is targeting her cousin, she could be next."

Darcy had a point. But Lizzie couldn't help but feel as though someone might have seen something in the park and she couldn't give up so quickly. "Go. You'll be able to ride faster without me."

"And leave you?"

"I'm hardly alone," Lizzie said, tilting her head toward where Bingley waited anxiously with the horses. "Go quickly. Call on me when you're finished."

They were surrounded by far too many people for Lizzie to dare reach out for him, despite her wish to cling to him for a moment, and feel the reassuring warmth of his solid chest and arms around her. Darcy held her gaze for a long moment, and she knew his thoughts were not far from her own. Finally, he nodded and mounted his horse, and kicked him into a canter, ignoring the cries of protest from other riders and the shocked gasps.

Bingley was left holding Violet. "Your sister is with Caroline and Louisa on the other side of the track," he told her. "Louisa became dizzy when she heard. . . ."

"That's all right," Lizzie said, doing some quick thinking. "Can the groom take Violet back to the stable? I need to see to a few more questions and arrangements. The young lady who was killed was connected to our case, and I need answers."

Bingley's eyes widened in alarm. "You intend to walk home? Miss Elizabeth, a young lady has been murdered!"

"And the killer is quite in the wind," Lizzie responded. "I can prevail upon one of the Runners to escort me to a carriage to take me home."

"I don't think Darcy would like this one bit," he said.

Lizzie appreciated Bingley's concern, but why were some men so chivalrous when others were so rotten? Not that Lizzie knew for certain that it was a *man* who had killed Leticia . . . after all, Lizzie had met at least one female killer. But somehow it was always other men that young ladies were taught to fear, even as they were told that men were their protectors.

It made very little sense.

"Please, see to your sisters. And mine, for that matter. I'm sure Jane is very upset. I can take care of myself." Lizzie pretended to wave a man behind Bingley's back. "Oh, in fact, I see a colleague now. Don't worry about me!"

"Are you absolutely certain?" Bingley asked, looking over his shoulder in the direction of Jane.

"Positively!"

Bingley reluctantly led Violet away, and Lizzie was rather relieved. There was not a chance that she'd be able to remount the horse with her dignity intact, and now she could move more easily in between the curious onlookers and the Runners who arrived on the scene. In her pocket, Leticia's necklace felt heavy, but Lizzie was now past surveying the murder scene— she blended seamlessly into the crowd of onlookers, crossed the grassy area shielded by the copse of trees, and emerged onto the clear slope above the track. She walked with a steady gait and kept her eyes forward until she drew close to the row of hedges that ran between the slope and footpath that followed Rotten Row. With a quick glance out of the corner of her eye, she judged her moment—and made her move.

Reaching down and over the hedges, her fist closed around the collar of a shabby green jacket. The small body in her grasp froze, then began to thrash; but Lizzie had made sure she grasped the boy's shirt beneath his jacket as well, so there was no easy way for him to shrug off her hold.

A pair of frightened blue eyes looked up at her and Lizzie looked down, stern but kind.

"Hello," she said. "I think it's time you and I had a proper chat."

NINE

*In Which Lizzie Consults an
Unconventional Source*

THE BOY'S NAME WAS Henry.

It had taken Lizzie a few minutes to convince him that she wasn't about to hurt him, haul him to the workhouse, or report him to the Runners, and another minute more to convince herself that he wasn't about to run off before she finally released him. The boy's eyes were wide, his face grimy, and his clothes were baggy, as if he'd begged for—or, more likely, stolen—them. He seemed no more comfortable standing in the middle of the park than Lizzie would be in the middle of a ballroom, so Lizzie said, "How about some mince pies?"

The boy's eyes widened, but he didn't say anything.

Lizzie took a gamble. "I know a good street vendor. Come along."

She began to walk toward the park's exit, hoping that if the boy had followed her halfway around London, he'd probably be willing to follow her a few blocks to a warm, free meal.

She was right.

Lizzie was silent as they walked to the closest market, and then found a vendor of mince pies whose hands and apron looked the cleanest. She bought two pies and took a seat on a nearby rough-hewn bench. Henry watched warily, out of arm's reach but he sat on the far end of the bench when Lizzie held out one of the pies, and accepted it with a nod, then wolfed it down.

Lizzie waited until his last bite before she said, "Now, maybe you'd be so kind as to tell me exactly why you've been following me?"

The boy froze, and then when he realized that she wasn't angry, he broke into a bashful smile. "You left your card," he said.

Lizzie raised an eyebrow. "That I did."

Henry shrugged, as if it was neither here nor there if she asked him stupid questions, but what he didn't realize was that he'd revealed something very interesting to Lizzie: he could read.

And now Lizzie was truly intrigued.

She'd had her fair share of interactions with street children and paid a number of them to run errands and keep an eye on various matters for her. One of her favorites, Fred, was now apprenticed to a printer, which was no small feat for him considering that before last year, he hadn't even known how to spell his own name.

Henry, she suspected, had not grown up on the streets.

Lizzie handed him her untouched mince pie, and he happily bit into it. "Do you live near the Mullins Brothers storehouse?" she asked.

"Don't live nowhere," the boy said around his second bite.

"But you hang about there at times? And you notice things."

Henry neither confirmed nor denied, but he stopped eating and regarded her warily.

"Perhaps you've seen that woman before, the one who was murdered in the park?"

"The French lady," the boy agreed. "She's nice to people like us."

People like us? "Children who live on the streets?"

Henry nodded. "Grown-ups, too."

Lizzie thought back to the previous day. Josette had admitted to helping refugees, but through a relief society. Had Leticia taken things one step further and gone to meet the émigrés in the streets? "Are you sure it was she, and not her cousin? They look alike."

He gave a noncommittal shrug. "There was only ever just one lady. She brought us food. And one time, mittens."

"Do you mean she brought them to you, where you lived?"

The boy nodded again, looking at Lizzie as if she were extremely dense.

Leticia Cavendish was a do-gooder, then. And more likely to help people where they were rather than dispense aid from a drawing room.

But why?

Perhaps she was a kind person. Or it could be that she had an ulterior motive. Lizzie thought of the challenging stance that Leticia had adopted when Lizzie and Darcy had revealed the reason for their visit, the way she seemed to needle Josette and Mr. Hughes. She hadn't been fearful at all but rather almost amused.

What had been her angle?

Henry had finished the second mince pie and was watching Lizzie warily. Lizzie found herself at a loss for words. Why on earth had this little boy decided to follow her? He appeared both hungry for her attention and skittish of what she might ask next.

Which led her to wonder . . . had he seen something?

"I don't think the men who own the storehouse that burned much like the people Miss Cavendish was helping."

"They don't like anyone," Henry countered, matter of fact.

"Oh?"

Lizzie waited. It didn't take long for Henry to fill the silence. "Everyone knows not to sleep on their side of the street. They kick at us and throw rocks. Sometimes buckets of filth."

Lizzie tried to control her sharp intake of breath but was unsuccessful. A part of her wanted to say, *But surely not Jack!* Instead, she said, "I'm sorry, Henry. That was very wrong of them."

"Do you have the dog?"

"The dog . . . Guy?" Lizzie asked.

He nodded.

"Yes, I took him home. Mr. Parry said no one wanted him, and he was going to turn him out into the streets."

Henry nodded, and looked down. "That's good, miss," he mumbled, sounding sad. "He's a good dog."

Lizzie was at a loss as she realized that if Henry were a dog, she would think nothing of sweeping him up in her arms and taking him home with her. But he wasn't a dog, he was a human boy. And it was the cruelest of ironies that some people treated dogs better than other human beings.

"You can always call on me if you need anything, you know," Lizzie began to say.

But she didn't get very far before Henry jumped to his feet and ran, faster than she thought possible. By the time she got to her feet, he was gone.

When Lizzie arrived home at Gracechurch Street, she was dissatisfied and distraught by the day's events. Therefore, her mood was not helped when Jane met her at the door with a worried expression.

"Darcy's here," she whispered to Lizzie as she stepped inside, "and Mama has been questioning him in the drawing room for almost a quarter of an hour!"

"She's asking him what his intentions are!"

Lizzie looked beyond Jane to see Lydia with her ear pressed to the closed door. "Lydia, stop eavesdropping!"

She pushed past her youngest sister and let herself into the drawing room.

Darcy was seated in the corner, looking incredibly uncomfortable, while Mrs. Bennet leaned forward in her chair, clearly in the middle of interrogating him. Darcy leapt to his feet upon spotting Lizzie, and Mrs. Bennet spun around to glare at her daughter.

"Mama! What are you doing?"

"How nice of you to join us, Elizabeth. I was just speaking with Mr. Darcy about your outing today."

"Oh?" Lizzie looked at Darcy, trying to discern whether he'd told her mother about Leticia.

"Am I to understand that he took you and Jane to the scene of a *murder*?" Mrs. Bennet screeched.

"That's hardly fair, Mama! We didn't know that Rotten Row would become a murder scene when we set out."

Mrs. Bennet turned to Darcy. "I cannot approve of you exposing my daughters to such things, sir!"

"I assure you, Mrs. Bennet, if I had known that such a thing would happen, and in Hyde Park, no less—"

"Darcy, please!" Lizzie interrupted. "Even you cannot predict when a suspect might be murdered! Besides, Bingley was there, too, and you don't hold him accountable, do you?"

Unfortunately, bringing up Mr. Bingley had been the wrong choice, for it seemed to remind Mrs. Bennet of marriage. "Mr. Darcy, you are spending an inordinate amount of time with my daughter, are you not?"

Lizzie tried to silently communicate with her eyes that Darcy should not answer that question, but he clearly didn't receive the message, for he responded with, "Er . . . yes?"

"And do you think that it is appropriate for you to do so when you have not called on Mr. Bennet and expressed your intentions? Even your friend Mr. Bingley calls frequently."

"Mama!" Lizzie admonished. "I'm a solicitor now, which

144

means I must conduct business with all sorts of people—some of them gentlemen, and, yes, some of them unmarried gentlemen. They cannot all come to Papa and ask for permission for me to merely have a conversation with them."

"Yes, but you're doing far more than having a conversation with Mr. Darcy, aren't you? You're . . . working! *Together.* So much time spent in each other's company—what will people think?"

"I don't care what the gossips say, Mama! I care about solving my cases."

"Wait until your father hears about this," Mrs. Bennet said. "Not a single one of you has any compassion for my nerves! This enterprise of yours is too much—you're in and out of the house at all hours, young men coming and going, and now you're arriving home unchaperoned when you were supposed to be with Jane."

Lizzie was not normally one without a rebuttal, but her mother's words stole the breath from her lungs. Her mother wouldn't bar her from working, would she? No, she couldn't. Papa wouldn't let her. But what if—

"Mrs. Bennet, if I may," Darcy cut in. "I apologize for any distress I might have caused you. I assure you that wasn't my intention, but I can see how the events of the day might be . . . alarming. What can I do to reassure you?"

Mrs. Bennet put both hands to her forehead. "I am not unfeeling, Mr. Darcy. I want nothing more than for my girls to be happy and cared for."

Lizzie rolled her eyes.

"But you must understand my position. I only catch glimpses of you, if ever, and my dear friends tell me they see you about town stepping out with my daughter; and in the meantime I have to pretend that I know anything about it!"

"Mama—"

"Hush, Lizzie! Mr. Darcy, we must see more of you socially. You'll come to dinner tomorrow."

"Of course, Mrs. Bennet," Darcy said. "I would be delighted."

"Mama. May I please consult with Darcy?" Lizzie asked through gritted teeth. "As you may be aware, our case has taken a dire turn."

Mrs. Bennet waved her hand, "Of course, of course. But, Lizzie—leave the door open, please! And Lydia and Kitty will stay in the hall."

Mrs. Bennet sailed out of the drawing room triumphantly, leaving Lizzie and Darcy mostly alone.

Lizzie sank into the nearest chair. "Well, that was a nightmare. I'm sorry about her."

"I wasn't aware our association bothered her quite that much," Darcy said quietly, taking the seat next to her. "You do realize that I am not averse to calling and coming to dinner?"

"It's not our association," Lizzie reassured him, eager to steer the subject away from social calls and the inevitable expectations that followed. "It's that we are here speaking of a murder case rather than . . . well, never mind. How did it go with Josette?"

It was as though a veil passed across Darcy's face and he

appeared even more somber than he had when she arrived. "It was awful, Lizzie."

Lizzie bit her lip, but she wasn't sure what to say. He took a moment to collect his thoughts and then continued. "She was surprised to see me, of course. Her butler very nearly didn't let me in. Mr. Hughes was calling, and so I had to tell them both that Leticia had been killed."

Lizzie could imagine the scene—the surprise, then shock. The shouted questions and disbelief. She reached out and took Darcy's hand in hers.

"Mr. Hughes thought I was playing a prank on Josette—as if I'd ever joke about someone's death. Josette was in a state of disbelief. Then the Runners arrived, along with the doctor they'd called and the wagon with her body, and well. That was that."

"I'm sorry," Lizzie whispered.

She couldn't read Darcy's expression just then—she sensed anguish, but something else lurking under the surface. Was there something more to his relationship with Josette that he wasn't saying? But before she could think of a way to broach that topic, he shook his head. "Where were you? I seem to remember a conversation in which you implied you'd stay with Jane and Bingley and come straight home."

"Was that implied? I don't recall—"

"Lizzie! Leticia was murdered in broad daylight."

"You're right, sorry. But remember our little shadow?"

"The boy? You spotted him?"

147

"I did, and I managed to have a conversation with him. He claims not to have seen anything, so don't get too excited. But he told me that Leticia has visited them in the streets before, talking with other refugees and bringing aid. I asked if he was sure if it was Leticia and not her cousin, and I didn't get a straight answer either way, but . . . I think I can imagine Leticia not being content to dole out aid from some parish hall, but I don't know if Josette would have the constitution to venture to the docks."

"Agreed," Darcy murmured. "Josette was a child when she left France, but if Leticia only recently joined her in London, perhaps she felt a greater connection to her fellow French émigrés and wished to visit them where they worked and lived."

"Which places her very near the storehouse," Lizzie concluded grimly. "So how did she get caught up in the mess of this case?"

"I would suggest asking Josette, but considering the circumstances, I think that would be . . . too much."

Lizzie agreed, but she really did want to know more about the young woman. In the hall, she heard a creak, followed by a smothered giggle, which reminded her of their little audience. Which reminded her of her mother. Which reminded her . . .

"I have an idea," she told him begrudgingly. "Prepare yourself." Sighing heavily, Lizzie called out, "Mama?"

Not ten seconds later, her mother poked her head into the doorway. "Yes, my dear? What is it?"

"May Darcy and I consult with you for a moment?"

"Consult? Why, Lizzie, what a funny way you have with

words. I shall ring for tea, and call in your sisters, and we can all have a nice visit—"

"No, Mama, I really do mean consult. Darcy and I have a question for you about our case. I think you may be able to shed some light on . . . a potential suspect."

"I shall call for tea," Mrs. Bennet repeated firmly, "and you two shall sit down in a civilized manner!"

Which was how Lizzie and Darcy found themselves sitting across from Mrs. Bennet as she poured tea and beamed at them. Lizzie took a tiny sip, and said, "Mama, do you recall that we went to visit Cavendish House yesterday?"

"Indeed. I trust it was a nice visit?"

Darcy grimaced, and Lizzie rushed to say, "It was a little sad, actually. Mama, did you know Mrs. Cavendish has passed away?"

"Oh, yes," she said. "It was in the papers—what was it, six months? Such a sad life she had, poor woman. She lost both of her children, you know?"

Lizzie saw Darcy lean forward just the tiniest bit. "And can you tell us about them?"

"Oh, I don't know, Lizzie—it was so long ago."

"You mentioned that her daughter ran off with a Frenchman," Lizzie prompted.

"Yes, it was quite the scandal at the time! She left in the middle of the night, and they didn't marry until they were in France, from what I heard! This was before their troubles, of course."

By troubles, she meant the Revolution.

"And they had a child?" Lizzie prompted. "Josette Beaufort."

"Is that her name? I do recall hearing about the girl, although not until years later when she returned to England. You see, what with all the *unpleasantness* happening in France, I believe her mother was never able to return to England. She died without ever having reconciled with her parents. Some attempts were made, of course, to get her and her child out of France, but well . . . such an unpleasant topic for tea, Lizzie!"

"Attempts?" Darcy asked.

"The Cavendishes were very wealthy, Mr. Darcy. They hired many people to try to return their daughter and granddaughter to them, all unsuccessful—why, even her son went in search of his sister."

Darcy and Lizzie glanced at each other. Leticia's father?

"What happened to him?" Lizzie asked.

Mrs. Bennet had just taken a sip of her tea, so they had to wait for her to swallow, lower her teacup, and delicately pat her lips with a handkerchief. "Oh, I don't know—there were some rumors that he found himself a French wife and decided to stay, but I can't remember. He was always a bit of a radical, I think. Either way, he never returned and I definitely remember reading that he'd passed."

"And . . . did he have any children?"

"How should I know?" Mrs. Bennet harrumphed. "So much interest in the past! I don't see how any of this ancient history is helpful for your case!"

"You've been incredibly helpful, madam," Darcy reassured

her. Mrs. Bennet preened at the praise, and then proceeded to take up the next quarter of an hour asking Darcy about the health of his sister, his father's travels, and their country estate.

Meanwhile, Lizzie was thinking. Leticia was the child of Mrs. Cavendish's lost son, but she had grown up with Josette, which implied that Leticia's father had reunited with his sister after all. And for whatever reason, they'd decided to stay in France rather than return to England—perhaps it had been safer to stay put than to risk life and freedom making the journey across the Channel to England. But why, then, had Josette found her way to London while Leticia had been left behind? And what had brought Leticia to England now?

When Mrs. Bennet was satisfied with her social visit with Mr. Darcy, he finally stood to take his leave. Lizzie saw him to the door. "I wish you could stay—I still have so many questions."

"If I impose upon your mother's hospitality any longer, she'll start planning a wedding," Darcy joked.

Lizzie's eyes widened in shock. "Never mind! We'll sort it out later."

"Lizzie, I was only joking—"

"We must speak with Mr. Mullins!" she interrupted, not eager to discuss her mother's hopes and dreams for her future. "I want to question him without him realizing we're questioning him."

Darcy didn't immediately agree, and Lizzie could tell he wanted to say something. *Please don't bring up my mother,* she thought, and was relieved when he nodded and said, "I'll be curious to see his reaction to the news that Leticia Cavendish is dead," he said, setting his hat upon his head. "Can you arrange a meeting for tomorrow? You can ask him questions under the guise of updating him about the case."

"I'll write him this evening," she said. "But can you come as well?"

He hesitated, but then nodded. "See if Mullins can meet in the morning, before I have to report to Pemberley."

His caginess gave her pause. "Darcy, is there something going on at work?"

"Nothing," he said. "Everything is fine—why do you ask?"

Because he hesitated whenever she brought up Pemberley. Because Mr. Tomlinson had seemed quite insistent that she not bother him. And because after nearly a year of working together, she had a sense for when he wasn't being entirely truthful.

But she smiled. "Never mind. I shall see you tomorrow."

TEN

In Which Darcy Receives a Threat, and Mr. Mullins Makes a Surprising Announcement

LIZZIE SUSPECTED.

Of course she did. She was the cleverest woman he knew, and he was an idiot for thinking she wouldn't. *Just tell her*, he thought. *No need to keep things from her. She'd understand, you fool.* She had to contend with working alongside Mr. Collins.

He arrived home to his mostly empty town house, his guilt and uncertainty nagging at him until he wondered if he ought to turn around and go back and tell Lizzie the whole story. But when he stepped into the hall past the foyer and spotted two letters on a tray, he stopped.

There was a letter from his father.

He broke into a cold sweat at the sight of his father's handwriting. It would be weeks before his lie about working a Pemberley case with Lizzie would reach him, but he had the feeling that Tomlinson hadn't been sending his father glowing reports of Darcy's work for months now. What would he say?

He looked at the second letter and relaxed when he saw it was from Georgiana. All manner of upsets and frustrations were made more tolerable with his sister's presence, and he missed her fiercely. He stepped into the study and sank into an armchair before a roaring fire, deciding he'd open Georgie's letter first.

Pemberley, Derbyshire
Dear Fitz,

How are you? How is your work? How is Bingley? How is London? Oh, I miss London! And you, of course. How much longer do you think Papa will be abroad? It's endlessly boring here, and I can't wait for the season to change and for summer to bring houseguests before I perish from monotony. Speaking of perishing, have you solved any more murders with Miss Bennet? Perhaps you will bring her here for a visit so I shall not wither away into nothing before my time.

Darcy laughed, hearing his sister's animated voice in his head. Sometimes she had to be reminded to take a breath between questions, and she left barely a space between sentences, as if she couldn't be bothered to lift her pen too far from paper for long.

Her letter continued on with updates from her time at their country estate, scant though they were. She'd reacquainted herself with their neighbors and spent most of her time calling on them and hosting teas, walking the grounds, and playing the pianoforte. Her one bright spot of happiness was that their father had relented that she was too old for a governess and had hired her a lady's companion by the name of Mrs. Watts, who was "old but not elderly" and "very proper, but not a bore."

Darcy made a mental note to write her a lengthy letter in return, and soon. Perhaps he'd confide in her—not about his troubles at work, Georgie mustn't know about that. But perhaps about Lizzie and how she seemed to balk at allowing him near her parents. Caroline Bingley hadn't been entirely wrong earlier that day, although it had been quite rude of her to point out how overzealous Mrs. Bennet could be. Perhaps that was it, and Lizzie was embarrassed by her mother's less than subtle attempts to see them together. He imagined what Georgie would say about that: *Who cares about her mother when it's the daughter you fancy?*

He couldn't argue with that.

Unfortunately, any good humor that Georgie's letter brought him immediately vanished upon opening his father's letter. It was brief, hardly worth the cost of postage.

Fitzwilliam,

    Tomlinson's updates on your work have not been satisfactory. I expect more from you. Perhaps you have too many distractions at Pemberley? Your association with Miss Bennet appears to no longer be suitable. Renew your focus on your cases, and cease

wasting time with Longbourn affairs, or I shall be required to
put you under my close personal supervision.
        Your father,
        Edward Darcy

His father's final sentence gave Darcy pause. His father hadn't said a word about when he'd return to London. Did that mean that he would return to London to oversee his work . . . or would he send for Darcy? The idea of leaving London, of leaving Lizzie, made his heart race and his fists clench, crumpling the letter. He wouldn't leave his home. He loved his job, and despite what Tomlinson thought, he worked hard. What did that man have against him?

He had to find out. Somehow, in between his caseload and helping Lizzie find Leticia's murderer and the Mullinses' arsonist, he had to discover a way to endear himself to Tomlinson.

Darcy tossed the letter into the fire and was satisfied to watch as the flames licked at his father's words. Then he shook himself out of his spiral of anxious thoughts and rang for dinner.

He had a lot of work to get through if he was to get caught up.

"You're late," Lizzie observed the next morning when he arrived at Longbourn & Sons, still bleary-eyed from a long night at his desk.

"Sorry," Darcy said, not offering an explanation. He nodded a greeting to Charlotte in the lobby. "Is Mr. Mullins here?"

"Not yet, but he's due any minute," Lizzie said, already herding him toward her office. "Quickly, I want to be situated and sure of our strategy before he arrives."

Normally, Darcy would have shared her desire to lay out an approach for interviewing a person of interest, but his mind was half on Tomlinson back at Pemberley & Associates. He'd managed to get through the entire backlog of paperwork he'd missed from taking time off the previous two days, but what punishment would Tomlinson have planned in the interim?

"Darcy, I need you to look relaxed," Lizzie said.

"I'm sorry, what?"

"Relaxed," Lizzie repeated, pushing him toward a chair in the corner. "Like you're simply dropping in to observe, but you don't really care either way how the case goes."

Darcy took a seat and tried to follow her instructions.

"I said relaxed, not like you're sitting on tacks!"

"Sorry," Darcy said. "It's hard to appear relaxed when a woman is dead."

"That's exactly why I need you to try—the stakes are too high." Lizzie looked through the window of her office and said, "He's here. Stay here; I'll bring him back."

Darcy watched her through the wavy glass that looked out into the main area of the office and tried to shake out any tension. Lizzie was far better at this aspect of their job than he—before meeting her it never would have occurred to him that he ought to affect various personas in an attempt to wring information from clients and witnesses. He approached every situation with his normal, straightforward attitude, making no attempt to obfuscate or curry favor. But her methods had a strange way of yielding results. He hoped this time would be no different.

As Jack Mullins followed Lizzie back to the office, Darcy evaluated him. The last time Darcy had seen him, he'd been rain-soaked and frantic, but now he appeared solemn and well-dressed, in clothing that fit him nicely, which meant he had coin enough to have replaced his wardrobe already. His expression when greeting Charlotte had been polite but restrained, and now he wore a grave look as he followed Lizzie. Darcy suspected that under normal circumstances, the gentleman was likely a very cheerful fellow—he had that air about him. But the task of burying his brother and salvaging his burned-out business appeared to have worn him down.

"So grateful you could make the time for us today," Lizzie said as she ushered Mr. Mullins into her office.

"Of course, I'm eager to hear your news." He spotted Darcy in the corner, and confusion clouded his face. "Hello?"

"Oh, my apologies," Lizzie said, sounding as if she'd forgotten Darcy was there. "This is my colleague Mr. Darcy. He often helps me out on cases, especially the more important ones."

Darcy made the decision not to rise to greet Mr. Mullins, and instead nodded at him. "My condolences for your loss."

"Thank you." Mr. Mullins was clearly flustered by Darcy's presence, but he tried to recover as Lizzie closed her office door and gestured to the empty seat opposite her desk. "I didn't know you'd be bringing in someone else."

"At no additional charge to you, I promise. Sometimes, for the very important cases, I like to have another set of eyes on things to ensure I miss nothing."

Mr. Mullins appeared mollified, though Darcy wasn't certain whether it was due to Lizzie's reassurances or because she'd emphasized twice that his case was important. He sat, giving Darcy a single sidelong glance before looking back at Lizzie. "All right, then."

"Excellent." Lizzie sat down at her desk and made a show of shuffling a few notes, which Darcy knew was an act. She was the most organized person he'd ever met. She moved a pile of papers, revealing a gold and pink-topaz necklace. "Do you recognize this necklace?"

Darcy felt his eyes widen in surprise as he leaned forward, momentarily forgetting his role. That was Leticia's necklace! He recalled she'd been wearing it the day they'd called. How had Lizzie gotten it?

"Er, no? Should I?" Mr. Mullins looked back at Darcy in confusion.

"Take a closer look," Lizzie encouraged. "Go ahead."

Baffled, Mr. Mullins leaned forward and took the necklace from her. He inspected it briefly, turning it about, and then handed it back. "I'm sorry. I don't think I've ever seen it. What does it have to do with the fire?"

Lizzie didn't answer him. "Jack, does the name Leticia Cavendish sound familiar to you?"

"Leticia Cavendish . . . no. I'm pretty certain I've never heard of her. Is she the lady who started the fire?"

"How about Josette Beaufort?"

That name gave Jack pause. "It does sound familiar. I'm not sure where I've heard it, though. She's French?"

"Yes," Lizzie confirmed.

"Is either of these women responsible for killing my brother?"

"I can't say," Lizzie said. "We've found no evidence of a tall, brunette lady who was in the vicinity of the storehouse on the day of the fire—"

"But this Miss Beaufort, and Miss Cav—Cavender?"

"Cavendish," Darcy corrected, unable to help himself.

"Cavendish. Why are you asking me about them? Who are they?"

"Their names came up in the course of the investigation," Lizzie confirmed. "But—and forgive me, Jack, because I know how much you want to find the person responsible—I cannot simply accuse someone without any evidence or even a motive. Why would a lady trespass upon your property and set fire to it?"

"I don't know!" Jack's fist came down on Lizzie's desk with a sharp bang. Darcy nearly leapt to his feet but a stern look from Lizzie kept him in his seat. Jack seemed to realize he'd gone too far. "I'm sorry."

Lizzie gave him one of her patient smiles, and if Darcy hadn't been so suspicious of Mr. Mullins at this moment, it would have been entertaining to sit back and watch her work her charm.

"It's all right, Jack. The thing is, we have very little to go on.

If you don't know why someone would want to set fire to your business, and you don't recognize the names we've uncovered, I'm afraid I have run out of leads. Your foreman wouldn't even let us into the building to inspect the damage."

"It's too dangerous," Jack said. "The building surveyor said no one but workmen are allowed in or out until repairs can be made. They've been working on it, but the surveyor won't be back for another week! As it is, I don't know if it'll be quick enough to receive our next shipment from the mills at the end of the month."

"So soon?" Lizzie sounded genuinely surprised, and Darcy was as well. He moved quickly.

"Time is money," Jack said. "If I have nowhere to store the cloth, then I can't arrange to sell it."

"It sounds difficult," Lizzie said, sounding sympathetic. "Have you had any trouble with your exporting business? Other clients have struggled with pirates in recent years."

Jack waved away Lizzie's worry. "Our ships are outfitted with carronades these days. I'm sorry, but have you investigated these ladies?"

Darcy watched Lizzie steel herself for the next part. "Yes, Jack. I have. And I'm afraid that they are quite shocked to hear of the fire and the suspicions. They are involved in relief efforts for the French émigrés in your neighborhood. But they say they've never been to your storehouse."

"So that's that? A dead end?"

"Not exactly." Lizzie looked at Darcy, and he nodded. She

refocused her gaze on Jack. "Jack, Leticia Cavendish was murdered yesterday."

A long silence followed Lizzie's words, and Darcy watched Mr. Mullins very carefully.

Liars tended to exaggerate their facial expressions or movements. They made a point of being shocked or devastated or made loud proclamations. But Jack Mullins did neither. His body went still, and his mouth fell open, although just slightly—his reaction was of surprise and confusion. "Are you serious?"

"Very."

The stunned silence stretched out for a few beats longer and Darcy was surprised when the man began to tremble, and then when that trembling turned into disbelieving laughter. "Murdered? The prime suspect of my brother's death was murdered?"

"I wouldn't go so far as to say she was the *prime* suspect," Lizzie corrected.

"But was she tall and brunette?" Jack demanded. "She could have been there."

"She fits the description you gave, but I cannot emphasize enough that we have no evidence placing her there. Even if she were still alive, we could hardly bring her before a court of law without proof."

"Is that her necklace?" Jack demanded. "Why did you ask me if I recognized it? Where did you find it? Do you suspect that I killed her?"

The thought had certainly crossed Darcy's mind, but Lizzie shook her head adamantly. "I asked if you recognized it in case you might have a connection to her that you didn't realize. The necklace wasn't anywhere near your storehouse."

"And what about the other lady? The French lady?"

"Miss Josette Beaufort," Lizzie said. "She is quite distraught about Miss Cavendish's death."

Jack muttered something that sounded to Darcy like "Bloody French."

Darcy was glad then that he was situated behind Mr. Mullins, for the thunderous thoughts that swirled in his head surely were showing on his face. *Composure*, he reminded himself. Even Lizzie looked aghast.

"Jack, I understand that you're upset. Truly, I do. But you must understand my position. I cannot conjure up a suspect out of nothing. If you could comb through your memories for anything your brother might have said for any sort of motive or clue—"

"So it's now my brother's fault he died?"

"Jack, no, that's not what I meant—"

"No, I think I understand." Jack rose to his feet, and Lizzie and Darcy scrambled to follow. "I thought you could help, but if there is truly nothing you can do for me—"

"That's not what I said! Leticia Cavendish was murdered, Jack. I don't believe that is a coincidence! But I need your help to—"

"No need," Mullins said. "This was a mistake. You may send me a bill for your time."

Lizzie's mouth dropped open. "Jack!"

"Good day, Miss Bennet. Mr. Darcy."

And with that, Jack Mullins strode out of Lizzie's office.

Lizzie wavered behind her desk, torn between running after him and staying put. "Let him go," Darcy advised. "I don't think you'll be able to talk any sense into him."

She sank into her seat. "He actually stormed out! I've had quite a few clients do that, but it's always been for trivial reasons, not because they're displeased with my work."

Darcy moved into Jack's vacated seat. "Don't take it personally. I'm sure he isn't dissatisfied. In fact, I'm convinced he's hiding something."

"Just because he's upset—"

"No, it's not that. Stop and think for a moment. The stupidest thing I've ever done in my life was challenge Wickham to a duel over my sister's honor. I knew it was foolish, but I did it because I care about Georgiana. Is there anything you wouldn't do for your sisters?"

That got Lizzie to pause. "Clearly he's upset over his brother's death."

"Yes, but if someone had killed Jane, you would go over every detail in your mind, every conversation, just in case there was any clue as to who was responsible."

She considered this. "Unless someone implied that Jane did anything wrong, in which case I wouldn't believe it because Jane has never done anything wrong in her entire life."

"Lizzie, I will not quibble with you about your sister's goodness, but really is this the time—"

"No, Darcy, you misunderstand me! I would defend my sister's honor because I know she's good." She looked at him significantly. "Jack didn't try to defend his brother . . ."

"Because perhaps he knows his brother did something wrong?" Darcy finished.

The suggestion sat between them for a long moment.

"If Simon was caught up in something bad, and it got him killed, then why would Jack hire me?" she asked.

It was a fair question. "Perhaps Jack doesn't know the full extent of it."

Lizzie shook her head. "Or maybe he does know the full extent of it, but he didn't know the details."

"What details?"

Lizzie held up the necklace. "We gave him names, Darcy! Josette Beaufort and Leticia Cavendish!"

Dread washed over Darcy. "Is Josette in danger?"

"Her cousin was murdered, and we don't know why. I think it's fair to say she's always been in danger."

"We have to warn her!"

"And what if in doing so, we tip off whoever is responsible? We suspect Jack, but don't forget that Leticia all but implied that her cousin and Mr. Hughes might not be trustworthy."

She was right, of course. And he hated it. "We can't do nothing."

"We won't," she said, already reaching for a sheet of paper. She picked up a pen. "I shall write to Miss Dashwood and enlist her help. I'll tell her the details of the case and request a meeting.

165

Does nine o'clock tomorrow work for you? I'm sure she'll clear her schedule for us and—"

A knock came at the doorway, and the two turned to find Mr. Bennet standing at the threshold of Lizzie's office. "Good day, Mr. Darcy," he said. "Consulting on a case, are we?"

Was it his imagination, or had Mr. Bennet's question sounded vaguely sarcastic? "Hello, Mr. Bennet. And . . . yes."

"Was that Jack Mullins I saw leaving just now?" he asked.

"Yes," Lizzie replied, looking up from her paper and setting down her pen. "He wasn't very satisfied with what we had to tell him."

"Ah. An occupational hazard, I'm afraid."

Darcy liked Mr. Bennet. He always had an unbothered air about him that seemed in contrast with Mrs. Bennet's harried nature, but he was reminded in this moment that Lizzie's father seldom missed the important things. Now he had the feeling that Mr. Bennet was about to say something neither of them would like.

"Lizzie, I'm afraid I need you."

"Can it wait? It seems as though the crimes we're investigating have increased and yet we are still in want of a clear suspect."

"As unfortunate as that is, no, it cannot wait. You have other cases, my dear."

"Papa, this is important! A woman has died."

"And that is very tragic, but I need you for a deposition."

"Papa—"

"Lizzie," he sternly. "I said you could take on this case as

166

long as you didn't neglect your other work. Now, is anyone in imminent danger?"

Lizzie sighed. "I don't think so, but a woman is dead—"

"No imminent danger, good. And you, young man—I imagine you also have other cases?"

Darcy resisted the urge to pull out his pocket watch and check the time. "Actually . . . yes."

Lizzie glared at him. *Traitor,* her gaze seemed to say.

He lifted his shoulders helplessly and thought of his father's threat. *Renew your focus on your cases.*

"There," Mr. Bennet said. "That's settled."

"Fine," Lizzie said, picking up her pen once more. She looked at Darcy before he left and said, "But remember—Miss Dashwood, nine o'clock tomorrow. I'm not giving up."

He smiled as he donned his hat. "I never thought you would."

ELEVEN

*In Which Mrs. Bennet's Dinner Party
Is Most Rudely Interrupted*

"JANE, ARE YOU WEARING the pink ribbon or the blue?" Mrs. Bennet asked.

"Blue, Mama."

"Wear the pink. It makes your cheeks look rosier. And, Lizzie! Why are you not dressed yet?"

Lizzie looked up from the book she had brought home from Longbourn, her mind lingering on the legal precedents involving cases of arson. She was dressed only in her shift and her hair fell across her shoulders and back, unbound. "I'm sorry?"

Mrs. Bennet crossed the room and wrenched the book from Lizzie's hands, snapping it shut. "Elizabeth! Do you mean to send me to an early grave? Mr. Bingley shall be here within the half hour, and if everything is to go perfectly, you need to be dressed and downstairs and ready to play your part!"

"I'm sorry," Lizzie said, knowing that apologizing was the

only course of action when Mrs. Bennet was this worked up. "I'm almost ready."

She reached for a cream-colored dress, only for Mrs. Bennet to cry out, "Not that one! It is too lovely for tonight—Jane must shine!"

"How about you see to preparations downstairs, and I'll make sure Lizzie is dressed and presentable?" Jane asked.

Mrs. Bennet took a steadying breath. "Fine. But, Lizzie, you better be ready in ten minutes. And I don't want to see that dog all evening!"

From his position on the bed, Guy cocked his head.

"We'll both be on our very best behavior tonight, Mama," Lizzie promised.

"My nerves, Lizzie, have compassion for my nerves! This is one of the most important nights of my life, and that dog isn't helping!"

And with that, she swept from the room.

"One would think she's the one about to be proposed to, not you," Lizzie said, reaching for her second-best dress, the brown-and-green-striped satin, and pulling it on.

"Yes, well . . . she's worked hard to make this evening come together." Jane began to remove the blue ribbon from the trim on her white lawn dress.

Lizzie laid a hand on her sister's, stilling it. "Leave the ribbons. It's your night—you ought to wear what you like. You look beautiful either way, and besides, I don't think Bingley will be noticing the color of your ribbons when he can scarcely take his eyes off your face."

Jane looked up at her. "Do you really mean that?"

"Of course," Lizzie said. "Have you not realized? The man is mad about you!"

"I'm surprised you've taken the time to notice Mr. Bingley's feelings," Jane said, and the rebuke was so mild that Lizzie couldn't have felt worse if Jane had offered her a cutting word instead.

"Janie." Lizzie reached out and took her sister's hands. "I'm sorry. I've been a rotten sister lately, haven't I? It's just this case . . . I've let it get to my head."

"You're not a rotten sister," Jane insisted, although Lizzie noticed she didn't refute Lizzie's claim that the case had been going to her head. "You've been very busy."

Lizzie had been consumed, but she could have asked Jane how she was feeling this morning, or made a point to come home sooner to help her get ready. "I'm sorry," she said. "I promise this evening shall be about you, and not about my case. I won't breathe a word of it!"

Jane hugged her. "Oh, Lizzie. I'm so nervous, I don't know how I can expect to eat a thing!"

"I think the only thing expected of you tonight is to say yes when the question is asked," Lizzie said. "But surely you don't doubt Bingley's feelings for you?"

"It's not that," Jane said. Lizzie struggled to recall the last time she'd seen her sister look so distressed—perhaps when Wickham had kidnapped Lizzie. "I suppose it's silly, but I was hoping for something rather more romantic."

"It's not silly," Lizzie insisted. "Perhaps Mama's manipulations don't exactly feel romantic now, but think about how happy you'll be."

That seemed to encourage Jane, and she grabbed hold of both of Lizzie's hands. "I want you to be happy, too."

Lizzie smiled brightly. "I'm incredibly happy."

"Yes, but you and Mr. Darcy . . ."

"We aren't talking about me this evening, remember?"

Lizzie didn't want to talk about yesterday and how embarrassing it had been to stand in her own drawing room and fend off her mother's rather obvious attempts at pressuring Darcy to propose marriage. Maybe she ought to have enjoyed it. After all, Darcy was quickly becoming one of her favorite people, alongside Jane. And he was a gentleman. There was nothing preventing a union between them. Nothing, except the undercurrent of fear and anxiety when she thought about giving up everything she'd worked for.

"Oh dear, it's as bad as that?" Jane asked.

Lizzie shook her head. "I don't know what you're talking about! Now, help me fasten my dress and let's go downstairs before Mama has a fit!"

Darcy was late.

Lizzie was unsurprised when Mr. Bingley arrived first, and then Charlotte. The gathering was a pleasant one, especially since Caroline and Louisa weren't present, and the conversation was lively as the minutes ticked by. But when the clock struck quarter past and Darcy had still not arrived, Lizzie had to start pretending not to see Mrs. Bennet's sharp, questioning looks. And when it was half past and dinner was announced, Mrs. Bennet shot Lizzie an accusatory look.

"No Mr. Darcy? I do hope that he is all right."

"He must have gotten caught up in court, Mama," Lizzie lied. She felt compelled to salvage his reputation before her mother, despite her own questions.

Mr. Bennet gave her a curious look, for he understood that no court would convene this late, but didn't contradict Lizzie's explanation. "Let us eat, and hope Mr. Darcy has a riveting explanation when he arrives."

Dinner was as carefully choreographed as a ballroom dance, with Jane and Bingley as the principal players. Lizzie was seated next to Bingley, and Jane was placed directly across from him, next to Charlotte. Her assorted sisters flanked them, while Mr. and Mrs. Bennet sat at either end of the table. Guy had slipped under the table when Mrs. Bennet wasn't looking, and Lizzie wasn't about to say anything as long as the dog stayed quiet. As the honored guest, Bingley was placed to the right of Mr. Bennet, and Mrs. Bennet was practically leaning into her soup in order to orchestrate the conversation from the other end, quizzing him on his latest social engagements and whether or not he had plans to visit his country estate that summer.

"I hear the countryside is lovely in June," Mrs. Bennet said, not allowing Mr. Bingley a chance to reply. "Not that we've been in quite a long while, of course."

That was accompanied by a pointed look at Mr. Bennet.

"Yes, well, I'm afraid that criminal activity only increases in the summer months," Mr. Bennet said, oblivious to his wife's attempts to steer the conversation. "It's the heat, you see. Drives most people mad."

"You avoid criminal cases," Lizzie pointed out.

"But they don't always avoid me."

"The weather would drive any sane person to commit heinous acts," Mr. Bingley agreed. "My sisters usually go, but as of late I've been far too busy to get away myself."

"When was the last time we were in the country, Mr. Bennet?" Mrs. Bennet asked, louder than necessary. "Why, it must have been for my brother's wedding! And what a lovely wedding it was! Summer weddings are always the height of fashion, in my opinion."

Lizzie would have laughed, if not for Jane practically swaying in her seat, looking ready to swoon from embarrassment. She cleared her throat and asked, "How is the shipping business, Mr. Bingley?"

"Well, thank you—not without its challenges, but much improved from this time last year."

Lizzie ignored her mother's dagger stare. "I am so glad to hear it."

"What challenges?" Mary asked. When her sisters glanced at her, her shoulders drew up defensively. "I'm just curious! I thought Lizzie took care of the pirate problem."

"We've had no trouble since my, ah, pirate problem, as Miss Mary put it." Bingley was quick to reassure the Bennets. "This time, it's France—Napoleon is determined to hobble us all when it comes to trading with the Continent. But the navy has been keeping up the good fight!"

"How awful," Mr. Bennet said. "I hope you haven't lost any more ships."

"None, thank goodness," Bingley said. "The waters have been a little bit safer as of late, thanks to Miss Elizabeth."

"I'm happy to hear it," Lizzie said. Clearing Mr. Bingley's name of murder the previous spring had been a winding case that involved tracing an insurance scam to a pirate by the name of Lady Catherine de Bourgh. She'd managed to evade Lizzie and Darcy in the end, but Darcy's contacts at the Royal Navy had assured them she wouldn't get far.

"Have you ever seen a pirate?" Lydia asked, directing her question at Mr. Bingley.

Mary tsked. "Don't be daft, Lydia—if he had, he'd not likely be telling us about it."

"Why not?" Kitty asked. "Are pirates indelicate topics?"

"No, silly, because if he'd encountered a pirate, he'd be *dead*."

Jane looked pained at the direction this conversation was taking. "I hardly like to think about how dangerous Mr. Bingley's job must be without you bringing pirates into the mix."

"You're forgetting that *I* met a pirate and lived to tell the tale," Lizzie said. She didn't point out that Lady Catherine might have shot her, too, because that did seem indelicate for a dinner party.

"The lady one," Lydia said with great disdain. "Not a handsome, dashing—"

"Lydia!" Jane admonished, cheeks now distinctly pink.

Lizzie sneaked a glance at her father, to see if he had any sort of reaction to Lydia airing her fantasies at the dinner table, but he was too busy sneaking a tiny piece of roast chicken to Guy.

"None of you must worry about my safety," Bingley hastened to reassure them. "The navy is doing its job, and I am in talks with a factory in Scotland to outfit Netherfield's ships with carronades."

"Are those like canons?" Mary asked.

Jane gasped. "Is that wise? Will you not become a target?"

"Don't worry, Miss Bennet—these carronades are for defense only. They're much smaller than the canons the navy uses, and we'd only use them in the event of an attack."

"I've read about these carronades in the paper," Charlotte said. "A good number of merchant ships are installing them."

"Yes, indeed," Bingley agreed. "One blast from a carronade and deadly damage is done to any privateer that might try to board, which allows the captains to steer our ships to safety."

"You'll get these carronades installed soon?" Jane inquired anxiously. "Before you set sail on another business trip?"

"As soon as I am able," Mr. Bingley promised.

"Sounds costly," Mr. Bennet observed.

"You can't put a price on safety. Besides, the carronades themselves will be easy to procure—finding cannonballs is the true challenge. They're in short supply, and all being requisitioned for the war effort."

"Why, that's just silly," Kitty said. "Why don't they make enough to shoot all the French and stop the war?"

Lizzie might have rolled her eyes at Kitty's simplification, but Mr. Bingley took her question in earnest. "It's not quite that easy, Miss Kitty. Cannonballs require certain materials, and they're hard to come by. Lead, iron, graphite . . ."

"I was reading in the papers that the French don't have enough graphite of their own," Charlotte added. "They're desperate for our supply. With such advantages, we can surely hope for a quick British victory."

Graphite. Why did that sound familiar?

"Indeed, England has some of the best deposits of graphite in all the world," Mr. Bingley agreed. "Now that it has become so dear, the Crown guards its supplies closely."

Lizzie gasped. Mr. Hughes owned a graphite mine! But what had he said about it? The vein had run dry, and now his mining days were over.

Jane looked at her, worried. "Are you all right, Lizzie?"

"I'm fine, thank you." She took a sip from her glass, and then said, "And where are these cannonballs made, Mr. Bingley?"

"Oh, I don't know precisely—but I believe there is a munitions factory here in London."

"Are you taking an interest in firearms, Lizzie?" Mr. Bennet asked. "I admit, I would prefer it if you chose less dangerous hobbies."

"I'm just curious about the graphite," she said, casting a glance at her older sister. She had promised Jane that tonight would be about her, and yet she couldn't help asking Mr. Bingley, "Is all the graphite in England controlled by the Crown?"

"Yes," Mr. Bennet answered instead. "Smuggling it is a felony."

Lizzie dropped her fork, which held a small bit of boiled potato, so great was her surprise. It clattered onto the floor, whereupon the potato was quickly claimed by Guy.

"Are you quite all right?" Jane asked.

Mrs. Bennet glared at her. "Lizzie! Is that dog in my dining room?"

"Sorry, Mama," she murmured. And then, "Oh, look, here comes the pudding!"

That was enough to distract the dinner party, and by the time everyone had been served and compliments were given, the conversation moved on. But Lizzie was still thinking of graphite, and carronades, and most of all, she was thinking of Mr. Hughes.

Mr. Hughes owned a graphite mine in the Lake District that was supposedly defunct.

Darcy had not been able to obtain a search permit for the Mullins Brothers storehouse due to official Crown business.

Were these two things related? If Mr. Hughes was moving his graphite through the Mullins Brothers storehouse, it could explain the secrecy and danger. But surely such an operation had to be illegal. And if a tall, dark-haired young lady, who was either Josette or Leticia, had discovered that Mr. Hughes was selling his graphite to the French . . . well, that was a secret worth killing for.

But why would Jack Mullins hire her to find an arsonist if the Crown was investigating his storehouse?

Unless . . . their suspicions were true and Jack Mullins wasn't aware of such an investigation.

A chill went through Lizzie then, and she missed Darcy fiercely. He would tell her if her imagination was running away with her. He would also be the first to tell her that the last thing they needed was to run afoul of the Crown if it was investigating felonies and possible *treason*.

Where was he?

"Shall we go through?" Mrs. Bennet asked, startling Lizzie out of her thoughts.

She looked around the table and realized that everyone was finished with their pudding, but Mrs. Bennet was not willing to wait on her account—this was the moment that she'd been waiting for all evening. She looked downright gleeful as she ushered the ladies away from the table, leaving Mr. Bennet and Mr. Bingley with their drinks.

Then Mr. Bennet said to Bingley, "It's just the two of us— unless you desperately want a brandy, how about we follow them?"

"No!" Mrs. Bennet cried, spinning around.

Bingley and Mr. Bennet looked at her, startled.

"No," she repeated, smiling. "Mr. Bennet, you simply must offer Mr. Bingley a drink! I will not have him saying that our hospitality is lacking!"

Beside Lizzie, Jane clutched at her hand. Lizzie squeezed it reassuringly, although she couldn't help but feel a wave of sympathy for her father—for all her mother's careful, diligent planning for this evening, she seemed to have failed to inform her husband to be prepared for any opportunity for Mr. Bingley to ask for Jane's hand.

"Well, all right," Mr. Bennet said. "But I have to warn you, this English brandy can't hold a candle to the French stuff."

"I shall happily receive it anyway," Bingley assured, and Mrs. Bennet shooed the girls out of the dining room and down the hall to the drawing room.

"Honestly," she seethed. "Your father is trying his best to send me to an early grave."

The ladies sat in tense silence in the drawing room, not allowed to even converse. They could just make out the murmur of the gentlemen's voices in the other room, but no amount of shushing or holding absolutely still rendered their voices audible enough to make out the conversation. Lizzie sat next to Jane, who had gone as pale as a sheet and was squeezing her hand tightly.

"It'll be fine," Lizzie whispered. "You know that Father won't say no."

"I know, but what if Mr. Bingley doesn't even ask at all?"

"Shush!" their mother hissed.

"Mama, this is silly—there's nothing we can do but wait. And besides, won't it look rather suspicious if they join us here and we're all just sitting in total silence?"

Mrs. Bennet seemed to consider this, then relented. "Mary, the piano."

Mary rolled her eyes but dutifully took her seat at the bench and began to pluck out notes. Lizzie tried to hide her wince.

"What's going on with you this evening?" Charlotte whispered from Lizzie's other side.

"What?"

"First of all, you and I both know that Mr. Darcy wouldn't still be in court at this hour, and you got a peculiar look on your face when Mr. Bingley began to discuss that business of carronades at dinner."

"I did not," Lizzie lied. She didn't want to ruin Jane's evening with talk about her case.

But Jane nodded. "You did."

"Fine," Lizzie relented. "But it's probably nothing. Someone involved in our case owns a graphite mine, that's all. And it got me thinking—"

But Lizzie didn't get a chance to say anything more, for the drawing room door opened and Mr. Bennet and Mr. Bingley appeared, Guy trotting on their heels. *That had to have been the quickest glass of brandy ever consumed,* Lizzie thought. The gaze of every lady in the room turned to them, and Mary abruptly stopped playing.

"Er, hello?" Bingley said.

"Hello." Jane was the only one to reply.

"What are you all staring at?" Mr. Bennet asked.

"Nothing!" Mrs. Bennet said. "Mary, why'd you stop playing?"

"I thought—"

"Never mind what you thought, keep playing!"

Mary picked up her shapeless tune once more and Mr. Bingley sat in the chair opposite the settee, where Lizzie, Jane, and Charlotte were seated while Mr. Bennet took his usual chair and, with a surreptitious look around, reached for his newspaper.

An inscrutable look seemed to pass between Jane and Bingley.

"Well, then," Mrs. Bennet began. "What did you two speak about—"

But Mrs. Bennet's matchmaking plans were abruptly cut short by the shattering glass that ripped through the drawing room.

At least four of the ladies screamed, and Guy immediately began barking, a high-pitched, alarmed yip that made Lizzie leap to her feet. Jane and Charlotte remained seated on the sofa, and Bingley had instinctively jumped in front of Jane, his arms raised protectively.

The drawing room window had been broken, letting in the cool night air. Glass littered the carpet, sparkling in the lamplight, and in the center of the room lay a heavy object—the projectile that had broken the glass. Beyond the broken window,

Lizzie could hear the sound of running feet on the cobblestones outside.

Without thinking, she picked up her skirts and bolted for the front door, ignoring the ruckus behind her and the crunch of glass under her slippers. She flung open the front door and ran down the steps, eyes searching for any sign of the vandal in the night. Next door and across the street her neighbors were emerging from their houses, and she ignored their inquiries as she stumbled out into the street and looked left, then right.

Whoever it was, they were gone.

"Elizabeth!" her father called from the front door. "Come inside."

"They're gone," she said, still looking about. Her eyes were beginning to adjust to the darkness, but she didn't see anything amiss. Her exposed skin prickled in the early spring cold.

"We'll send for the Runners," he said. "But come inside before you catch a chill or your mother's nerves do her in, whichever occurs first."

Inside, Mrs. Bennet was working herself up to full-blown hysterics, attended by her daughters, while a maid nervously tried to clean up the glass and Bingley stood before the open window as if ready to defend the Bennets from any more projectiles. Guy was barking like mad, but Lizzie was relieved to see in the mayhem that he'd leapt up on Mr. Bennet's chair, so at least she didn't need to worry about him cutting himself on the broken glass.

"We're under attack! Oh, who would do such a thing?" Mrs. Bennet wailed.

"Are we about to be robbed?" Lydia asked.

"No, you fool," Mary snapped. "Does it look like we're about to be robbed?"

"Someone threw a brick through our window—how should I know?"

"I am going to swoon!" Mrs. Bennet cried out.

"You sound quite alert to me, ma'am," Mr. Bennet said, following Lizzie back into the drawing room. "Now, if you all would just be quiet!"

They all hushed, except for Guy. "Sit! Quiet!" Lizzie hissed at him, and to her surprise he sat obediently in Mr. Bennet's chair.

"Right," he said. "Girls, get your mother upstairs, then go to your rooms and stay there. I have to fetch the Runners and we'll need to file an official report. Bingley, would you—"

"I'll stay right here and ensure everyone is safe," he promised, and Lizzie noticed him looking at Jane as he said it.

"Very well," Mr. Bennet said, casting one longing look at his newspaper before saying, "Now!"

The younger Bennet sisters escorted their mother upstairs and Jane followed. Lizzie felt a pang of regret for Jane. Her poor sister! She thought she was getting engaged tonight, and now she'd likely spend the next three hours comforting their distraught mother. Charlotte sidled up to Lizzie and whispered, "I think you ought to look at the brick."

Lizzie had been far more interested in the damage caused by the projectile and trying to catch whoever was responsible, so she was surprised by Charlotte's grave suggestion. She took a step forward, glass crunching underfoot, and found the brick where it had landed on the carpet. It was an entirely normal-looking brick, as far as Lizzie was concerned, but already her thoughts were racing—why a brick? Bricks had value when a stone would have been free and done the job just as well.

"Miss Elizabeth, I don't think . . ." Mr. Bingley began, but then seemed to think better of what he was about to say. Lizzie had gotten him cleared of murder charges, after all.

When she drew close, she realized that the brick had dark marks slashed across it. As her racing heart settled a bit, she stopped cold. "Does that say . . ."

"Yes," Charlotte said. "Is *that* connected to your case?"

But Lizzie could not speak. Across the broad surface of the brick, someone had used a black, smudgy substance to scratch out the word *STOP*.

Bingley leaned forward to read it. His face drained of all color. "Stop? Stop what?"

Lizzie withdrew a handkerchief, embroidered with her own haphazard strawberries, and picked up the brick gingerly. Her heart was hammering in her chest now. *Darcy*, she thought. *Where are you?*

"I'm not sure, exactly, but I think I have an idea."

TWELVE

In Which Darcy Finds Himself Unavoidably
Detained and Receives Romantic Advice

"IF YOU INTEND TO be a dandy and keep a social schedule, why don't you do all of us a favor and inform us now?"

Mr. Tomlinson's voice rang out across the office as soon as Darcy arrived at Pemberley. Any stray conversations fell immediately silent. Darcy looked up to find his supervisor standing at the threshold of his office, staring at him with a smirk.

"My apologies," Darcy said, keeping his voice even. "I had an early appointment."

"What appointment?"

"That's confidential," he said.

Darcy was aware that all eyes were on him. Mr. Tomlinson had an audience now, and Darcy dreaded what he'd do next. "Randall had to step in for you at court yesterday," his supervisor said, "seeing as you didn't deign to show up to work."

Leticia Cavendish's lifeless face haunted his memory. "I sent a note explaining my absence. Which case?"

He looked around for Randall, but Mr. Tomlinson snorted. "Oh, you sent a note—well, you aren't a schoolboy anymore. Writing a note doesn't excuse your absences!"

Darcy spotted Randall at his desk, trying his best to appear as though he wasn't listening to this very public dressing down. "Randall, which case?"

"The Covington case, sir," Randall said, looking up.

"Don't call him sir!" Tomlinson snapped. "He is not deserving of the title."

No one in the office said a word. Darcy knew what they were all thinking—no one would dare speak to Darcy like that if his father were here. But his father wasn't here.

"The Covington case shouldn't have gone before the magistrate until next week," Darcy said, failing to keep the frustration from his voice.

"The court date was moved up, sir," Randall said, then gulped. "I mean . . . well. Yes. It was moved up."

"And now do you see what happens when you're off frolicking with that woman?" Tomlinson asked.

"She is a lady, and you'd best remember it," Darcy shot back.

Tomlinson recoiled as if Darcy had slapped him. In all the weeks of underhanded slights and abuses, Darcy hadn't once talked back to Tomlinson. But now he didn't care—Tomlinson could disparage or humiliate him all he wanted in front of his father's employees, but he wasn't about to stand by and let him disrespect Lizzie.

"Get back to work," Tomlinson finally sneered. "And if I

catch you slacking off or sneaking away one more time, I'll lock you in here myself."

Darcy returned to his desk, stone-faced. He supposed that to all the men in the office, it looked as though he might be seething. In reality, he burned with shame. Because Tomlinson was not particularly wrong about one thing—Darcy had been shunning work in favor of assisting Lizzie on her case. He should have been in the office to receive word that the hearing had been moved up.

This was his job. His future. His dream.

So why was it that he was all too willing to throw it aside in favor of helping Lizzie at the drop of a hat?

Even now, as he spent the rest of the afternoon throwing himself vigorously into his work and getting caught up, he couldn't let go of the case. Mr. Mullins was hiding something. Leticia Cavendish was dead.

And Josette—Josette was heartbroken.

He couldn't help but think about her shock at seeing him for the first time in two years. It had almost been as great as his shock at finding her in mourning. Old Mrs. Cavendish had always been kind to him, and it felt wrong that she'd died and he hadn't known. Despite how things had ended between him and Josette, he would have attended the funeral, at the very least. When people die, there are so many details to see to, and they can be overwhelming. He would have offered to help with the estate, the will . . . well, he supposed she had Mr. Hughes for all that now.

The will.

It came to him suddenly—who had settled Mrs. Cavendish's will?

If Darcy hadn't just been publicly scolded by Tomlinson, he would have leapt to his feet and gone straight to the records room. But he knew if he made the slightest motion away from his desk, Tomlinson would demand to know what he was doing; and some instinct told him that he needed to keep his questions to himself, at least for now.

And so he spent the next few hours at his desk, trying his very best to look the part of the busy, industrious worker. But really, he kept an eye out for Tomlinson. The man spent most of the time in his office, with the door closed while one of the clerks, Maxwell, scuttled in and out of the office, doing his bidding. Tomlinson stayed put all day, which meant that Darcy spent a long afternoon at his desk, catching up on the backlog of work and keeping one eye on Tomlinson's office door.

He waited it out until the other solicitors stood and put on their hats to go home. He lit a lamp he kept at his desk, even as the last of his colleagues finally set down the pens for the night. *Just go*, he though impatiently.

Tomlinson watched him from his office door as he put on his coat and donned his hat. "Don't think that you can make up for the last few days by staying late one night."

"No, sir," Darcy said, feeling a certain amount of satisfaction when Tomlinson finally took his leave.

He forced himself to wait ten minutes more before standing from his desk and stretching his aching limbs. Then he hurried to the records room and withdrew his key. Most junior solicitors were not allowed their own key to this room, but this was one advantage to being the son of the founding senior partner and heir apparent to the Pemberley legacy. Darcy let himself in and shut the door firmly behind him.

He could not come in here anymore without thinking of Lizzie. They'd been locked in this room together while working on Bingley's case; and even now, with a lamp in his hand, he got short of breath thinking about the darkness pressing in on him, close and claustrophobic, and the feel of Lizzie's hand taking his for the first time.

He felt himself shiver. Damn it all, Lizzie had ruined him for this room.

He was aware that he was cutting it close if he expected to arrive at the Bennets' in time for dinner, but he pictured how happy Lizzie would be if he could procure another clue to this case. Maybe she'd be pleased enough to kiss him when no one was looking, even if it was just a quick brush of her lips against his cheek. He liked it when she took the liberty of initiating, and her eyes gleamed with a fierceness as she went after what she wanted. . . .

Not now, he reminded himself.

Darcy wound his way through the files, starting at the *B*s. He got to *Bitely, John* before realizing that any files regarding

Josette and her grandmother wouldn't be under *Beaufort*, but under *Cavendish*, her grandmother's name. Cursing his lack of focus, he moved on to the *C*s.

Of course, there were more than a few Cavendish case files, and none of them were labeled *Cavendish, Amelia*. They all had male names attached to them. "Albert, Frederick, George, Matthew, Phineas, Reginald," he muttered as he paged through them all. But no Amelia. What the devil? Was her case file missing? Perhaps someone else had pulled it? He glanced at the log near the door, where every clerk was supposed to record whichever file they had removed from the room, so as to keep track of them all. Perhaps it was listed there?

Then, he heard Lizzie's voice in the back of his head saying, *It's absurd, really, that a woman gives up everything, even her name, when she marries.*

Of course! How stupid of him—they rarely labeled case files under women's names if they were otherwise attached to a male. He pulled all the Cavendish files and set them down, and began to page through them. Under *Cavendish, Reginald*, he found what he was looking for: a sheet of paper with the man's information. Name, address, business contacts, and family members. Wife: Amelia Cavendish, née Holt. A copy of the burial register from the week she'd died was the next document and, next to her name and date of burial, the cause of death was listed: "rheumatism." The six-month anniversary of her death would be next week.

But other than that, the file was empty.

That couldn't be right. He went through all the other

Cavendish files, in case someone had made a mistake in filing, but there was nothing else there. Then he began searching the files in the drawer near *Cavendish, Reginald*'s file, but nothing turned up.

Where were the wills? The business contracts, the insurance policies, the years' worth of history and paperwork?

He stalked over to the records logs and paged through them slowly, going back seven months—before the date of Mrs. Cavendish's death—but there was nothing to indicate that the files had been removed.

Which meant that someone must have taken them.

But why?

Tomlinson was a brute to him, and he was clearly drunk with power. But Darcy had never seriously thought that he was anything more than a bully who enjoyed making a privileged son feel small when his father's back was turned. What if he was responsible for something more nefarious? Lost files, unhappy clients . . . was Tomlinson trying to hurt the firm?

Darcy turned to the door and wrenched the door handle, but it didn't budge. Immediately, panic closed around his throat like a vise. He twisted the knob, but the door wasn't locked—it simply wouldn't move. Something was blocking it on the other side.

Darcy shoved his entire weight against the door, but it was to no avail. Someone had trapped him in. From the other side of the door, he thought he heard the sound of footsteps, and he knocked on the door and called out, "Hello? Is anyone there?"

No answer came, and try as he might, he couldn't hear any

more sounds beyond the door. He was stuck for the second time in this blasted room, and panic made his heartbeat gallop. Was this some kind of joke? A prank? Or was it a punishment? *If I catch you slacking off or sneaking away one more time, I'll lock you in here myself,* Tomlinson had said. Darcy hadn't thought he'd literally lock him in the office overnight.

He looked at the lamp, which glowed brightly, and took deep, even breaths. Already the walls around him felt too close and tight now that he knew there was no way out. He tried to think of Lizzie, when they'd been trapped in this room in total darkness and they'd loathed each other but her hand found his in the dark and she had calmed his nerves.

Oh, Lizzie. He wished she were here now to distract from the panic that was crawling up his body to grab him by the throat. He could imagine her now saying, *At least we've got a lamp this time.* Or, *What secrets do you suppose we'll find in these files? Who shall we look up first?* Or maybe even simply, *Someone at Pemberley really ought to reconsider the design of this room.*

He choked on a small bit of laughter. Many horrible situations were much improved upon with Lizzie's presence, or even just the thought of her. He could only hope that she felt the same way, although there was still that niggling, uncomfortable feeling that she wished to keep him as far away from her mother as possible. Would his absence be a worry or relief for her this evening?

The lamp flickered, and he noted with unease that it would not likely last the next hour. He settled himself on the floor, leaning against the closed door. Thoughts of Lizzie had distracted him momentarily from his panic. He tried to recall every detail of her appearance, catalogue each of her smiles.

If she was embarrassed about her mother, then he simply had to tell her that it didn't matter. If she was worried about what her father might say, then he'd tell her he'd do whatever Mr. Bennet required to gain his approval. Darcy didn't care what Tomlinson thought, what his own father thought—his life was far more interesting with her in it. A fair bit more complicated, too, but Darcy didn't mind that. He'd once thought that in order to be successful, he had to be proper and follow the rules. That he had to stick to the path laid out before him by his father. But that path held no temptation for him now.

What was the law without justice? And what use was all his training if he never showed any bit of curiosity about the cases presented to him?

What good was life without Lizzie in it?

The lamp went out suddenly, and in the inky darkness, Darcy laughed. Not with panic or nerves, but with genuine surprise. Because it was only in the dark of the records room that he was finally able to see what was obvious.

He was in love with Lizzie Bennet.

It was Randall who let him out the following morning.

Darcy had fallen asleep at some point and he came awake slowly to a filmy gray light and a very sore back and bottom. He heard the murmur of voices beyond the door and as he scrambled to his feet, the door swung open.

"Sir? I mean—Mr. Darcy?" Randall asked, bewildered.

"Randall!" Darcy dusted himself off, as if it were perfectly natural for him to be trapped in the room at such an early hour.

"There was a chair wedged against the door, sir. Did you spend the night here?"

"I did indeed, Randall, but no matter—what time is it?"

"But why—are you all right, sir? Should I call someone?"

"No need, I'm out now. The time, Randall!"

"Half past eight—sir, where are you going?"

Darcy had already pushed past him and rushed to his desk. He picked up his jacket and hat and turned to Randall. "I have an appointment!"

"But Mr. Tomlinson—"

"I'll be back!" he called over his shoulder, bursting out of the offices. If Tomlinson was responsible for his night in the records room, then Darcy would deal with that later. Outside, he hailed a carriage and tried to straighten his appearance on the ride to Brower Street, where the Dashwoods kept a shop, and hoped that Lizzie still planned to meet him there.

The shop's front was a perfumery, which allowed all sorts of clients to come and go discreetly. The bell above the door tinkled when he let himself in, and there was only one other customer at the counter, head bent over the perfume samples displayed against a stretch of shockingly pink velvet. The young lady wore a wide straw bonnet trimmed with pink ribbon, and she paid

Darcy no mind as she continued her hushed conversation with the young lady behind the counter.

"Now, this one is floral, with deliberately light notes of vanilla and musk, and—oh, don't worry, we can speak plainly." Marianne Dashwood smiled broadly in his direction. "Mr. Darcy! We've not seen you in a while."

"Good day, Miss Dashwood." He bowed in her direction, and gave the young lady she was assisting a polite nod but said nothing to her as they were not acquainted. Blond ringlets framed her porcelain face from under her bonnet and she regarded him coolly but similarly held her tongue.

"Elinor, come see who's here!" Marianne called out, then turned back to her customer. "Sorry about that, Miss Woodhouse."

"Don't trouble yourself on my account," she said, casting Darcy a sidelong glance.

"Where's Miss Bennet?" Marianne asked, peering behind him as if she expected Lizzie to pop out.

The door behind the counter swung open and the oldest Dashwood sister, Elinor, came bustling out, wiping her hands on her apron. "Mr. Darcy, hello," she said, and smiled gently in his direction. Elinor was the more soft-spoken Dashwood sister; and while she was not prone to the same dramatic outbursts that Marianne was known for, her eyes held genuine warmth as she regarded him. "Oh—is Miss Bennet not with you?"

"That's what I asked," Marianne said. "He has yet to respond."

"Well, give him a moment," Elinor told her sister.

Miss Woodhouse, whoever she was, was watching this exchange with great interest.

"Good day, ladies," Mr. Darcy said. "Is Lizzie not here yet?"

"I'm afraid not," Elinor said.

At the same time, Marianne asked, "Is everything all right? I don't think I've ever seen either of you on your own."

"We do operate independently on occasion," Darcy noted, with a trace of irony in his voice.

Marianne was unimpressed. "If you'll excuse me saying so, you look dreadful."

"Marianne!"

"Oh, Mr. Darcy appreciates honesty!"

As a matter of course, this was true, but he was not sure he appreciated this brand of honesty. "I'm fine, Miss Dashwood. I had a rough night."

The sisters exchanged knowing looks, which immediately made Darcy suspicious.

"Is everything all right between you and Lizzie?" Marianne asked.

"What? Of course."

"It's just that this is highly unusual."

"Everything is fine," he insisted. "Except, well . . . our case has gotten complicated, and I went looking for information last night and found myself locked in the records room—it's a long story—and I missed a very important dinner last night, so she's likely a bit irritated with me at the moment. But once I explain the matter, it should be fine."

"You were locked in a records room?" Marianne asked.

"What important dinner?" Elinor added.

"A dinner her mother hosted, for my friend Bingley—you know Bingley?"

"Accused of murder, the man who brought you together!" Marianne said. "And very sweet on Jane Bennet, correct?"

"Cleared of murder," Darcy reminded them, more for the sake of Miss Woodhouse, who was watching this exchange with curiosity. "Mrs. Bennet is hoping Bingley will propose—which he absolutely will do, the man is lovesick—but to force the matter she hosted a dinner party last night. I was supposed to be there. Or rather, I think I was."

"You think?" Marianne asked.

"Mr. Darcy, let me fetch you a cup of tea while we wait for Lizzie," Elinor said. "And sit. You look absolutely wrung out."

Which was how Darcy found himself sitting in a chair, sipping a bracingly sweet cup of tea, while the Misses Dashwood and Miss Woodhouse quizzed him about Lizzie. "Is this the first time you've missed an important social function?" Marianne asked.

"Yes," he replied. "Although we don't attend many. Important social functions, that is."

"Why not?" Elinor asked.

"Well, we don't often have reason to spend time together socially."

The Dashwoods and Miss Woodhouse all exchanged looks. "Why not?" asked Miss Woodhouse.

He wasn't sure he appreciated her interest in the case—she was a total stranger! But Marianne waved a hand. "Don't mind Miss Woodhouse. She dispenses the best advice."

Miss Woodhouse smiled. "I do."

"Um, well . . ." Darcy glanced longingly at the door but was trapped. "I suppose it's because we're both very busy? I have my own work, which I've been neglecting lately, and Lizzie is London's first female solicitor—she must always work twice as hard."

"London's first female solicitor! That's impressive," Miss Woodhouse said.

"But you must *make* the time," Marianne protested.

"It is not for lack of interest! But it always seems . . ." Darcy hesitated to say anything more. It felt almost like a betrayal, speaking of his relationship with Lizzie with their mutual friends.

"It's all right," Elinor urged. "You don't have to tell us if you don't want."

She gave her sister and Miss Woodhouse stern looks that seemed to say, *Don't press.*

"It's likely silly," he finally admitted. "Except that I get the sense at times she doesn't wish to socialize with me. She doesn't even want me to walk her to her front door. And when her mother invited me to dinner, Lizzie seemed resigned."

The ladies all gasped in shock.

"But you're perfect together," Marianne moaned.

"Have you asked her how she feels?" Elinor asked.

"Well . . . not exactly. But Lizzie is very straightforward. She wouldn't hesitate to tell me how she feels."

All three ladies gave him a look.

"Wouldn't she?" Darcy asked.

"And how are things when you are working together professionally?" Miss Woodhouse asked. "Does she welcome your help?"

"Of course," Darcy said. "I've been absent from my job more days than not this last week because of this case—her case! I care for her deeply. And I have to say, until recently, I never doubted her feelings either. It's just that she doesn't seem to want me anywhere near her parents!"

"Ah," said Elinor knowingly. "So it might not be about you at all."

Marianne and Miss Woodhouse were nodding knowingly. "Well?" Darcy demanded. "Are you going to explain it to me?"

"I suspect that it isn't that Lizzie doesn't care to spend time with you outside of your professional duties, but that she is struggling with the consequences of such a close arrangement," Elinor said.

Marianne was much more forthright. "Her parents expect you to propose."

This was not entirely shocking news. No one who'd ever met Mrs. Bennet would fail to realize that obtaining husbands for each of her daughters was her chief mission in life. That didn't frighten him off like it might some young gentlemen— last night's revelation that he loved her was no passing fancy. He smiled at the mere thought of her, despite the discomfort of this conversation. "Well, naturally I want to marry her."

The Dashwoods let out identical squeals. "I knew it!" Marianne proclaimed. "Elinor, you owe me ten shillings!"

"You had a bet on whether or not I would propose?" Darcy was aghast.

"Not on whether or not you would," Marianne said, triumphant. "That has never been in question. Just on how soon you would admit it."

Miss Woodhouse was studying him. "Young ladies do not have the sort of freedom that you enjoy, Mr. Darcy. And enterprising young ladies such as your Miss Bennet must struggle with the constraints of society even more so than those who are content to stay close to home."

"I know that," Darcy said, a tad defensively.

"As long as most people believe we ought to be kept in the drawing room, stitching samplers and pouring tea, our lives will always be difficult," Marianne grumbled. "The trick is to ask how you can make her life easier!"

Darcy felt he knew where this was going. "So I should . . . propose?"

All three ladies, including Miss Woodhouse, gasped—and not in a good way.

"What?" Darcy knew it was a bit of a hasty thought, but he didn't think it warranted that level of amazement. "If we were married, then no one would be upset about how much time we spend together!"

"True," Elinor said, "but marriage is a big step. Have you spoken with her about the matter?"

"Oh, well . . ." He'd always assumed that marriage was the logical next step—clearly, they were fond of each other, and if Mrs. Bennet knew about even one of the kisses they'd shared, she'd force a marriage that very week. But they'd never talked about it. He'd always just *assumed* that eventually they'd get around to it.

"I think that's a no, ladies," Miss Woodhouse said. "If I may dispense some advice, Mr. Darcy? Just because you admire her and you spend time together doesn't mean she is obligated to commit her life to you. She is her own person."

"I know that!" Darcy felt more condescended to in this moment than he had in the last three months of working with Mr. Tomlinson. "I like that she's her own person!"

Miss Woodhouse continued, undeterred. "Good. Now, marriage *can* be very advantageous, but even with the obvious benefits there are some drawbacks. Personally, I don't see the point of it. For example, could she still be her own person, if she were to marry you?"

"Of course!" Why, the mere notion that Darcy would control Lizzie if they were to get married was insulting. "She knows I would never force her to do anything she doesn't want to do! If I were to marry her, it would be because it would make her life easier, so she wouldn't be the subject of gossip!"

Marianne gave him a pitying look. "Yes, because that's the sort of marriage proposal all young ladies dream of."

Darcy opened his mouth to retort that Lizzie didn't care about things like that, but then he shut it once more. He thought back to that moment in the drawing room with Josette—not this week, but two years ago. He really, really thought about it, which was something he generally avoided doing.

Oh.

Elinor bit her lip. "Mr. Darcy, I'm sorry—you shouldn't listen to us. You really ought to talk with Lizzie herself."

"No," he said. "This has been . . . rather humiliating. But enlightening."

"Good," Miss Woodhouse said, clearly satisfied. "Miss Dashwood, Miss Marianne, I must depart—but thank you for your help." To Darcy, she said, "Good luck." She gathered her things and left promptly, the bell above the door tinkling as she departed.

"Pardon me," Darcy heard a familiar voice say, and he turned to see Lizzie herself stepping past Miss Woodhouse to enter the shop, a market basket over one arm and Guy at her heels.

"Lizzie!" Darcy exclaimed, setting down his tea and standing. "There you are!"

His heart swelled at the sight of her. Her brows were furrowed, and her mouth was slightly downturned, which was common when she was worried about something. Even with the dark circles under her eyes and her drawn expression, Darcy thought her the most beautiful young lady in all of London.

But when her eyes landed on him, she didn't light up with happiness. "*You!*" she shouted. "*Where were you?*"

Stunned, Darcy merely gaped at her. "I'm sorry about last night, I was detained—"

"You didn't come! You didn't send a note! And when I sent Bingley to your house, your butler said you hadn't come home! We thought you were dead and dumped in the Thames!"

Darcy crossed the space between them and gathered her up in his arms. "I'm not dead! I'm all right! Someone locked me in the records room, I just got out this morning and came straight here."

Lizzie held herself rigid for a moment and then relaxed into his embrace. Her arms came around him and squeezed tightly. "I am very cross with you," she said into his jacket.

But now Darcy was truly alarmed, for her reaction to seeing him seemed awfully drastic considering he had missed one dinner. "Lizzie, did something happen?"

She inhaled one more time, then stepped back. Guy danced between them, clearly happy to see him as well. "Yes," she said, and carefully withdrew a heavy object wrapped in a length of muslin from her basket.

Lizzie set it on the pink velvet counter and unwrapped it. At the center was a brick, with the word *stop* scrawled in black letters on its wide side. Darcy's heart plummeted.

Lizzie looked at Elinor Dashwood. "Someone threw this through my front window yesterday evening, and I need to know everything about where it came from."

THIRTEEN

*In Which Lizzie and Darcy Consult
the Misses Dashwood*

LIZZIE'S RELIEF AT FINDING Darcy safe and sound was quickly overshadowed by his alarm and Elinor's and Marianne's shock at the sight of the brick.

"Good heavens," Elinor proclaimed.

"Are you all right?" Marianne asked.

"We're all unharmed," Lizzie assured them. Darcy was staring at the brick with a clenched jaw, so she could only imagine what sort of angry thoughts were brewing in his mind. "The brick didn't land anywhere near us."

"You don't throw something like this through a drawing room window unless you're content with the idea of causing harm," he said darkly.

Guy began barking, an excited, happy sound as he lunged toward one of the shop's displays.

"Guy, shush! This is quite unbecoming!" Lizzie scolded. But then Guy dove under the table's cloth, and a peal of laughter came from beneath the table. The tablecloth flipped up, revealing the youngest Dashwood sister, Margaret. Guy licked her face and danced in happiness.

"Hello, Miss Bennet. Did the window make an awful mess?" Margaret asked.

"Margaret! You're not supposed to eavesdrop!" Elinor scolded.

"It's a public shop," Margaret protested as she crawled out. "I like your dog."

"Thank you," Lizzie said. "And, yes, it made an awful mess. We'll be picking glass out of the carpet for weeks."

Darcy made a strangled sort of noise just then, and his face was twisted in misery. "Lizzie."

"He's been very worried about you," Margaret said.

"Margaret," Elinor said with a warning in her voice.

"Oh?" Lizzie looked between the sisters and Darcy. "What were you all discussing just now?"

"Romantic woes," Margaret quipped as she tussled with Guy.

"Margaret!" Elinor clapped her hands. "That's it! In the back!"

Margaret protested but was pulled along by her oldest sister. Marianne went to the front of the shop, locked the door, and flipped their sign so it read *Closed*. "Lizzie, I think you'd better start from the very beginning."

Lizzie was not entirely convinced that they hadn't been talking about her, but she quickly recounted the previous evening's events. Darcy listened with horror, and when she had finished he looked miserable. "I'm so sorry I wasn't there."

She wished they were alone so she could step closer to him. "What is this about being locked in the records room?"

"I stayed late to look at a file," he said. "Mrs. Cavendish's file, actually. And someone locked me in the room—I didn't get out until this morning."

"Why on earth would someone lock you in?" Lizzie demanded. "And what did you find in Mrs. Cavendish's file?"

"That's just it . . . it was practically empty."

Lizzie let that news sink in. "But what does that mean?"

"It means someone has stolen it," Darcy said darkly. "Or misplaced it."

"But why would anyone at Pemberley have reason to take the file? This isn't a Pemberley case—it's our case!"

Darcy shook his head, and Lizzie had a sense that there was more he wasn't sharing. But before she could press him on that, Elinor asked, "I presume you brought this brick for me to analyze?"

"Yes, please." Lizzie turned her attention to the brick. "What is the message written in?

"Hmm, it could be a few things," Elinor said, removing a pair of spectacles from her apron pocket. "Come on back."

They followed her through a doorway leading to the back of the shop, which turned out to be Elinor's workroom. Stepping through the doorway felt like being transported into another world, far from the bustling streets outside. The space felt like a combination of cozy parlor and laboratory, with an overstuffed couch and shelves of books on one end, and a stove, worktable, and cabinets and shelves stuffed full of glass beakers, jars, and various pots on the other. Margaret was slumped on the couch but perked up when Elinor came bustling in.

"It looks like soot," Marianne said, peering over her sister's shoulder.

"I don't think so," Elinor said. She picked up a half-burned log next to the stove and a metal instrument. She scraped a bit of the blackened end of the log into a small piece of scrap paper. "This is soot. It flakes easily, see?" It spread like fine dust.

She turned to the substance on the brick and repeated her actions on the dark line of the *T.* The substance didn't flake like the soot had, although it did smear against the paper in greasy streaks. "And this . . . it's definitely not soot."

"Elinor . . . could it be graphite?" Lizzie had been up half the night, thinking about Mr. Hughes and his graphite mines.

"Oh! Like from a pencil?"

"Is that what pencils are made out of?" Lizzie asked.

"Yes, fine pencils—they're very expensive. But let me run a few tests. . . ." Elinor turned to her stove, muttering to herself.

"Lizzie," Darcy said apprehensively. "Why do you think it's graphite?"

"Because Mr. Hughes owns a graphite mine," Lizzie said. "And last night at dinner, I learned that it is a highly valuable resource, guarded closely by the Crown, and it is a felony to possess it unlawfully."

Darcy stared at her, dumbfounded. "I'm sorry—you found this out over dinner?"

"Yes, you can imagine how pleased my mother was about our choice of conversation. But Darcy—think about it. Mr. Hughes allegedly has a graphite mine that's run dry. And we suspect that something suspicious is being run out of the Mullins Brothers storehouse. What if—"

"They were smuggling graphite," Darcy finished. He was quiet as her absorbed this information. "But who set the fire? And who killed Leticia?"

"I don't know, but it seems that we've gone from a dearth of suspects to a good many, except that there is no one clue that links them definitively to the crime."

The party was silent as they pondered this, and then Marianne said, "You know what this calls for?"

"What?" Lizzie asked.

"A slate!" Marianne rustled through a pile of papers, books, and other miscellaneous items on a desk, and returned with a slate and a nub of chalk in hand. "When I am stuck, I write things down on a slate. It helps me to be able to puzzle through things more easily."

"Also, Elinor said that she was running through the paper budget too quickly," Margaret added.

"Shut up, you," Marianne said fondly. "You go through more paper than any of us."

Lizzie had not used a slate since she was small and learning her numbers, but she was willing to give anything a try. "All right, where do you want to start?"

"Your suspects," Marianne said, laying the slate down on the table between them.

"Leticia Cavendish, Jack Mullins, Richard Hughes, and"—Lizzie looked at Darcy—"Josette Beaufort?"

He nodded, although he didn't look happy about it.

Marianne wrote their names across the top of the wide edge of the slate. "Now, what are the reasons we have to suspect Miss Cavendish?"

"A woman fitting her description was seen at the storehouse and was accused of starting the fire, she indicated that she had information for us, and then she was murdered before she could meet with us," Lizzie said. Marianne rushed to list the reasons.

"Doesn't the fact that she was murdered mean that she wasn't guilty?" Margaret asked.

"Not necessarily. She could have started the fire." Lizzie thought of the sight of Leticia, strangled in the park, and tried not to shudder. "But she certainly isn't responsible for her own murder."

"Double crimes," Margaret whispered with excitement, and scrawled something in her own journal.

"Don't forget, Miss Cavendish has dubious origins," Darcy added. "Not much is known about her early life or how and why she came to London. We don't know her motivations."

Marianne nodded, listing all the reasons in shorthand. "And Jack Mullins?"

Lizzie sighed. "He accused a dark-haired, tall young lady of setting the fire, but didn't actually *see* her start the fire. He's been cagey about letting us inspect the premises, although he claims it's for our safety."

"Vengeful?" Marianne asked.

"Perhaps. When he learned that Leticia had been murdered, he seemed . . . upset, but not despondent. He also claims not to know who she is. But he didn't disclose that there is a Crown investigation into his storehouse, and we don't know if he's unaware or if he's keeping it from us."

"So he might be responsible for the murder, but it seems unlikely he was responsible for the fire that caused his brother's death?" Marianne asked. "And he's keeping secrets, possibly."

"Likely," Darcy corrected.

Lizzie sighed. "I suppose that's fair—but he relieved me from the case yesterday, so he really has no reason to toss a brick through my front window."

Marianne wrote *Brick?* under Jack's name. "All right, Mr. Hughes next. He's Josette's fiancé?"

"Yes," Darcy said. "He owns graphite mines. He was not pleased to see us in Josette's drawing room when we first went to speak with her."

"That could have just been because you once courted Josette," Lizzie pointed out.

"Oh *really*?" Marianne asked, and all three Dashwoods looked at Darcy with keen interest.

"It was ages ago!" he protested. "And it ended amicably."

"But I hardly think that's reason enough for Mr. Hughes to turn to villainy, so I suppose it's irrelevant," Lizzie said. "Let's suppose he's lying and his graphite mines haven't dried up. What if he's selling it on the black market out of the Mullins Brothers storehouse?"

"That's a felony," Darcy pointed out. "But if he were selling to the French, that would be treason."

"Exactly."

"But would he set fire to a storehouse where his illegal goods are?"

"Maybe," Lizzie conceded, "if he were on the verge of getting caught. Losing out on all that money is likely preferable to being arrested and facing treason charges. Elinor, what would happen to graphite if it was set on fire?"

"It wouldn't burn," she said confidently.

"Oh," Lizzie said.

"But it would become explosive."

"*Oh.*"

Lizzie considered that, reviewing her memories of that day. "There was a rather large crash, wasn't there, Darcy? Do you remember?"

"Yes, but I don't think it was an explosion," he said slowly.

"I suppose there's no way of knowing for certain, not without getting inside." Which, of course, they hadn't been able to do.

"Why else might someone set fire to the storehouse?" Marianne asked. "What else might they want to destroy?"

"Wool? But that seems hardly worth all this effort." Lizzie

thought about how despondent Jack had seemed, his business on the brink of ruin. "Or maybe it's not about the goods, but the building itself."

"The fire has certainly rendered the storehouse useless for storing goods, illegal or otherwise," Darcy pointed out. "Mullins said as much the other day—without a place to store goods, he can't sell them."

"So it's possible that someone might have set the fire to stop the exchange," Lizzie said. "But who?"

"And would that same person murder to keep their secrets?" Marianne asked, tapping on Leticia's name.

That made them all pause.

"I suppose we must assume any of our suspects is capable of anything," Lizzie murmured, looking at Darcy.

"Agreed," he said, although it was clear he was uncomfortable with the idea. "Although Mr. Hughes was already at Cavendish House when I arrived that day, to inform Josette of her cousin's murder."

"That's hardly an alibi. If he left right after killing her and had a horse, he could have gotten there a good fifteen minutes before you arrived, at least." Lizzie hesitated. "Josette would be able to tell you definitively when he called upon her that day."

"Speaking of Josette," Marianne said, "are we going to consider her?"

"We must," Lizzie said, although she was hard-pressed to come up with reasons why Josette would want to kill her only living relative. "She might have discovered that her fiancé was engaged in illegal activity, and set fire to the storehouse to stop it. Although it does seem unlikely. She doesn't seem to have the constitution for it. And why would she kill her own cousin?"

"She wouldn't," Darcy said. "I promise you, she was truly devastated when I informed her of Leticia's death."

Marianne, however, wasn't willing to give up so easily. "Maybe she didn't want to share her inheritance?"

"Maybe," Darcy conceded. "Except I don't know what she did or didn't inherit because her grandmother's will is missing."

Marianne drew a large question mark under Josette's name. "So we can all agree that Josette as either the arsonist or the murderer makes the least sense, but she might be at the center of things. And whoever is responsible for the fire may not be the same person who is responsible for the murder," Marianne said, scribbling *more than one perpetrator* at the bottom of the slate. "What else do we know?"

"The necklace," Lizzie said, opening her reticule. She withdrew Leticia's gold necklace. "I found it near her body. Someone removed it from her person—forcibly, because the clasp is broken."

"It could have been any one of these suspects trying to make it look like a robbery," Darcy pointed out.

"I don't suppose you can tell me anything about it?" Lizzie asked Elinor.

"I'm afraid not," she said. "I'm no jeweler. It's a lovely piece, though, and it looks expensive."

"May I?" Marianne asked. Lizzie handed over the necklace and Marianne inspected it carefully. She held it closer to the lamp as she turned it one way and then the next. "I could be mistaken, but this appears to be a locket."

"What?" Lizzie leaned forward. "I didn't see a latch."

Marianne tapped the pendant. "It's hidden by the filigree, I'm fairly certain. I only know because last week I recovered some stolen jewelry from a lady who lives in— Oh, well, never mind that. But I went to an awful lot of jewelers, and I met one who makes pendants that are secret lockets. Apparently they're all the rage among the society set."

Lizzie recalled now one of Lydia's dramatic spells. What was it she had said? Felicity Carlton had a splendid necklace given to her by her fiancé that looked like an opal pendant but opened into a locket that contained a lock of his hair. "Can you open it?" she asked Marianne.

"Maybe," she said, trying to dig her fingernails in between the finely wrought lines of the pendant. She tapped, pulled, pressed, and pried at the various seams and edges, but it didn't budge. Reluctantly, Marianne passed it to Elinor, who had a go at it, and then Lizzie, and finally Darcy. Neither of them had any success, and Lizzie felt the frustration in her very fingertips.

"What if there is something in this locket that provides a clue as to what Leticia was really up to?" she said. "Lockets are made to conceal."

"The jeweler who made it will know how to open it," Marianne said. "We just need to find him."

"We need to split up," Lizzie announced. "It will take too

long for us all to follow each lead individually, and we have no way to know who we ought to be focusing on first. I don't want whoever is responsible to wiggle away. Darcy, you need to call on Josette—offer your condolences, and then try to figure out what she knows about her fiancé's business and what Leticia might have wanted to tell us."

"What are you going to do?" he asked, clearly concerned.

"I'm going to see if any of the London jewelers made this necklace. A lady doesn't buy this sort of thing for herself. This is something a suitor or a lover gives a lady. Don't worry, Darcy—I can hardly come to any harm while in a shop."

"I'm sure you'd prove to be the exception," he said, which earned him a small smile.

"And what do you want us to do?" Elinor asked.

Lizzie considered a moment, then said, "Can you confirm that the substance on the brick is graphite? Whatever tests you must run, please run them. This brick might link us to the killer. Marianne, can you track down and follow Jack Mullins? I can give you a description and the address of his temporary lodgings. I would like to know what he's up to now that he has dismissed me from the case."

"Of course."

"What about Hughes?" Darcy asked.

"Leave him alone for now," Lizzie said. "If he's the one who threw that brick through my window, let's not get too close. Let him think his intimidation worked."

"And if he wasn't responsible for the brick?" Darcy asked.

Lizzie looked at the offending object with its crudely drawn message. Stop? Never.

"Then I suppose we all better watch our backs."

FOURTEEN

In Which Darcy Makes a Long-Overdue Apology

FOR THE THIRD TIME in a week, Darcy found himself approaching Josette's front door. He held Guy's leash and looked down at the dog while he rang the bell. "You have to be on your very best behavior here, understand?"

The dog cocked his head to the side, and Darcy got the eerie feeling the dog was casting judgment on him. Margaret had mounted a strong argument for keeping him at her sisters' shop while Lizzie and Darcy went on their errands; but Elinor had put her foot down, which left the dog with Darcy as Lizzie could hardly bring him with her into the various jewelers she intended to visit.

"There will be a treat in it for you if you're good, understand? What do you eat, anyway? I haven't the faintest clue, so I hope Lizzie fed you a good breakfast—"

The door opened, revealing the disapproving face of Mr. Dupont. Before Darcy could draw breath, he said, "Miss Beaufort is not accepting callers—"

"She'll see me," Darcy cut him off. "It's about her cousin's death."

Mr. Dupont's expression was doubtful; but after a long pause, Darcy and Guy were admitted into the foyer. The dog's nails clicked on the shiny marble and Mr. Dupont looked down at the dog with a pained expression. "Perhaps you'd like to entrust your dog to a footman while you call upon Miss Beaufort?"

"Yes, thank you," Darcy said, passing the leash to a hovering footman. He gave Guy a look that he hoped said, *Be good.*

Moments later, he was ushered down the hall, past the drawing room, and to a morning room. Josette, wearing a black mourning gown, sat in a chair by the window, which overlooked a small garden.

"Josette," Darcy said as he entered. "How are you?"

Josette managed an indifferent shrug. "What are you doing here?"

Darcy was not offended by her bluntness. "I have some news."

"You know who killed Leticia?"

She looked up at him with such raw hope that Darcy felt horrible as he shook his head. "Not exactly. The man who said he saw someone who looked like Leticia . . . Jack Mullins? He's decided to drop the case. I'm sorry."

"Is that supposed to make me happy?"

"Well, no. But I thought it might bring you some relief."

"Relief. Ha." She looked back out the window. "I have no relief. Even if you presented her murderer before me, I still wouldn't have any relief. My cousin is dead."

"I know," Darcy said quietly. And even though he hadn't been invited, he sat across from Josette.

"What are you doing?" Josette demanded.

"Sitting."

"Why?"

"Because you're sad, and I thought you could use a friend."

"We are friends?"

He deserved that. "Josette . . . I'm sorry."

"You already said that."

"No, I know . . . I mean, I'm sorry for before." That got her attention. She turned to look at him, pinning him in place with her wide, red-rimmed eyes. Darcy couldn't stop now. "I'm sorry about the way I asked you to marry me. I knew I had missed the mark afterward, but it wasn't until very recently that I've taken into consideration how my proposal must have come across."

Josette's mouth had fallen open in shock. "That is not what I expected you to say."

"I didn't mean to cause you any more distress." He looked away, wishing he could leave. As a rule, he tended to barrel through awkward conversations with steely composure. Sitting with his own discomfort was not at all pleasant.

"No, Darcy . . . thank you." She touched his arm. "For whatever it's worth, I was very cross at the time, but I've long since let go of any anger. You are honorable, Darcy. We were just ill-suited."

A weight he hadn't realized he'd been carrying seemed to

lift slowly, and then all at once. He *really* hoped that she was not culpable for either the fire or the murder. "Thank you, Josette. I'm happy you had enough sense for the both of us back then. And . . . I'm happy you have found Mr. Hughes."

She smiled a little then. "I am very lucky."

Darcy hated himself for what he was about to say next. "I was especially happy he was here . . . that day. I did not want you to be alone."

She looked back out the window again. "He's barely left me alone since then. He's only gone at the moment to obtain a special license."

Darcy wasn't sure he'd heard her correctly. "A special license! But you don't mean . . ."

"We'll marry first thing tomorrow morning," she said shortly. "I don't want to wait. What use do I have for parties and celebrations now? At least after tomorrow, I won't have to be alone."

Some instinct in him wanted to beg her not to marry Richard Hughes—but what right did he have to ask her to delay her wedding? It wasn't as though he could say, *Don't marry him until I can clear him as a suspect.*

"You never told me about Leticia," he blurted out. "I didn't even know you had a cousin."

"There is a great deal you don't know about me, Darcy, which is why I am marrying Mr. Hughes tomorrow, not you." Her barbed look was not as sharp as when he'd first walked into the room, but Darcy took it as a warning.

"It's just that . . . you must promise me you'll be careful, Josette."

"I've been careful my whole life," Josette said with a scoff. "Why are you so concerned now?"

"Because whoever killed Leticia might come after you next."

There, he'd said it. But now that the fear was voiced, Josette didn't appear especially worried or shocked. "As far as I am concerned, that snake Jack Mullins is likely the cause of her death. I don't have proof, but he wanted to accuse someone—a French someone. And you led him straight to us."

Her words hit in harder than a blow. "If that's true, then I am eternally sorry. But forgive me, I have to ask . . . is there any reason that Mr. Mullins may have to despise Mr. Hughes?"

"What? Mr. Hughes is above reproach, sir!"

Darcy didn't want to press her, but he had to. "Perhaps not necessarily on purpose. But if they'd had a disagreement, for example—"

"Absolutely not! Mr. Hughes hardly knows the man!"

"Something to do with his mines?"

Josette blinked rapidly. "His mines? I know nothing about his mines. Darcy, what are you implying?"

"Nothing! But if there is some connection, some stone yet unturned—"

But Darcy could tell that he'd lost control of the situation. Josette stood. "I want you to leave."

He also stood but didn't make any move for the door. "I don't mean to sound uncaring, but it is my job to inquire. I care about you—"

"You care? What fine words! Where were you when my grandmother was dying? Why did you not care then?"

"Josette, I—"

The door to the sitting room opened and Dupont appeared, likely drawn by the sound of raised voice. "Miss Beaufort?"

"Mr. Darcy is leaving!"

"Josette—"

"Good day!"

The butler held up an arm to indicate that Darcy should follow him. "This way, sir," he said, a core of steel in his voice.

"I'm sorry," he said to Josette again, but she had turned her back on him.

In the foyer, Dupont handed him his hat and a footman came forward with Guy. Darcy took the dog's leash and made one last entreaty to the butler. "I do care for her, despite what she might say. And I fear she's in terrible danger still. Please, keep a close eye on her."

The butler's expression was withering. "I *always* keep a close eye on Miss Beaufort."

Darcy felt somehow chastened, but he forced himself to hold Dupont's gaze. His unyielding gray eyes held . . . not scorn, but condescension, to be sure. As if Darcy were just a little boy and he was the grown-up. His face softened a bit, and he nodded. "I know you do."

Outside of Cavendish House, Guy wagged his tail and

looked up expectantly at Darcy. "I don't know what's next," he said. "She didn't really tell me anything, and I doubt she will now."

Guy sat.

"I've made a mess of things," Darcy told him.

The little dog tilted his head, as if he understood what Darcy was saying. But even Guy couldn't distract Darcy from Josette's parting words. *Where were you when my grandmother was dying? Why did you not care then?*

He thought of the empty file at Pemberley.

Why would Josette expect him to have shown up at her grandmother's deathbed?

Unless . . .

He looked down at Guy. "How discreet can you be?"

FIFTEEN

*In Which Lizzie Discovers a Most
Shocking Connection*

THE BELL ABOVE THE door of the fourth jeweler's shop tinkled as Lizzie stepped inside, assuming the role of a harried, anxious young lady.

She'd perfected her persona at the last shop, so now it was easy to hover near the counter, casting her gaze about for a free clerk while taking in the shop's displays of earrings, bracelets, rings, brooches, and necklaces. But no necklaces looked like the pendant that was growing warm in her gloved hand. She also took in the clerks—she wanted someone a little timid looking, the most junior person she could find. She thought she spotted her mark, a sandy-haired young man wearing an ill-fitting jacket and speaking earnestly to a well-dressed matron. He seemed like the type that was eager to please and would answer all of Lizzie's questions—

"May I help you, miss?"

Lizzie jumped and turned to find a poised and polished clerk standing behind her, watching her coolly. He was old enough to have creases around his eyes, but not quite as old as her parents. Not exactly who she'd been hoping for, but beggars couldn't be choosers. "Oh, hello!" she squeaked out.

"Good afternoon. Is there something you would like to take a closer look at?"

The clerk nodded at the jewelry under its glass cases, and Lizzie forced herself to emit a high, nervous laugh. "No, no. I do need help, though." She held up the necklace and noted the glint of interest in the clerk's eyes as he took in the gold and topaz. "My fiancé gave it to me, but I don't know how to open it!"

The clerk pulled on a pair of white gloves and held out his hand. She carefully placed the necklace in the man's hand. He cradled the small object like one would hold a newborn kitten as he inspected it. "Ah, yes," he said. "Pink topaz. I recall this commission."

"Can you help me?" Lizzie asked, and she didn't even have to pretend to sound hopeful and anxious all at once, even though she was desperate to know if he remembered *who* had commissioned the necklace.

"Certainly," the man said. "Miss . . . ?"

"Bennet," Lizzie said, for she had no calling cards but her own on her person, and if asked for proof of identity, it would look awfully suspicious if she couldn't come up with a card. "I feel so silly!"

"Not at all, miss," the clerk said, guiding her to a nearby

counter. He pulled out a velvet-lined tray and set the necklace down with a small tsk. "I see that your clasp has been damaged, miss."

"Yes, I was terribly clumsy the other day," she lied. "It caught on my hairbrush."

"I'm sorry to hear that, Miss. You must know that we pride ourselves on the quality of our jewelry, and for such a thing to happen . . . well, I'm not at all satisfied, miss."

Was it Lizzie's imagination, or was he eyeing her with suspicion as he arranged the broken necklace on the tray? Lizzie felt her heartbeat pick up, but she brazened her way through. "Oh, I'm sure your quality is excellent, sir. It's me. Why, I shattered a vase the other day and I thought my poor mama would faint!"

The clerk gave her an obligatory polite smile. He picked up a small magnifying glass and turned the pendant around to the back, and then to the front, making small hmm sounds.

"You see, my fiancé gave it to me, and he told me that it contained a surprise! Only, I hadn't the faintest idea what he meant until my dear friend Miss Carlton told me about her locket. But hers looks different from mine, and I'm terribly afraid I'll break it by trying to force anything, so I decided to just ask an expert. Is it a locket?"

She batted her eyelashes at him, hoping he'd be taken in by feminine charms and flattery, but the clerk wore a peculiar expression. "I see," he said. "It is most definitely ours, and you're correct, miss, it is a locket. They've been incredibly popular."

"Oh, thank goodness!" Lizzie cried, and she truly was

relieved. "I'm afraid he's beginning to suspect that I haven't fig-ured it out!"

The clerk smiled politely, but he was still examining the necklace. "And what is your fiancé's name, Miss Bennet?"

A twinge of panic ran through Lizzie. "Oh, I hope you don't plan on telling him I was here! He'll think I'm awfully dim!"

"No, no," the clerk assured in a tone that she found far from reassuring. "But I do like to know all of our customers, and I make it a point to remember everyone."

I'm sure you do, Lizzie thought. This was a test—he wouldn't open it for her unless she could name the man who commis-sioned it. And if she was wrong, he'd likely accuse her of stealing. Lizzie felt a thin sheen of sweat break out across her body. If she gave the wrong name, could she snatch the necklace and make a run for it? Not likely, at least not without drawing the Runners.

"Hu-Hughes," she stuttered, and forced a fond smile. "Not much longer now, and I'll be Mrs. Hughes!"

"Excellent, Miss Bennet," he said. Then, so quickly that she almost missed it, the clerk squeezed the rounded edge of the fil-igree, and the pink topaz at the center moved on a hidden hinge, then pressed inward. There was a small click, and then the hid-den hinge opened to reveal a small compartment.

"Oh!" Lizzie cried, leaning forward to inspect it. "How clever!"

"Yes, it is," the clerk said, clearly pleased with the design. "Now, for your 'secret,' Miss Bennet."

He stepped aside so that she could see the inside of the

locket. Lizzie supposed it was a bit much to hope for a tiny note that contained all of Leticia's secrets, but she was nonetheless surprised to find that the locket was . . . empty. Empty, that is, except for a bit of engraving in the center of the locket.

To L.B. with all my love and adoration. —R.H.

"*Oh*," Lizzie said, aware that she sounded confused, and not at all thrilled.

"Were you expecting something else, miss?"

"No! I'm merely surprised, that's all!"

"It's quite the moving declaration, isn't it?"

It was indeed, but not for the reason the clerk thought. For a dizzying moment, Lizzie had thought that the necklace had actually been meant for her, when she saw the L.B. But when she saw the R.H. her heartbeat galloped out of her chest.

R.H. Richard Hughes! She had guessed correctly!

But who was L.B.? Not Leticia Cavendish? Unless . . .

Leticia Beaufort?

But that wasn't her surname.

"If I may ask, miss," the clerk said, "might I see your card?"

Lizzie barely managed to keep from sucking in a sharp breath. She looked up and blinked innocently at him. "My card? Why, whatever for?"

"Please pardon my insolence, but you see . . . we've had quite the rash of stolen jewelry showing up in the oddest of places," he said. "Now, I don't believe that this necklace is stolen at all! But given the circumstances, I feel duty bound to write to Mr. Hughes and tell him of your visit."

"Well, I never!" Lizzie wanted to refuse, but if she did so, she suspected that the Runners would definitely be called. She reached into her reticule and extracted a card, thankful that she hadn't given a false name. She slapped it down on the counter and stared the clerk down as his blue eyes dropped to the counter and took in her name.

"Miss *Elizabeth* Bennet? Why not E.B.?"

"I go by Lizzie," she told him with a sniff.

She hoped—no, expected—for him to back off after that. Instead, he smiled wanly. "My apologies, Miss Bennet. I expect you'll want the clasp repaired?"

"I—" Lizzie had been about to tell him no, because she wanted to get back to the Dashwoods and Darcy and tell them that Richard Hughes had given Leticia Cavendish a necklace with a romantic inscription in it. But if she were truly an embarrassed fiancée, she'd want the chain repaired.

"I'm not sure I have the time today," she said lamely. "I have an appointment."

"It should take no more than fifteen minutes, miss," the clerk assured her. "Please, make yourself comfortable. Would you like some tea?"

Lizzie declined but resigned herself to waiting. She hated seeing the clerk whisk the necklace behind a door to the workshop.

After only several minutes, the clerk reemerged from the back room, wearing a solicitous expression that put Lizzie immediately on edge. "Miss Bennet," he said, an apology in his voice.

"I'm terribly sorry to tell you this, but . . . your fiancé commissioned this necklace nearly a year ago."

"Oh?" Lizzie raised her eyebrows at the news, but she mentally filed away the knowledge. How long had Mr. Hughes been engaged to Josette? Had he been betraying her their entire engagement? "Well, that is surprising! I had no idea his affection went back that far."

"Yes, and during that time, I'm afraid . . . well, this is rather indelicate. Please forgive me for bringing it up, but you see, he's *neglected to pay his bill.*"

Lizzie had no trouble looking shocked, which was exactly what the fiancée of a supposedly rich man would be, should a clerk steep so low as to speak of money with her. "I don't know what you mean!"

"I mean, Miss Bennet, that Mr. Hughes still owes us a significant amount of money for this necklace."

That was when she realized he didn't have the necklace in hand. Panic shot through her. She *needed* that necklace back. It was her only evidence tying Leticia and Richard Hughes together. It pained her to think about what she had to do next, for it wasn't this clerk's fault that his shop and its owners were out the money that Hughes owed.

"I don't see how that is *my* problem, and it is highly inappropriate that you should bring it up with me!"

"I am sorry, Miss Bennet. But nonetheless, I'm afraid that until Mr. Hughes has paid his outstanding bill—"

"Absolutely not! I demand you bring me my property this instant!"

She let her voice rise in volume—not quite yelling, but certainly louder than the clerk would wish, given that the shop contained more than a few customers. He looked around nervously but held his ground. "I cannot do that. I understand you are upset, but the best thing you can do is tell your fiancé—"

"Do I look like a common messenger?" Lizzie demanded. Inside, she was cringing at the haughty tone she'd adopted. She leaned toward the man and whispered, "If you do not return my necklace, I will cause a scene and your shop will be in all the society papers as the one who held an innocent young lady's property ransom!"

Lizzie stared him down and narrowed her eyes. Let him try to outlast her.

Finally, he looked away. "Very well, miss," he said shortly.

He disappeared into the back, and Lizzie tried to get her breathing under control. If that wretched Mr. Hughes had never paid his bill, then she had to wonder whether he was as successful as he would have his true fiancée believe.

What else was he hiding?

The clerk returned after a minute, all false smiles. "Here you are, Miss Bennet. I'm afraid we won't be able to repair that clasp after all. But please do feel free to come back at a later date."

"I shall," she said, smiling. She felt a wave of relief wash over her when the necklace was back in her possession. Mimicking the clerk, she pressed the pad of her forefinger into the filigree on the side of the necklace and felt the satisfying give of a hidden latch. The locket revealed its message inside. She snapped it shut and tucked it into her pocket. "Good day, sir. You've been most helpful."

As she left the shop, her mind spun with what this new connection meant. Hughes and Leticia? Were they working together? But what about Josette?

Lizzie walked away quickly, almost afraid that the clerk would come running after her. But no one from the jeweler came out, and she turned down a side street, feeling the need to get away as quickly as possible. She'd gone three blocks when a pang in her stomach reminded her it was far past luncheon, which she'd missed. It was no use puzzling these things out on an empty stomach. She found a vendor selling buns and approached.

"One, please," she said, and opened her reticule. But when she looked down, she caught a flash of movement to her right. "Actually, make it two."

She accepted the buns and wound her way to the edge of the market until she found a spot between two stout barrels and a donkey hitched to a small cart. She bit into one of the buns, and waited until Henry appeared beside her, almost sheepishly.

"Good day." She greeted the boy.

"G'day, miss," he said. Now that she was paying attention, she realized he almost sounded like one of the street children, but not quite. It was as if Henry was playacting at sounding uneducated. Lizzie doubted she would have picked up on the difference in his speech if he hadn't tipped her off by admitting he knew how to read.

"Tell me, Henry—have you been following my every move since we last spoke?"

His eyes widened in surprise at Lizzie's boldness, and he shook his head unconvincingly. "No, miss!"

"Hmm," was all Lizzie said, but her thoughts were racing. He seemed too smart to attach himself to any person who showed him kindness. "Surely I cannot be so interesting that you've followed me all around London for fun?"

He shrugged. "Are you still trying to find out what happened with the fire, miss?"

"I am." Why was he curious about that?

"Why?"

"What do you mean?"

"Just . . . why?"

"People hire me to help them," Lizzie said.

Henry made an ugly face. "People like the men who own the storehouse that burned?"

"Yes," she said slowly. "But also . . . if I see something wrong or unjust, I try to help the people in need. Mr. Mullins no longer wants me to look into the fire, actually."

"Why not?"

"I have no idea. Do you?"

Henry looked at her with suspicion. *Too close*, Lizzie told herself. She had to gain his trust. "You're not going to stop?" he asked.

"No, I'm not. A woman was murdered, Henry. I simply cannot let that go."

"Why not?" Henry's question was a challenge, but there was something else in his voice that tugged at Lizzie's heart.

"Because looking away when bad things happen is wrong," she said. "And because if I stop trying to find out who killed her, then whoever did will likely get away with it."

Lizzie felt the truth of her words sink in, even after she spoke them. This case wasn't like last time, when, yes, she wanted to find Hurst's killer, but she mostly wanted to prove to her father that she had what it took to be a barrister. Now she still wanted to prove to her father, to the courts, to the men of the world that she had what it took to succeed. But that felt secondary to getting justice for the deaths of Simon Mullins and Leticia Cavendish.

"Mr. Mullins doesn't just have cloth in his storehouse," Henry announced.

Lizzie went very still. She wanted to swing around and grab the boy by the shoulders and beg him to tell her everything he knew, but she was aware of how skittish he could be. "Oh?" she asked.

Henry shrugged. "Cloth doesn't ship in crates with straw."

Lizzie stared at him as she absorbed his meaning. "You're right. How very astute of you."

"His storehouse is mostly cloth," the boy continued. "But he also gets special shipments."

Lizzie trembled with excitement. "And these special shipments, you've seen them?"

Henry nodded. "They come at night."

Lizzie swallowed hard. Her mouth had gone dry, but she tried not to show it. "Do you know what time? Closer to midnight, or closer to morning?"

"I don't know," the boy said. "But on the nights that they come, they don't like us sleeping anywhere nearby. Men with pistols come by and they chase us off."

Lizzie thought of Henry's nest in the alley, and what it must be like to have only a bed of refuse to lie on each chilly night. Then she pictured men coming by, shaking him awake, forcing him off into the cold darkness. Her blood began to boil.

"That's awful," she told him. "And you lingered then, to see what they're up to?"

"Got curious," he mumbled. "I climbed the tree, before the smith cut the branches so I couldn't. I could see 'em, and . . ."

Lizzie didn't want to push him, but she had to know. "What did you see, Henry?

"Crates," he repeated. "They moved 'em in and out."

"Could you see what was in the crates?"

He shook his head. "I don't know. But like I said—not cloth."

This was it—the confirmation Lizzie needed that they were hiding something. A child of the streets was hardly a reliable witness in a court of law, but Lizzie would worry about that later—she had been right! Someone had been moving goods through the Mullinses' storehouse!

"Henry, why are you telling me this now?" she asked, trying

to sound gentle and not accusatory. "You've been following me for days, but you never said a word."

He shrugged. "I wasn't sure you'd believe me. But they came last night."

Lizzie's breath caught. "They? The people who bring the crates?"

He nodded.

"And are the crates still there now, Henry?"

"I think so," he said. "They don't move them in the middle of the day. And besides, the storehouse is still closed down. But the workmen didn't come today."

"Henry, you're a saint," Lizzie said. She could have hugged the boy if she didn't think it would have scared him off. "I need you to deliver a message for me. Do you know the firm Pemberley and Associates?"

"I followed you there," he reminded her. "Four days ago."

"Right," Lizzie said. "No wonder I've felt eyes on my back for days. Well, Mr. Darcy will be headed there—I need you give him a message to me."

Henry looked doubtful, and Lizzie was afraid for a moment he'd refuse. "I'll pay you, just as I would anyone else."

Still, he hesitated.

"Mr. Darcy has Guy at the moment. I'm sure he'd love to see you again."

That seemed to convince him. "All right," he said. "What should I say?"

SIXTEEN

In Which Darcy Loses All Composure

GUY, AS IT TURNED out, did not have a talent for being discreet.

The moment that Darcy walked through the doors with him, the little dog began to pull at his leash and sniff about with great excitement. Reeves widened his eyes at the sight of them, and Darcy thought for a moment that the man would tell him dogs weren't allowed in his own firm.

Darcy cut his gaze down at Guy. So much for sneaking in.

"Reeves," Darcy said, making a split-second decision. "I was wondering if you could do me a small favor and hold this dog while I run to my desk?"

"Is that Miss Bennet's dog, sir?"

"Yes, he is. I'm afraid if I bring him back, he'll cause all sorts of mayhem."

"Yes, sir," Reeves said, and Darcy wasn't sure if he was agreeing that the dog would cause mayhem or agreeing to watch him. Darcy held out the leash hopefully.

The man took it and gave the dog a tentative smile. "Mr. Tomlinson will return soon, sir."

Tomlinson wasn't there! That was the first bit of luck Darcy had had in a while. "I'll be quick," he promised.

Recognizing he'd get no better opportunity, Darcy walked toward the office, keeping his head down. From his pocket, he withdrew his key. It was the same that let him into the records room, but it was also a master key that opened even office doors. He'd never abused the privilege of carrying this key before and he could only imagine his father's horror at finding out that Darcy had used it to enter the office of another employee—a superior!—to rifle through his paperwork.

But Darcy didn't hesitate to insert the key into the lock and open the door.

The office was dim, with only a bit of daylight coming in through the drawn curtains. Darcy closed the door behind him, eyes searching for a place to start. The desk held a mountain of paperwork, and there were filing cabinets against the back wall. Darcy decided to start there.

None of the files were labeled, however, which meant that as Darcy paged through the folders he had to open each one and scan the documents within to get a sense for what they were. He kept his eyes open for the names Amelia or Reginald Cavendish, Josette Beaufort, even Leticia Cavendish, but found nothing. A voice inside him that sounded suspiciously like Lizzie whispered, *Hurry.*

He shifted his focus to the desk. This was more precarious.

If he moved any of the files, Tomlinson might suspect that some-one had been in here poking about. Darcy tried to memorize the exact position of the piles before he reached for the first file, but quickly realized how futile it was. He was in too much of a hurry. He'd have to just try to be careful.

The files on the desk were mostly familiar. Insurance claims, a libel case he was on, new business contracts, a loan agreement he'd reviewed last week. He even picked up a stray letter that appeared to be from Mr. Tomlinson's mother in Milnthorpe—he caught a glimpse of a sentence that read "proud you are making something of yourself" and an entreaty to come visit before he tossed it aside as well.

This was useless. If Tomlinson was keeping files in his office that should be in the records room, then where would they be? Not on the desk. Anyone could come into the office at any time and lay eyes on anything that was left out. No, these files would be hidden.

He moved to the drawers of the desk, testing each of them. There were six, and five of them slid open, revealing various tools, nibs, jars of ink, and bundles of letters. But the bottom right-hand drawer was locked.

Darcy cursed, not even wasting his time on the other draw-ers. The lock was too small for his master key. He cast about the room, looking for any place that might be a hiding spot for a key but to no avail. Besides, if this drawer held very important documents, Mr. Tomlinson wouldn't be as careless as to leave the key in his office.

There was nothing to do but pick the locks.

Marianne Dashwood had given them a lesson once. Lizzie had been rather enthusiastic about it, and Darcy had barely paid any attention because gentlemen did not pick locks. But today was proving to be the exception.

Darcy grabbed Mr. Tomlinson's penknife and slid it between the drawer and its casing. It was a rather crude and rough way of breaking the lock, and a distant part of him realized there was no going back now. He was going to scuff the wood and possibly break the lock, and Tomlinson would know someone had broken in. He might even suspect him. But Darcy didn't care anymore.

Click.

The lock gave and Darcy yanked the drawer open.

There weren't very many files in the drawer, which surprised him. But the very first document he picked up was the last will and testament of Mrs. Amelia Cavendish. Excitement coursed through his veins as he thumbed through the rest of the documents. It was here! It was all here and . . .

He came across a letter with a broken seal.

A letter addressed to Mr. Fitzwilliam Darcy.

August 23, 18—
Cavendish House
Dear Mr. Darcy,

  I hope you can forgive an elderly lady for the impudence of writing you when a handful of years have passed since we were last acquainted. I write not for myself, but the sake of my granddaughter Josette. Despite the fact she has turned down your offer of marriage, Josette assures me you remain honorable. I know my days are near their end. Very soon my affairs will be exposed by solicitors and creditors, and all my secrets will come to light. I do not fear for this, except in one matter that I entrust to you. It is my hope that you still care for Josette enough to protect her future.

As you are likely aware, my daughter, Anne, Josette's mother, fell for Joseph Beaufort, a Frenchman who visited London before the Revolution. I was against their marriage, as was my husband, but she eloped with him to France. In the weeks following the news of the Revolution, we had no word, no address, and no reason to believe that she was safe. Joseph's family was nobility, and we feared the worst. I was so disheartened that my son, Jacob, became determined to travel to France and discover the fate of his sister. It was dangerous and his father tried to dissuade him. I, to my everlasting regret, did not. I hoped he would defy the odds and both of my children would return to me safely.

But months passed without a word, then years. By then my husband had passed and I had very little hope I'd ever see either of my children in this life. Five years passed, and one day a man arrived on my doorstep with a little girl who was a mirror image of my Anne. The girl, as you may have guessed, was Josette, and her guardian angel was Dupont. He was Joseph's dearest friend, and he bore the tragic news of Joseph's and Anne's deaths, but he also brought their daughter to me, and for that I am eternally grateful, and I immediately gave him employment.

Josette, as you likely have inferred, has lived a difficult life.

She speaks little of the things she saw before she arrived in London. Dupont has told me about my daughter's life in France and her last days, and I believe that she was too ashamed of her elopement to return home to us when circumstances in France became dangerous. That, too, is a regret I carry to my grave. But Dupont also told me of Joseph's family, particularly of his brother François, who had a girl of his own, just a little younger than my Josette. They were close as children, and I knew that Josette missed her cousin and worried about her as she grew older. It was an ache that I understood well, and Dupont convinced me it was one that I could do something about.

Not long after your attachment to Josette ended, Dupont received word from friends in France that Leticia was still alive. With my blessing and full support, he left London to retrieve the girl. To Josette's everlasting joy and my eternal relief, he was successful. He returned with Leticia within a matter of weeks, and I agreed to shelter her.

But given the popular opinion toward the French and Napoleon's encroaching war, Josette and I recognized that introducing Leticia to society was, in its own way, a risk. Not to mention, her status in London was precarious as a French citizen, and with the increase in anti-French sentiment, we worried about her becoming detained, or worse, deported. It was becoming increasingly evident that Leticia would not allow herself to be pushed aside or hidden away—you will see what I mean when you meet her. And so we concocted a story, only slightly less scandalous than the truth. We said that Leticia was the illegitimate daughter of Jacob and a woman he met on his ill-fated journey. We said that I had long suspected I had another grandchild, but I had lost track of her and her mother in the ensuing war. We said that she had surfaced and had proven to my satisfaction that she was kin, so she was granted the safety of British citizenship. It was only a matter of planting a few well-placed rumors and soon the entire ton accepted the story. If anyone doubted it, then Josette was able to convince them with the level of affection and sisterly care she shows her cousin.

Which brings me to the reason for my writing. Everyone will assume that I have amended my will to include Leticia, for they all know her as the daughter of my only son. But I fear doing so would prompt a probe into her parentage and a close inspection into Leticia's past would ruin her reputation, and Josette's—she is a devoted cousin, and she will not cut ties with Leticia. Therefore, I am not leaving Leticia anything, and I need a solicitor who understands the delicate nature of this unique circumstance.

Leticia will not dispute the will. Josette does not need the law to do right by her cousin, so you should not worry there. My only concern is that recently Leticia has attached herself to a young man—she thinks I do not know, but although I may struggle to grip a pen or soupspoon these days, there is nothing wrong with my eyes. I'm sure she'll have confided in Josette, but I fear I have too little time to properly meet her young man and ascertain that he can be trusted with our secret. If he is an honorable gentleman, then he shall make her very happy. If not, then I fear he cannot be trusted—and under no circumstances should he learn that Leticia shall have no inheritance from me.

243

I am entrusting you, Mr. Darcy, to see to these affairs. You remind me of my Jacob, and I was very happy to see you and Josette together for the short time you enjoyed each other's company. I am very sorry it did not lead to a union, but I hope that even after all this time, you still care for her well-being. She will need someone she can trust in the coming weeks.

Expect her letter upon my death. I am in your debt.

Sincerely,

Mrs. Amelia Cavendish

The hand that held Mrs. Cavendish's letter trembled.

She had written Darcy, mere weeks before her death. And Josette—she had likely written him after her death, expecting that Darcy would know her situation and help. But he'd never gotten either letter. They'd been intercepted—intercepted by Mr. Tomlinson before his father had even left for the Continent!

Suddenly, he became aware of a high-pitched barking sound. Guy! And it was definitely his angry bark, not his excited bark. He tucked Mrs. Cavendish's letter in his inner jacket pocket, not bothering with the rest of the files. Beyond the door, a voice began to yell—not just any voice, either. Tomlinson's voice. *Bloody hell.*

He was trapped. If Tomlinson was back, there was no way that Darcy could slip out unnoticed, and the window of his office didn't open. He looked down at the scratched wood of the drawer he'd forced open. He still wasn't certain what exactly Tomlinson's ploy was, and he wasn't ready to confront the man.

Lizzie's voice came to him: *So create a diversion.*

He pushed the previously locked drawer shut and picked up the nearest stack of files, only to toss them on the floor. And then the next stack, and then the next. It was rather satisfying, actually, to hear the whomp! of the files falling to the floor, the skittering of paper across the waxed surface. He reached for the next stack, even as he could hear Tomlinson's voice coming closer. "Where is he? That dog is here, so he can't be far! Bring him to me at once!"

The office door swung open, just as Darcy tossed an entire armful of paper into the air.

"Darcy! What is the meaning of this?"

If he hadn't just been caught ransacking his supervisor's office, he might have laughed at Tomlinson's shocked expression. Behind him stood Reeves, struggling to keep hold of Guy's leash as the dog strained toward Darcy, yapping away.

"Oh," Darcy said, dropping the paper he held. "You're back."

"Darcy, I demand to know what you are doing in my office!"

"You know, I find that I prefer a messy office," Darcy said. 'To me, it shows that you're in the thick of it, you're accomplishing things."

"I don't know what you think you're doing in my private office—"

"Going through files," he interrupted. "Isn't it obvious?"

"You have no right—"

"I think I have every right," Darcy corrected him. "This is, after all, my father's firm. My father's office. My father's desk, my father's inkpot, my father's files . . . well, you get the idea."

"Your father isn't here right now." Tomlinson stormed toward him, and grabbed a fistful of his jacket. "While he's gone, I'm in charge, and you have crossed a line—"

"I don't actually think I am as bad of an employee as you make me out to be," Darcy interrupted, pulling out of Tomlinson's grasp. "In fact, I think you've been misplacing my work for weeks to discredit me."

If Darcy had known how it would feel to simply call out Tomlinson, he might have done it weeks ago. The man sputtered for a moment, but Darcy would have guessed it was for the benefit of all the men listening just outside the door. His eyes were cold, and Darcy knew that he'd crossed a line. "You're speaking nonsense, Darcy. The fact that your father founded this firm doesn't give you leave to ransack my office!"

Darcy dropped the other papers he'd been holding and walked toward the office door. Tomlinson blocked him, puffing up his chest to seem larger than he really was. He glared down at Darcy, but there was a flicker of something in his eyes—oh. He was enjoying this, Darcy realized. Perhaps he thought that Darcy would hit him. That surely would bring down his father's wrath, more than anything. The idea of his own son, brawling with the man he'd left in charge in their very proper law firm . . . the image of it nearly made Darcy laugh.

Darcy wasn't about to lose his composure. Not because his father would have been disappointed in him, but because Tomlinson, for all his height, was just a small man who enjoyed making others feel smaller than him. And he was, quite frankly, not worth Darcy's time.

"Consider this my notice," Darcy said. He stepped around Tomlinson and headed for the door.

"Your father will hear of this!" Tomlinson yelled after him.

"I imagine he will," Darcy agreed.

Darcy took Guy's leash from Reeves and clapped him on the shoulder. As he walked out of Pemberley & Associates, more than a few solicitors and clerks got to their feet and nodded at him. This touched Darcy more than he realized it would, and he nodded at them all in return as Tomlinson ordered someone to clean up the mess in his office. Mrs. Cavendish's letter smoldered next to his heart as he reached the lobby. With a small pang, he realized he'd left his favorite writing box back at his desk, but no matter—it would quite ruin the effect if he went back now for it.

No use ruining a perfectly good dramatic exit, he could imagine Lizzie agreeing. His lips almost quirked into a smile.

And then the front door of Pemberley & Associates banged open.

Mr. Hughes strode in. "I demand to see whoever's in charge!" he roared. "I am filing a complaint against Mr. Darcy!"

In the silence that followed, one might have been able to hear a pin drop. Mr. Hughes looked about and spotted Darcy. "You!" he spat.

Darcy sighed. The last person he wanted to deal with at the moment was Josette's bombastic fiancé. "I'm not sure why you felt the need to make such a loud entry, but I am sure whatever it is we can discuss it in a civilized manner."

Hughes advanced toward him. "You are to stop harassing my fiancée immediately! She was in tears after you left, all because of some insane theory that the person who killed her cousin is out to get her!"

"It's hardly insane," Darcy began to say, but then Tomlinson appeared, inserting himself.

"I can assure you, sir, whatever concerns you have will be addressed immediately!"

Mr. Hughes turned to a more willing ear. "Tomlinson, your employee has been harassing my fiancée, causing her extreme distress during her time of grief with wild and false accusations! I want him restrained!"

"Of course, absolutely," Tomlinson was groveling. "Darcy, let's handle this like gentlemen. There's no reason your father needs to hear about this if we all act sensibly."

Darcy actually laughed then. He didn't care about saving face or what his father might think. He cared about the truth. About justice. About honoring his commitments. About being dependable. He had disappointed Josette twice, and he wouldn't allow it to happen for a third time.

"No," he said, and continued to the door.

"*No?* Darcy, you have been corrupted by that Bennet woman!"

But Darcy kept walking. He stepped out into the street, carried by the exhilaration of the moment. He had never been one to get carried away by anything before, and now he could understand why people let their emotions override sense. The momentum of the confrontation propelled him at least thirty paces before he thought about the reality of what he'd just done.

He faltered.

What *would* his father say? Nothing good, that was for certain. Would the news reach him via letter, or would he return to London and hear the news from Tomlinson himself? Would it be in the papers?

Heaven help him if his father discovered that he'd abandoned his birthright in a *newspaper*.

He looked down at Guy, who was trotting alongside him with his small pink tongue hanging out. The little dog seemed totally unbothered by the theatrics they'd just left behind. Darcy stopped, and Guy did, too, looking up at him. He felt a bit at a loss.

"Good dog," he told him. Then, he bent over and tentatively patted the dog's head. Guy shrank back from the touch, so Darcy changed tactics and petted his back instead. The dog arched his back into Darcy's hand, so he supposed he liked it. He smiled. "If it hadn't been for you barking, Tomlinson might have caught me in his locked drawer. Good boy."

Pedestrians swerved past him, except one. Darcy looked up and was surprised to find the boy in the threadbare green coat. Henry.

He became alert at once. "Hello," he said. "Has something happened to Lizzie?"

The boy seemed skittish at being addressed in such a forth-right manner. He shook his head and whispered something.

Darcy took a step forward. "Sorry, I didn't catch that."

"She sent a message," the boy said.

But before Henry could relay it, Darcy heard a sharp voice call out behind him: "Darcy!"

He turned instinctively and saw Mr. Tomlinson and Mr. Hughes standing in front of Pemberley. Tomlinson was seeing Mr. Hughes to his carriage, and his groom had the door open. Hughes stood with one foot on the running board, carrying an elegant ebony cane. He pointed it at him as he said, "Stay away from my fiancée!"

A number of possible replies came to mind, but before Darcy had the opportunity to decide which one to deliver, he saw movement out of the corner of his eye. Henry had spotted Mr. Hughes, and he shrank back, trying to hide behind Darcy.

"Henry?" Darcy asked, but that was all he managed to say before Henry shook his head vigorously, turned, and ran.

Darcy gaped for a moment, but then the leather leash in his hand pulled taut, and Guy yanked right of his grasp.

"Hey!" he called. Darcy left a bellowing Hughes behind him—served him right, for thinking that he owned anyone, let alone Josette—and took off after them. The boy was *fast*. But Guy was on his heels. They wound their way in between pedestrians and carriages, eliciting shouts of anger and surprise, and it was all Darcy could do to keep from losing sight of them.

Darcy soon found himself short of breath and was in danger

of losing both Henry and Guy as he chased them through a tight alley and down another packed street. He spotted the boy turning down yet another alley and he put all his effort into closing the distance between them as he turned the corner. An old cart sat on its side, and laundry lines sagging with the day's wash hung above him. "Henry, wait!" Darcy gasped out. "I just want to talk!"

Henry ducked between the hanging laundry, but Guy, being so low to the ground, was not slowed down in the same way. He caught up with Henry and ran in circles around the boy, causing him to falter. His cap fell to the ground as he attempted to get away, and he didn't even stop to grab it. Darcy jogged forward and picked up the cap as he continued after the boy, swatting at hanging sheets and linens until he came out on the other side.

It was a dead end.

Darcy slowed to a walk. Guy was sitting at the edge of a heap of building materials and what appeared to be rubbish, tongue lolling, looking very proud of himself. Darcy didn't see Henry.

"I'm sorry for scaring you," he called out, looking around for the boy's hiding spot. "I don't want to hurt you. I just want to hear the message from Lizzie. And to return your hat."

He looked down at the hat he had picked up without thinking. It was threadbare in places and, like everything else the child wore, not the cleanest. It was also much larger than Darcy would have expected—a hat made for an adult head, not a child's. It hadn't looked that large on Henry.

A scuttling sound drew Darcy's attention. "Guy, come here,"

Darcy said, and to his surprise the dog trotted over and looked up at him expectantly. Darcy picked up his leash, now grimy from its drag through the streets. "The dog won't hurt you either. I've got a hold of his leash."

"I know."

The small voice came from behind the pile of rubbish. Darcy took a few steps closer, and soon spotted Henry. The boy had his arms covering his head, as if he expected Darcy to rain down a series of blows. Anger lit in his chest at the thought of how and why Henry had learned this instinct—who had hurt him in the past? "Henry?" he asked.

"Don't come any closer!" he said, his voice sounding almost shrill with panic.

"All right, I won't." Darcy lifted up his hands in a placating gesture. "Maybe you can give me your message and I'll toss your hat over to you? And then if you want me to, I'll be on my way."

He considered this a long moment. Darcy couldn't see his face. But Henry must have decided this sounded reasonable, for he said, "Toss the hat first."

Darcy took one step forward and lightly tossed the cap in Henry's direction. It fell just short of him, landing in the muck below their feet. Darcy winced—he hadn't meant for the hat to fall in the mud—he'd have thought that Henry would have caught it. But he kept his arms over his head. After a moment of hesitation, he reached down, feeling about for his fallen hat.

And a long plait fell over his shoulder.

"Oh," Darcy said.

Henry snatched the hat from the ground. Despite appearing as though it had been a good number of weeks since Henry had had a bath, his hair was recently combed and tightly plaited. He'd clearly taken great care to keep it neat, and as Darcy watched him wind the hair into a tight coil and ram the hat back on his head, Darcy realized that this was a routine.

He'd never seen a boy with hair like that. Only girls . . .

Which meant . . .

Oh.

"What are you looking at?" Henry snarled.

"I beg your pardon," Darcy said, because in the absence of sense, his manners never deserted him. "I didn't mean to stare."

"Are you going to tell?"

The demand caught him off guard. Was Darcy going to tell anyone that Henry . . . what? Had a long plait of hair? Was a girl?

"Is your name really Henry?" Darcy asked.

He was treated with a magnificent scowl. "Henrietta."

"Ah."

"But I prefer Henry."

"Fair enough," Darcy said.

The silence between them stretched out, and Henry continued to glare at him. Darcy had the peculiar sensation that he was still missing something. How did Lizzie manage to do it? She never seemed to have any trouble winning over the street children with kind questions, small praises, and the perfect little odd job or bit of encouragement. But she wasn't here now, and Darcy had the feeling that Henry was one wrong word away from bolting again, and Darcy really didn't think he was up for another chase.

"I understand that," he said awkwardly. "Going by a nick-name, that is."

No reaction.

"Sometimes our parents can saddle us with the most absurd names. Do you want to know my given name?"

No reaction, but Darcy could swear Henry's glare was soft-ening.

He made a big deal of looking left and right as if checking for witnesses. "It's not a secret, only you have to promise not to laugh, all right? It's . . . Fitzwilliam."

Henry's mouth quivered with what Darcy suspected might be the beginning of a smile.

"I know. Now, it's not the worst name you've ever heard. I have a great uncle Archibald, you know, and I'm lucky my mother didn't want to name me after him. And William is a nice, solid name. William sounds like a dependable sort, you know? But Fitzwilliam? I always thought it was a bit pretentious. Can you just picture a dandy named Fitzwilliam?"

Henry nodded. Progress.

"And heaven help me if anyone were to ever describe me as a dandy." Darcy played up his dramatic shudder, although the sentiment was honest enough. "That's why everyone, even Liz-zie, calls me Darcy. Not as fussy, not as dramatic. It feels more like . . . me."

His words seemed to have softened Henry's hard exterior somewhat. The boy looked down at his hands and said, "Henry is who I am. But it's more than a name. It's . . ." Darcy waited for more, but Henry seemed at a loss for words. Finally, he asked, "Does Miss Bennet ever wish she was a boy?"

Darcy was so surprised by the question that he stumbled into a reply without thinking it through. "At times, I'm sure she wishes that she commanded the presence and respect of a man, but I've not heard her say she wishes she *were* a man. Although . . . I mean . . . maybe you better ask her."

Henry considered that for a moment, then nodded. "I always wanted to be a boy, ever since I was big enough to know the difference between boys and girls. And now . . . I'm a boy. And my name's Henry."

Darcy let Henry's words sink in slowly. Before he'd met Lizzie, he might have laughed at the idea that Henry could just decide to be a boy, but there was something about associating with an unconventional lady like her that opened his mind, like a cabinet whose doors had always been locked, but she had turned the key. *Why not?* he found himself wondering. Life, he knew, was seldom easy or fair. It took courage to reach for what you wanted out of life—Lizzie had taught him that. If being a boy was what made sense to Henry, was what she—no, he—wanted, then . . .

"All right," Darcy said. "Nice to meet you, Henry."

There was a brief moment where Henry's entire body seemed to relax. Darcy hadn't been aware that up until that moment Henry had likely been tensed to fight, run, do whatever he needed. And that broke something inside Darcy, to realize that he'd already faced such cruelty and hardship that he had honed an instinct for how to fight, even in the face of kindness.

But in a flash, that softness was gone and Henry demanded, "You aren't going to tell Miss Bennet, are you?"

"Er, well . . . no?" Darcy said. He might have, but given Henry's reaction, Darcy guessed that it wouldn't be welcome. "That is, it appears that this is information you wish to keep private. And a gentleman always has discretion. So, no, I won't if you don't wish me to."

Henry nodded, and Darcy felt as though he'd made the right decision. But his curiosity—and concern—got the better of him. "I must say, and I hope you'll forgive this overstep, but keeping your hair long like that is a risk. Why not cut it?"

Henry gave him the most magnificent scowl, as if Darcy were a first-rate fool. "I know that. But I don't got a knife or scissors, and if I go to the wigmaker she'll know, and . . ."

"Ah," Darcy said. So it was a matter of poverty, and not carelessness. "I only have a penknife on me, and it's not particularly sharp . . . but I can get you a pair of barber scissors, if you like."

"Really?" Henry was suspicious but hopeful.

"It would be no bother," Darcy promised. "But first, if you don't mind—would you care to tell me the message from Lizzie?"

"Oh, right." Henry crossed his skinny arms. "She said you weren't going to be very happy to hear it."

Darcy rolled his eyes. "Of course not."

"But you don't seem the type to get angry enough to hurt the messenger."

"I'd never," Darcy promised solemnly.

"She said to tell you she was meeting the Dashwoods and she'd find the truth tonight, at the storehouse."

"Find the truth?" Whatever did that mean? "She didn't say anything more?"

He looked at Henry, who didn't respond. He'd crept forward close enough that Guy trotted up to him and sat. Henry was petting the dog; he looked happy for attention. Like that was what he was hoping for all along, and now he'd finally gotten it.

"You know Guy," Darcy said.

Henry looked up at him, shrugged. "He was Mr. Simon's dog."

"Henry," Darcy said, his voice very serious. "I'm not upset, but . . . please tell me the real reason why you've been following Lizzie around. It's not just because she was kind to you, is it?"

For a moment, Darcy was afraid Henry would bolt again. He stared up, wide-eyed. But then Guy nudged his hand and moved closer to Henry, begging for more attention. Henry looked at the dog and mumbled, "It's not fair."

"What isn't fair, Henry?"

"I wasn't sneaking or spying, but I saw what they were doing! I didn't mean to!"

"What were they doing?" Darcy asked urgently.

But Henry didn't answer, at least not directly. "They always come at night. They move crates and boxes in, a whole lot of them. Mr. Simon walks around the outside, with Guy. Guy always finds me, but on the nights the crates come, Mr. Simon yells and chases me away."

"And Lizzie is going there tonight?" he asked. "To see what's in the crates?"

Henry nodded miserably.

"Is there something else you've not said, Henry? Something more to it?"

"They always come, the next night," Henry whispered. "They take the crates somewhere else. They're bad people. Even Mr. Simon doesn't like them. One of them kicked Guy once."

A sick, icy feeling replaced the confusion. "Who, Henry?"

"The man," he said. "The man at your office."

SEVENTEEN

In Which Lizzie and the Dashwoods Make
a Series of Inadvisable Decisions

"LIZZIE, I DON'T THINK he's coming," Marianne whispered.

Lizzie repressed a sigh, even though she knew Marianne was right. "Just a few minutes more."

It had not been difficult to convince the Dashwood sisters to join her on a nighttime stakeout of the Mullins Brothers storehouse. Marianne and Margaret had been downright eager, and Elinor reluctant, and then there had been the small matter of telling Margaret that she wouldn't be joining them. The row that ensued had made Lizzie's arguments with Lydia look like child's play, but eventually Elinor and Marianne had overruled their younger sister, and she had sullenly agreed that Lizzie's case was too important for her to rat them out to Mrs. Dashwood.

Which was how they'd found themselves sneaking out of their respective homes in the middle of the night and meeting on a darkened street corner before making their way to the Mullins Brothers storehouse. Lizzie had not given up hope that Darcy would appear at the Dashwoods' shop or meet them there—had he not gotten her message? Had something happened to him, or to Henry?

The worry was eating her alive.

"Lizzie, I think we really ought not to wait any longer," Marianne said. "We run the risk of getting caught."

Lizzie knew she was right. And what's more, she could feel Elinor and Marianne's nervous energy as they huddled together, just out of sight from the storehouse down the street. They'd been standing there for more than a half hour, their cloaks woefully insufficient against the early spring chill, which still held the bite of winter.

If Darcy wasn't coming, there was no use wasting precious time. "All right," she conceded.

"I just want to state for the record that I am not fond of this plan," Elinor hissed.

"Noted," Marianne and Lizzie said in unison. Nonetheless, the trio approached with caution.

Earlier, Marianne had made Lizzie draw them a crude map of the storehouse, its entrances, the scaffolding surrounding it, and the nearby buildings so they'd know how to approach in the dark. Lizzie wasn't sure what to expect when they got inside, but they decided they'd cross that bridge when they came to it.

"Ready?" Marianne asked.

"Ready," Lizzie confirmed, pushing Darcy to the back of her mind.

"I suppose," Elinor said, resigned.

The trio kept to the shadows close to the buildings, creeping up to the alleyway between the storehouse and the blacksmith, where Lizzie had first spotted Henry. They slipped farther down the alley, taking care not to stumble over the uneven ground. Just like the last time she'd been here, the scaffolding and flimsy wall was still erect around the side of the building, but the smell of newly cut wood hung in the air.

Lizzie searched for the best spot to get past the wall while the Dashwoods kept watch. Even in the alley they were too exposed to risk lighting any of the candles they'd brought with them, so Lizzie had to go by feel alone, search for any weakness or possible foothold for climbing over. She found a gap between two boards and pushed. The wall wobbled but held.

"Here," she whispered.

But she'd no sooner uttered the words than a weak light lit up the darkness. All three ladies stilled, and Lizzie's heart flew into her throat.

"Oy, who's there?" called a voice.

Lizzie recognized the voice—it was Parry, the foreman. They'd known there was a chance that someone would be standing guard, but they hadn't seen him at all in their reconnaissance. From the direction of his voice and the weak light, he was at the front of the building, but the light was moving closer to them.

"Go," Marianne whispered. "I'll distract him!"

Before Lizzie could question her, Marianne was trotting toward the street. "Marianne!" Elinor hissed after her, but her sister disappeared around the corner.

Never one to waste an opportunity, Lizzie refocused her attention on the foothold she found. It was at approximately hip height. "Elinor, give me a boost."

"Hurry," Elinor said, kneeling in the mud to offer her knee and hand to Lizzie. In the distance, they could hear the sound of Marianne's voice calling out a greeting. She sounded merry, and although Lizzie couldn't quite make out what she was saying as she hoisted herself up on Elinor's knee, she could hear Marianne's words slur together.

Elinor let out a small grunt, but Lizzie worked quickly. From there, she wedged her foot into the foothold and stretched to reach the top of the fence. She wobbled, but her fingers couldn't quite reach. As she braced her palms against the rough wood, she felt her center of balance tip.

"Got it?" Elinor huffed.

"Not . . . quite!"

"Hold on." And before Lizzie could guess at what would come next, Elinor's hands came beneath her foot and she lifted Lizzie the last little stretch she needed to grasp the top of the wall—and just in time, too. Elinor let go with a small "oof" but between her grasp on the top of the wall and her foothold, Lizzie was able to push up with her leg and pull up with both arms. Muscles she had not realized she had screamed in protest, and once she had lifted herself up, Lizzie realized that she now had to find a way *over*. And then down.

"Surely you're jesting!" Marianne protested. "Why, a big building like that and there's nowhere for a lady to relieve herself inside?"

Lizzie had to gulp back a laugh. Marianne sounded drunk.

"No," came Parry's gruff response. "Move along."

Lizzie kicked her free foot over the edge of the fence, gritting her teeth as the hard edge of the board cut into the softness of her belly. But luckily for her, the drop was not far, for there was a platform a mere two feet down on the other side. She fell shakily onto it.

"No? But surely you aren't being entirely forthcoming?" Marianne's voice sounded cajoling. "I know you don't let in just anyone off the streets, but I am not just anyone, sir!"

"Lizzie?" Elinor whispered.

Lizzie's heart was racing but she sat up and peered over the edge. "Fine!"

"You're trouble!" Parry said, sounding louder. "You look like you come from around here, but that don't mean you're not trouble like the rest of them."

"How dare you!" Marianne exclaimed, and Lizzie noticed that she sounded closer, too. She rose to a crouch and looked toward the street. The corner of the building obstructed her view, despite the advantage of her elevation, but she could see light bobbing about, like a lantern being carried by someone approaching.

"Elinor!" she whispered, looking down. "You have to come up! Now!"

"I can't!" came the scandalized response.

"See here," Marianne shouted. "Do you mean to march me up this street, sir?"

That was as good of a warning as any.

Lizzie missed Parry's response. She kneeled on the platform of the scaffolding and reached her hand down to Elinor. The other young lady looked wildly about, as if there were any other option to be found in a dark alley. Out of the corner of her eye Lizzie could see the lantern light drawing closer. "Hurry!"

Elinor was taller than Lizzie, with longer legs, so she hoped it would be enough that she could reach and pull her up. But Elinor's foot could not reach the foothold that Lizzie had used without getting hopelessly tangled in her skirts. Lizzie looked on desperately as she heard Parry say, "I aim to march you 'round the perimeter of this buildin' and see what sort of distraction you believe yourself to be!"

Elinor heard his words, too. And in a move that shocked Lizzie, she reached down, pulled her skirts up to her waist, exposing her drawers, and placed her foot in the hold. Then, she hopped from her other foot, giving herself the boost she needed to catch Lizzie's outstretched hand.

Lizzie had thought she was prepared to haul Elinor up, but despite being rather willowy in build, Elinor was much heavier than Lizzie had anticipated. She gritted her teeth and clenched Elinor's hand while Elinor's other hand came to clutch Lizzie's wrist in return. Using the exhilaration that came with the fear of being caught, Lizzie hauled Elinor up until she was close enough that Lizzie could grab her waist and pull her over the wall. They dropped onto their bellies on the gritty platform and tried to breathe silently as they heard Marianne protest, "Sir, what is down this dark alley? I hope you aren't about to take advantage of a lady! I warn you, I shall scream."

Parry didn't respond immediately, but Lizzie could sense his confusion as she heard his boots tromp down the alley and saw the light from the lantern throw wild shadows against the wall. Elinor and Lizzie stayed absolutely still. They were out of sight and Lizzie was certain that as long as they didn't move or make a noise, they would be safe.

"Thought I heard something," Parry said finally, although he seemed to linger in the alley.

"Rats," Marianne pronounced with disgust. "Or stray cats, maybe?"

"Maybe," Parry said. "Either way, you best move on now. There's no privy behind this fence, and this street is no place for a so-called lady after dark."

"You're no fun!" they heard Marianne say, and Lizzie could easily imagine her pout. But the sound of their voices was moving away, and Lizzie felt her shoulders relax, even as the muscles in her back and shoulder still burned.

"Are you all right?" she whispered.

"I shall recover," came Elinor's response.

"Excellent." Lizzie slowly rose to her hands and knees and

began moving gingerly. "I think there's a ladder."

As quickly as they dared, Elinor and Lizzie made their way down to the ground, making as little noise as possible. As Lizzie had suspected, repair work had already begun on the storehouse, and the wooden frames of the windows had been replaced, although the glass had yet to be installed. From the inside, new wooden shutters blocked out the night, but Lizzie quietly tested one by pushing on it. It was latched, but the latch was easy enough to flip open by shimmying the blade of Elinor's pocketknife between the crack in the shutters.

"Here," she whispered, indicating that they ought to climb through the opening. "Do you need a boost, or—"

"I think that I've had enough boosts for the evening," Elinor replied. "Although I am not sure I feel comfortable breaking in through a window."

"We've already climbed their fence," Lizzie pointed out. "And there isn't any glass."

"I was just supposed to stand watch! Perhaps I'll keep watch out here."

Lizzie hoisted herself up on the windowsill. "Best not. Out there, you had plausible deniability—you could claim you were simply out for an evening stroll. On this side, you've already trespassed." She dropped down onto the wooden floor of the storehouse and turned to face Elinor. "Besides, the shutters weren't locked. We broke nothing."

She could sense rather than see Elinor's eye roll. "And I suppose you're the legal expert."

But despite Lizzie's stretch of the truth, Elinor followed her, and soon both ladies were standing in the storehouse, Lizzie gently closing the shutters behind her. It was completely black inside, and there was no adjusting to the gloom when there was no light to be had. A memory rose, unbidden, of the last time Lizzie had found herself shut in absolute darkness, in the records room at Pemberley & Associates. Darcy had been at her side, and she had followed him into Pemberley without thinking things through properly, and they'd been locked inside with no way out. But they'd held hands for the first time, and if Lizzie concentrated, she could still feel the warmth of his hand around hers, and the strength of his presence, which filled up all the dark corners and put her at ease, even as he was struggling not to panic at his own claustrophobia.

The scrape of a tinderbox jolted Lizzie back to reality.

"Sorry," Elinor said, lighting a candle. "But we aren't getting anywhere without some light."

"You're right," Lizzie said, forcing her thoughts to the matter at hand and away from the memory of Darcy and his intoxicating scent. She withdrew her own candle from her pocket and lit the wick on Elinor's flame. "I hope Marianne managed to get away."

"I'm sure she'll be fine," Elinor whispered as they moved carefully through the storehouse. There were tables and a workbench on this end, and beyond that, stacks of crates huddled in the dark. "If anything, she'll be peeved that she missed out on this little venture and complain about it for a week."

"I will not!"

The whisper from ahead made both Elinor and Lizzie jump, but then Marianne herself appeared between the stacks of crates, hair in disarray and skirts streaked with mud.

"Marianne!" Elinor and Lizzie both exclaimed in a whisper.

"If you thought I was about to let you two do the fun bits after I did the hard work, then you both don't know me at all!" She joined them and withdrew her own candle from her pocket.

"How did you get past the guard?" Elinor asked, lighting her candle.

"As soon as we got back around the front, he left me on the street," she said. "But then there was a whistle, and he went running in the other direction. I was able to squeeze under the gate he'd been guarding and walked right through the front door. But we better hurry. It could be that someone is here for whatever they're hiding."

That got the three of them moving.

The storehouse consisted of an open space on the first level where they received crates of wares—mostly wool broadcloth and linen from the weavers in the countryside—before it was shipped to its final destinations all around the world. Lizzie knew from Jack that they kept back a percentage of their wares to be sold here in London, in the Western Exchange, where the Mullinses had booths. There had been a system, she recalled, of sorting, labeling, and processing the wares.

But in the dark, all the crates looked the same.

"We need to open one of these," Lizzie said to Marianne.

"Can you find something—"

"Here," Marianne said, and there was the sound of her skirts rustling followed by the metallic clang of something. Lizzie heard Elinor say, "Oh dear," and then Marianne returned in the circle of light, grinning and wielding a crowbar. Elinor followed, carrying both her candle and Marianne's, and she and Lizzie held up the light while Marianne went to work, trying to pry open the nearest crate.

"These crates aren't damaged, so they've been delivered since the fire," Lizzie observed.

"If not for the stink of smoke, you wouldn't know that a fire had taken place," Elinor agreed, looking at the newly laid wood planks on the floor. "Where did the fire break out?"

"Toward the back, I think," Lizzie said. "We can go looking there next."

"Priorities," Marianne reminded them with a grunt as she leveled her weight onto the crowbar. The lid gave way with a loud squeak and all three ladies pressed close, eager for a good look.

"Careful of the nails," Elinor warned as Marianne lifted the lid and Lizzie hoisted the candles, only to reveal . . .

"Cloth," Marianne said dryly.

"All right," Lizzie said. "So, he's a dealer in wool. Well, we knew that. I mean, of course there is cloth here."

"We don't have time to open every crate," Marianne said.

"Let's keep looking," Lizzie said, afraid that Marianne was right.

From there, they split up. Lizzie tried to focus on what she could see, making note of how many crates were stacked on the main floor, memorizing the painted labels on the sides of the crates, and noting their position. Toward the back of the storehouse, soot streaked the brick walls of the perimeter of the building, and tools and building supplies were stacked near a brand-new desk, table, and cabinet. It was a makeshift office, and Lizzie guessed that the builders hadn't had time to erect walls and a door here yet. Marianne tried to open the cabinet, but it was locked, and there was nothing to find in the desk drawers. Elinor walked very carefully, almost catlike, around the perimeter of the storeroom, almost as if she were hoping to get a clear view of the entire operation.

It was when Elinor had disappeared from view and Lizzie was growing more and more frustrated that she heard what sounded like a faint crunching. Then Elinor's voice called out in a loud whisper, "Here! I think I found something!"

Marianne and Lizzie both hurried toward her. Elinor was in the far corner of the storehouse, near a contraption that looked like a large box encased with ropes that hung from the ceiling. Lizzie lifted her candle and tried to look up to see where the ropes were attached, but her flame was too feeble.

"There's a bit of broken glass back here," Elinor said, drawing her attention to the back wall. "And see here, all the floorboards have been replaced? I think there might have been a wall concealing all of this at one time—do you see where there used to be studs here?"

"Scorch marks on the brick here, too," Marianne added, looking at the back wall.

Elinor held up a shard of glass, and beneath the soot, it glinted in the candlelight.

"It looks like a bottle?" Lizzie asked, uncertain.

"Indeed," Elinor agreed. "And there's more."

The ladies peered at a pile of rubbish that had been swept aside, beyond the scorch marks on the brick and the freshly replaced wooden floors. There were charred hunks of wood, a few broken bricks, and heaps of broken glass, all appearing to be from bottles. Some of it was burnt, but Marianne plucked one piece that wasn't.

"This remind you of anything?" she asked them.

Lizzie stared at the broken bottle. "Well, a bottle, of course."

"But what sort of bottle?" she asked.

Lizzie looked at the sisters. "A spirits bottle," Elinor said.

"Oh."

Marianne's triumphant smile flashed bright in the weak light. "Exactly. What sort of storehouse of linen and broadcloth would have this much broken glass?"

"It's not totally unreasonable to find *some* broken glass," Lizzie said, but her heart was beginning to thump with excitement. "In fact, anyone could argue that a group of working men kept a store of spirits for after the workday. Perhaps not the most prudent move, but hardly illegal."

Marianne raised the shard to her nose and snuffed. "Spirits for certain. But I think . . . maybe brandy?"

"How can you tell?"

"Marianne has a very keen sense of smell," Elinor explained, as though it pained her.

"And it's saved my life before, thank you!" Marianne looked about. "I am fairly certain that this is a brandy bottle. Good brandy, too. Now tell me, why would a storehouse keep a large collection of fine brandy? Not for their day laborers."

"Perhaps they're distilling it?" Lizzie suggested. She couldn't believe that she'd been wrong and there was no evidence of graphite here. What if they'd taken this terrible risk of breaking in for nothing?

"I don't see a distillery," Elinor whispered. "But I think there's something upstairs."

"Why do you say that?"

"Because of the lift."

"Come again?" Marianne asked.

"A lift," Elinor repeated. "They're like dumbwaiters, but large enough for people or goods. You see, you place boxes of cargo within it, and then you pull on the ropes—they're attached to pulleys somewhere above, I imagine—and then the whole thing lifts itself. I've never seen one in person, actually. I think the wall that used to be here concealed it from view from the rest of the storehouse."

Suddenly, Lizzie remembered what Henry had said—he climbed the tree and saw through the windows. If they'd been moving illicit goods, they wouldn't be foolish enough to leave the shutters open on the first floor. But if Henry was in the tree, and they left an upstairs shutter open . . . "Of course," she muttered. "They're moving their illicit goods upstairs. They must have been using this lift to bring them up."

"Heavy goods," Marianne noted.

"Does it look like it was damaged in the fire?" Lizzie asked. The tremendous crash—what if that had been the contraption falling, and not some explosion caused by graphite?

Elinor stepped closer, holding her candle aloft. "Likely. All the wood has been replaced or repaired. You see, the ropes here are connected to that support, which looks new. And this over here . . ."

Marianne's and Lizzie's eyes met while Elinor continued speaking about lifts and inventions, and in unison their gazes shifted upward. "We need to get upstairs," Marianne said.

Lizzie and Marianne went searching for the stairs in opposite directions, Elinor scrambling after them. Lizzie would have settled for even a ladder, but Marianne and Elinor found an open doorway leading to a staircase, tucked away in shadows near the office area. "Lizzie!" Marianne called out, just a touch too loud. Lizzie turned and was about to join the Dashwoods when the unmistakable sound of a door swinging open stilled her.

Acting instinctively, all three ladies immediately blew out their candles. Lizzie ducked behind the cabinet in the office area, and looked to Marianne and Elinor, whom she could just make out, thanks to the light shed by the newcomers. She waved at them to go, for there was no way for her to make her way to them without walking across an exposed swath of the storehouse floor. Marianne hesitated for a moment, but then the sound of approaching footsteps convinced her. She and Elinor stepped into the stairwell and closed the door.

Lizzie had no time to feel relief. Her heart was pounding in her chest, and her position was far too exposed for comfort. Peering around the cabinet, she saw the figures of three men approaching, carrying heavy lanterns. One was Jack Mullins, and one, she thought, was Parry. But she couldn't get a good look at the third man's face.

"I want it all out, tonight," Jack was saying. "And then consider us closed for business."

"It doesn't work that way," came the stranger's voice. "You can't simply decide enough is enough."

"I didn't decide anything, if you'll recall!"

Lizzie felt a cold fear wash over her—not because the men were drawing closer but because Jack sounded *scared*.

"You, your brother, doesn't matter. You're indebted now."

"I'm in debt all right! No thanks to you!"

"I wasn't the one who torched the place! But you'll have far bigger worries if you displease her yet again."

Her? Was he referring to the lady that Jack claimed set fire to the building?

As much as Lizzie would have loved to sit and puzzle out the mystery, they were getting far too close for comfort. She began to edge her way around the side of the cabinet that was still cast in shadow—and just in time, too. The trio of men stopped mere paces away from where Lizzie had first hid, the stranger so close to Lizzie's last hiding spot that she might have been able to reach out and touch his coat if she'd still been there.

"I'll turn you over to the Crown!" Jack said suddenly. There was a small waver in his voice. "Unless you let me walk away, I'll do it!"

The strange man laughed. It was the low, delighted laugh of a man who found amusement in Jack's panic, and it chilled Lizzie. "No, I don't think you will. If you do, that hole you've dug yourself will become your grave."

Something about that turn of phrase sent a shiver down Lizzie's spine. It wasn't just the dark imagery, though. She'd heard someone say that before.

"I'll expose your operation," Jack said, though he sounded less certain. "Goods are one thing, but I never signed up for—"

"Shut up!"

Lizzie's blood ran cold.

"What's that smell?" the stranger asked.

"Well, I don't know if ya noticed, but we had a wee fire last week," Parry said sarcastically.

"No, I don't smell old smoke. It's as if . . . someone just blew out a candle."

Lizzie let out the softest exhale, her only outward sign of panic.

The men were quiet and very, very still. "No one's here," Parry said finally. "I've been guardin' the place myself all day. No one in, no one out."

"And you never once stepped a single foot away from the gate?" the stranger demanded.

"I was always within sight!" Parry lied, and even if Lizzie hadn't known the truth, she would have suspected it from the panicked note to his voice. "Sir, I would never—"

"Quiet!" the man ordered.

Lizzie had been trying to ease away from the cabinet and toward the stacks of crates, but part of her knew it was useless. There was no place to hide where she couldn't easily be found, and no way of getting to the other side of the storehouse without exposing herself. She was moments away from discovery. Her only hope would be to use the shadows of the storehouse to her advantage and try to make a run for it. It would give the Dashwood sisters enough time to hopefully find whatever was upstairs and make their own escape.

Above her, there was a tiny creak.

"Someone's upstairs," Jack whispered.

"Quiet," the stranger ordered. "You better not have set a trap for me, boy."

"I didn't!" Jack protested. "I swear! I don't want to hang any more than you do!"

There was another creak. She heard the stranger say, "Upstairs, but quietly," and she readied to make her move.

The trio of men had just started up the stairs when Lizzie launched into action. Since they already suspected they weren't alone, she chose speed over stealth, making a run for the front doors. If she could escape into the night, raise the alarm, and bring the Runners back to the storehouse before the men could hurt the Dashwoods, then they had a decent chance of getting out of this unscathed.

A grunt of surprise, followed by the stranger's voice shouting, "There!" let her know that that she had been spotted, and she heard the footsteps of someone racing after her. At the same time, she realized she had miscalculated the distance she needed to cover between her hiding spot and the door, and just how many obstacles were in her way. She was forced to detour around them, slowing down her progress. She didn't dare look back, though, weaving in between crates and holding her skirts high enough to jump over a stack of tools and bricks until finally the door was in sight.

But doing so had cost her precious time, and her pursuer had seemed to know exactly what was in her way and what her destination would be and opted not to follow her. Instead, he retraced his own steps and loomed suddenly to her right, intent on cutting her off. Above, Lizzie heard the unmistakable sound of a pistol being fired, and she instinctively screamed.

"*Don't shoot!*" the stranger bellowed, and then she felt an extraordinary flash of hot pain break across her entire head as she was violently pulled back by her hair.

Lizzie managed one more scream, and then the man threw her to the ground.

Climbing over the wall and pulling Elinor up after her had not hurt as much as it did to be yanked by one's hair and tossed like a rag doll. Lizzie tried to get to her feet, but before she could fully regain her faculties, the man was hauling her up sharply by her elbow and threw her roughly against three stacked crates. He took a step between her and her escape, and, inexplicably, began to chuckle.

"Miss Bennet. I must admit, even I did not think you'd be so foolhardy. Yet you continue to surprise me."

It was at that precise moment that Lizzie placed his voice, but even still she had to raise her gaze to his leering face in order to confirm it really was him, so great was her disbelief.

"Mr. Tomlinson?"

EIGHTEEN

In Which Lizzie Takes a Beating and the
Dashwoods Discover the Mullins Brothers' Secret

MR. TOMLINSON LEERED DOWN at her, seeming amused by Lizzie's shock.

"But," Lizzie said, "what . . . ? Why?"

"Not as smart as you think you are," he observed. "There's a reason why I didn't want Darcy consorting with you, and it's not just because you're damn meddlesome!"

"I believe the word you're looking for is *consulting*, not *consorting*," Lizzie said, which earned her a hard slap across the face.

"Shut up," Tomlinson spat.

"Darcy knows I'm here," Lizzie said, and prayed that it was true. "So whatever you're going to do, you won't get away with it."

"Darcy is a self-centered child who can't see what's right in front of his eyes, so I doubt very much that he'll manage to save you this time," Tomlinson said, and the assurance in his voice made Lizzie even more frightened than she already was.

"You don't know—"

Another slap. This one sent her head spinning and brought tears to her eyes. "No, Miss Bennet, *you* don't know."

He yanked her to her feet once more and Lizzie stumbled. It felt as though her ears were ringing, and above her she heard a loud clatter followed by some shouts. "That will be your friends getting rounded up, I imagine. I do hope that bullet hit at least one of them."

That, more than anything, brought Lizzie's anger bubbling to the surface, and Lizzie did the only thing she could—she gave Mr. Tomlinson a swift kick in the shin.

She knew that her assault would likely anger him rather than cause injury, but it still felt good to kick that horrid man. He sucked in a sharp breath, and then shoved her against two stacked crates. They were heavy enough that they didn't tumble as she crashed into them, but Lizzie felt her feet go out beneath her. Now her ears were truly ringing.

"If you want to play it that way, Miss Bennet, then we can," Mr. Tomlinson said, taking an ominous step closer. "I admit that I've often wanted to smack that smug expression off your face. You won't be able to charm the magistrates with a broken nose."

He drew back his foot to kick her and Lizzie instinctively curled around herself. His boot connected with her upper arm with stunning force, pain blooming from her chest to the tips of her fingers, and Lizzie couldn't help it—she cried out. She had to get on her feet. She had to defend herself somehow. But how could she when she could barely catch her breath and her feet were sprawled out and her skirts tangled and Tomlinson was standing above her, an eager grin cracking his face in two?

"This was easier than I thought it would be," he said, sounding pleased. "Jack Mullins didn't want to kidnap you—said it would be too difficult. But you walked right in."

Lizzie coughed, feeling every single ache and pain and her body as she struggled to her hands and knees. "You wanted to kidnap . . . me? Sir, I'm flattered."

He shoved her back to the ground, and Lizzie was only grateful that he'd pushed her rather than kicked her. "Shut up. You won't be making jokes soon enough when she gets her hands on you."

She? Lizzie would have been afraid, if everything didn't already hurt so much. Above her, she heard heavy footsteps and felt a spike of fear for Elinor and Marianne. At least they had each other . . . but they were facing two men, not one.

"And what is your part in all of this?" Lizzie asked, choosing not to try to get up just then. In fact, lying still was nice. Almost pleasant, if not for all the aches and bruises. "You're orchestrating whatever business is going in and out of this storehouse?"

"Shut up," Tomlinson snapped.

But Lizzie was never one to take orders from unreasonable men. "I don't know all the details, but I think I can make a few guesses. You're involved in some sort of illegal smuggling ring. You work at Pemberley, so surely you must be familiar with Josette Beaufort. She's engaged to Mr. Hughes, who claims his graphite mines are spent."

"If you know what's good for you, you will shut *up*." Tomlinson took another step toward her, and Lizzie flinched, preparing herself for a blow—but it never came. So she kept going, speaking almost as quickly as she put the pieces together.

"But I don't actually think they are! I think he's selling graphite illegally. I think he's selling it to the French! You're a solicitor; you know that doing so would be treason. Hughes couldn't exactly make that sort of deal out of his own buildings—graphite mines are too closely watched. So he dragged the Mullins brothers into it. They receive shipments of cloth from the countryside on a regular basis—no one would question a few extra crates, correct?"

Tomlinson was glowering at her, and Lizzie decided to try to sit up slowly. Her muscles screamed, but Tomlinson didn't stop her. He seemed to be looking toward the entrance, as if waiting for something—or someone.

"It all started to fall apart when the storehouse was set on fire, didn't it? Did you lose some of your product? Perhaps just the idea of losing out on a convenient place to stash whatever you're dealing was a big enough blow. And then Jack came to me, asking me to find the woman who set the fire. He was trying to find out who was responsible for his brother's death and for getting them into this mess. Am I right?"

"You don't know what you're saying. Your sense is addled."

"You look scared," Lizzie said. She wasn't certain if he was, or if she was merely dizzy. "Is it because I'm close to the truth?"

"You don't know what you're talking about! You think you're

so clever and you've worked it all out, but she's much smarter than you and she's been watching you this entire time! You never suspected, did you? And now because you've been so stupid, you'll never see Darcy or your family again, you idiotic girl!"

What on earth did he mean? Lizzie felt like her thoughts were moving through a thick syrup. "Darcy knows where I am," she repeated. "And so does my father, for that matter."

"I don't believe you," Tomlinson hissed, crouching down so his face was disconcertingly close to her. "I think you're a fool who decided to poke her nose where it didn't belong and—"

Thwack!

Tomlinson fell forward, right into Lizzie's lap. She cried out in alarm and attempted to shove his heavy body off of her, and he didn't struggle. Lizzie looked up.

Elinor Dashwood stood before her, holding a crowbar, wearing a stricken look.

"Good job, Elinor!" Marianne cheered. "Now, the rope—tie him up! Lizzie, are you all right?"

Lizzie was speechless as Elinor grabbed some rope and approached Mr. Tomlinson. "I've never done this before," she said. "Do you suppose I start with the hands, or the feet?"

"Hands," Lizzie said faintly, and recovered her wits enough to push herself into a kneeling position and roll him over. "Here."

They quickly bound Tomlinson's hands and then his feet. Elinor looked nervously at the back of his head. "Did I kill him?"

"I don't think so," Lizzie said slowly. Her head still felt a bit fuzzy, and she kept hearing the echo of the thwack of Elinor hitting him across the back of head. There was no blood, and Lizzie could feel the rise and fall of his chest when she rolled him over. "I think he's just lost consciousness."

"Are you done?" Marianne asked anxiously.

"Yes," Elinor said, and gave Lizzie her hand. "Can you stand?"

"I think so," Lizzie said, getting to her feet with an unlady-like grunt. The act of standing was incredibly painful, but once she was on her feet, Lizzie found that the aches were quite manageable. "Nothing broken."

"Good," Marianne said. "Now we have to decide what to do with these three."

Lizzie could see now that Jack and Mr. Parry were standing nearby, hands bound and mouths gagged, although their feet remained free. They were standing rather nicely in place . . . and Lizzie realized it was because Marianne was two paces away, wielding a pistol in each hand.

"How on earth did you manage this?" Lizzie asked, rubbing her aching head. Her ears were still ringing, and every small sound was making her jumpy.

"I have my ways," Marianne said.

"We set up a trip wire," Elinor said at the same time.

"Ah." Lizzie looked at Jack and shook her head. "I see."

"You don't look so good," Marianne said, sounding alarmed. "Did you hit your head? Brandon says that when one hits their head very hard, it can be dangerous. You aren't sleepy, are you?"

Lizzie wasn't sure who Brandon was, but she shook her head, which did cause it to ache. "No. But am I hearing things, or is a dog barking?"

All three ladies went still, and then Lizzie heard it again—and judging by Marianne and Elinor's reactions, they heard it, too. Hope flamed in Lizzie's chest.

She hobbled toward the door but hadn't made it halfway when Guy came tearing through, barking at the sight of Lizzie. "Guy!" she cried out, bending down to pet the dog. But he was too excited to stop—he zipped around the storehouse, circling the Dashwoods and their captives as if it were his job to keep them all in order. A moment later, three frantic gentlemen came tumbling through the door.

"Darcy!"

He ran straight to her and threw his arms around her. She hugged him back; so great was her relief that she didn't even care that his embrace was putting pressure on her newly forming bruises. "You came," she said.

"I will always come for you," he whispered. "I'm sorry we were delayed."

She looked beyond him to his companions. A gentleman with curly brown hair wore an appalled expression and wrapped an arm around Elinor's waist, and the darker-haired gentlemen with spectacles stood next to Marianne, who didn't let her attention slip from Jack and Mr. Parry despite the commotion of their new arrivals.

"Mr. Farrows and Mr. Brandon," Darcy said by way of explanation. "Associates of the Dashwoods, apparently. We thought you all could use some help."

"How on earth did you get roped into this?" Elinor asked Mr. Farrows.

"Ah, well . . . a little bird told us that you were planning on doing something dangerous tonight," Mr. Farrows said, avoiding Elinor's gaze.

"Margaret!" Marianne exclaimed. "That brat!"

"She was reasonably worried," Mr. Brandon told her, although he seemed less distressed than Mr. Farrows to find them in a darkened storehouse in the middle of the night. Then again, Marianne did look rather fierce, wielding those two pistols.

She scowled at him, though Lizzie didn't sense any anger in her stance. "It's always nice to see you, darling. But we are not some damsels in need of rescuing."

"Clearly," Brandon replied. "But you mistake the situation, beloved. This isn't a rescue mission. We are simply here to inquire if you need assistance."

"*I'm* happy to see you," Elinor said to Mr. Farrows.

"Are you all right? All three of you?" Darcy asked.

"Elinor and I are fine," Marianne answered. "I'm afraid that brute roughed up Lizzie a bit, but don't worry, Darcy—Elinor hit him in the back of the head."

Darcy's entire body tensed as he looked directly at Mr. Tomlinson. "It's him," Lizzie confirmed. "He's involved in this somehow. I'm not quite sure, exactly, but I think he's responsible for whisking the goods away to the buyers."

Darcy didn't relax—in fact, his body seemed to tremble with barely controlled fury, and Lizzie knew that Darcy was trying very hard not to lose his temper. "He's not worth it," she whispered. "Besides, now you can haul him off to Newgate, where he belongs."

Darcy blinked a few moments, his expression utterly unreadable.

And then he leaned down and kissed her.

It was not one of the gentle kisses he usually bestowed upon her in stolen moments when no one was about to witness their impropriety, nor was it as tentative as their first kiss. This was a hungry kiss, almost rough. As Lizzie's lips parted and she returned it, she felt all his fear and anguish, and utter relief in that moment.

They finally separated when both needed to draw breath, and the shock of it all left Lizzie panting lightly. But also, every bit of her was engulfed in heat, and all she wanted to do was draw his lips back to her own for more. . . .

"Ahem," Marianne said, not subtle in the least. "Now that we've gotten that out of the way, Lizzie, I really think you ought to see what we found upstairs."

"Right," she said, and she knew without looking in a mirror that her cheeks were flushed. "What's that?"

"Go," Mr. Farrows urged them, taking one of the pistols from Marianne. "I'll guard these criminals." The criminals in question glowered but were unable to speak thanks to their gags.

Elinor gave him a quick, grateful smile, and then gestured at the group to follow her. "Back here, near the lift."

"The what?" Darcy asked.

"You'll see," Lizzie assured him. "It's like a very large dumb-waiter."

They brought their lanterns to the back corner, where it was much more apparent that the floor and wooden trim had been replaced recently. In the better light, Lizzie could see that the brick around the repaired lift was still scorched black and all the wooden planks of the floor and ceiling had been replaced.

"The fire clearly started back here," Elinor continued. "It burned fast and hot, and there was some damage to the floor above."

"Can you tell what started it?"

"I cannot say definitively," Elinor admitted, "but I can hazard a guess that I'd be willing to stake my reputation on."

She strode over to where they'd found the pile of refuse, and picked a glass shard up and held it aloft. "I believe these bottles held spirits, and when they broke, they acted as an accelerant."

"Isn't this a wool storehouse?" Brandon asked. "Why would there be spirits here?"

"Because the Mullins brothers were smuggling French contraband," Marianne said with wicked satisfaction.

"I was working up to that," Elinor said, giving her sister a long-suffering look.

"Sorry!" Marianne didn't appear to be sorry, though. "I got excited."

"Do go on," Elinor told her.

"Well, while we were sneaking off upstairs, I wondered— why on earth would the Mullins brothers need such an elaborate contraption?"

"To move heavy crates upstairs," Lizzie said.

"And why keep their stores up there when that was where they lived?"

Darcy looked at the lift. "Because they didn't want anything illegal down here, in plain view of their workers or any visitors."

"Come see," Marianne said, leading them to the stairs. They opened up into a large room that appeared to be a makeshift living area. On the far wall, the same side as the lift, there stood a mess of crates that had clearly been moved to the second level with the assistance of the contraption, for they were far too large to have been carried up the stairs. Marianne walked up to the nearest one and reached inside. She lifted a glass bottle, and Lizzie saw it was filled with amber liquid.

"Brandy," she announced.

Brandon took the bottle from her and inspected the label before letting out a low whistle. "*French* brandy."

"There's more," Elinor said, leading them to another crate, almost identical to the ones downstairs. She shoved the lid off. "This one has silks. Smoke damaged, but . . ."

"I'm guessing French?" Darcy asked.

"Undoubtedly," Marianne said. "Now, I am no expert, but

Mama has a gorgeous pelisse made from French silk that Papa gave her before it was impossible to get and—well, never matter. But I believe we've found your illegal goods."

"Not graphite," Lizzie murmured. "I thought for sure Mr. Hughes was involved."

"Lizzie, only you would be disappointed by uncovering a smuggling ring," Darcy said.

"Yes, because it's not proof of treason," she said with exasperation. "Although . . . good work, ladies."

"Chin up," Darcy said. "This is still more than enough to put those scoundrels downstairs away."

"But why were we denied a search permit?" Lizzie asked. "The Crown has to suspect something here."

"Perhaps they had their own investigation? Either that or Mullins is paying someone a large amount of money to look the other way—" He stopped speaking abruptly, and his mouth hardened into an unforgiving line. "Not Mullins. Tomlinson."

Lizzie didn't want Darcy to harden into the scary person he'd been downstairs, but she had to ask. "You don't seem especially shocked to find him here."

"I broke into his office this afternoon," he said proudly.

"You did *what*?"

"Yes, right before I quit my job."

Lizzie rubbed her temple. "I know I've hit my head, but did you just say *you quit your job*?"

He grinned. "That's not the best part—I found proof that Leticia and Josette have a secret. Mrs. Cavendish wrote me about it. Only, I never got the letter because Tomlinson intercepted it."

"What secret?" Lizzie demanded.

"Leticia and Josette are cousins, but Leticia isn't related to Mrs. Cavendish at all—she's entirely French. And before she died, it seemed that Mrs. Cavendish suspected that Leticia had a secret beau."

Lizzie needed a moment to make sense of this new information. "Wait—are you saying that Mrs. Cavendish worried that Leticia couldn't be trusted?"

"She didn't say it in so many words, but she was worried that he'd find out Leticia's secret and ruin Josette's reputat—"

"Richard Hughes!" Lizzie spat out.

"What?"

"He gave Leticia the necklace, Darcy! At the jeweler's—he got the locket to open! It said 'to L.B.'—Leticia Beaufort, *of course*, he knew that she wasn't a Cavendish—'with all my love and adoration, R.H.'! The jeweler said the necklace was commissioned a year ago, but Mr. Hughes has neglected to pay for it!"

"But he's engaged to Josette!" Darcy shook his head, and then stopped just as quickly. "Oh God."

"What?"

"Leticia didn't inherit a single penny from Mrs. Cavendish! It all went to Josette."

"And so he threw Leticia over for her cousin?" Lizzie asked. "How . . . diabolical."

"More likely for her cousin's fortune," Marianne said practically. "It was likely a plot to steal Josette's fortune, if Leticia was still wearing his token of affection. And perhaps Mr. Hughes decided he didn't want to share with Leticia after all."

"Oh, you're able to follow all of this?" Mr. Brandon asked Marianne.

"Yes, darling, I'll explain it all later," she said, patting his shoulder fondly. "Now, in case you've forgotten, we've got three of those villains tied up downstairs. We could ask them a few questions, if that would help?"

"Right," Lizzie said, with one last glance at the French contraband. "I suppose the least Jack Mullins owes us is the truth."

Downstairs, Tomlinson was still unconscious, but Jack and Parry were very much alert and glaring at Mr. Farrows. Jack began to struggle against his bonds when Lizzie approached. She held up her hand, and he stopped. "I'm going to remove your gag, and then we'll have a civilized conversation. But if you scream or tell me a single lie, I'll have this gentleman gag you once more. Fair enough?"

Jack nodded eagerly.

Lizzie unknotted the gag, and as soon as it fell away, Jack began speaking. "Lizzie, you have to believe me—I never had any part of this! I never meant for anyone to get hurt!"

Lizzie held up a finger, and to her surprise, Jack quieted. "Did you know about this plot when you hired me?"

"I . . . yes. But Lizzie, it's not that simple!"

There was little Lizzie liked less than being played a fool. "Explain."

"I didn't know what Simon was doing. You can ask

Parry—he'll confirm that it's true. Our business has been slow lately—nothing dire, but . . . not good. And then, all of a sudden, we have money again, and there are all of these crates everywhere that Simon says to leave alone, he'll handle them. He was being secretive, so one day I looked inside one, and I thought, well—that's definitely not broadcloth. But I didn't know what to do—and so finally, I decided to confront him."

"And?" Lizzie prompted.

Jack gulped. "The day of the fire, I found Simon and Parry moving crates from upstairs, and Simon told me he had to—we'd lose the business unless we held the crates. He didn't say who owned them or who we were holding them for. I told him it had to stop, but Simon said it was too late for that, he couldn't stop. And then . . ."

Lizzie waited for him to go on, but he seemed to have lost his voice. He swallowed hard, twice.

"And then Leticia Cavendish showed up," Darcy said.

Lizzie looked to him in surprise, but Jack said, "I had no idea who she was or why she was there, I promise you—but she saw what we were moving. One of the crates was open. That day it was . . . brandy. She grew incensed. She picked up bottles, and she started hurling them every which way, screaming at us. You know the French, they're hysterical and violent—"

"Enough," Lizzie told him. "I could say the same thing about a good many British. You don't think that a displaced Frenchwoman who has lost her home might become upset upon finding that you were smuggling French goods?"

"She's the reason for the fire," Jack insisted, a fire in his own eyes. "Simon went to grab her, to stop her . . . a lamp was knocked over. The fire spread—the brandy. She escaped, but Simon . . ." Jack was crying now, and Lizzie didn't think that his emotion was contrived. "He was trying to save the goods. He wouldn't listen to reason."

"Simon died because the fire spread," Lizzie stated. "But the fire was an accident."

"It was her fault! It never would have started if she hadn't been there!"

"And you hired me to find her so you could get revenge," Lizzie deduced. "Did you kill her?"

"No!" Jack hiccupped. "Lizzie, I never killed anyone, I swear it on my brother's grave! I simply wanted her to *pay*. I'm not upset she's dead, but I would have settled to see her in Newgate."

Lizzie looked to Darcy, unsure whether she should believe him. Darcy looked shaken, and behind him the Dashwood sisters watched the scene with solemn eyes.

"Where were you two afternoons ago?" Darcy asked.

"Here! I swear to it—and Parry can vouch for me!"

Lizzie looked at Parry, who was glaring at her with so much hate that a lesser woman might have faltered. "Is this true? Nod or shake your head, and if you lie, I'll ensure you face the highest penalties under the law for smuggling!"

Parry nodded.

The fire was an accident. A horrific, tragic accident. But the consequences of the fire had brought upon more heartache—all of which could have been avoided if Jack Mullins had just been honest with her from the outset.

"When you told me that the woman was dead, I got scared—clearly she'd been punished for what she'd ruined, and I don't want to be involved with people who will kill a lady like that! But then Parry got word that another shipment was coming in last night, and I had to take it or they'd kill me! I never wanted any of this!"

"Who is they?" Lizzie asked. She pointed at Tomlinson. "This man?"

"He's a part of it, but he's not at the top," Jack said, and Parry nodded his vigorous agreement. "We never saw anyone else, I swear, Lizzie—just him."

Lizzie looked down at Tomlinson. He was awake now, and he glared up at Lizzie with such hatred in his eyes that Lizzie shivered. What had he said? *She's much smarter than you. She's been watching you this entire time.*

"Who is your boss?" she asked him, crouching down to look him in the eye.

Mr. Farrows loosened Tomlinson's gag so he could reply. But as soon as it fell from his mouth, he spat in Lizzie's face. "Go to hell, you b—"

Darcy decked him.

In short order, Mr. Farrows and Marianne had Mr. Tomlinson gagged and Elinor handed Lizzie a handkerchief. "Don't worry, that's the least of what he's done tonight," she reassured her friends. "I shall survive."

"Lizzie, I didn't mean for this to happen," Jack said. "You have to believe me. That man wanted to kidnap you, and I said that it was a bad idea. I was trying to protect you!"

"I do believe that you never meant for this to happen," Lizzie said. "But you didn't protect me. You put us all in danger tonight." She nodded to Mr. Farrows, who stepped forward to gag Jack once more.

But then something came to her.

"Wait! I have one question. You said the day of the fire, one of the crates was open and that day it was brandy. But when you first looked into the crates, and it wasn't broadcloth—what was it?"

She expected him to say brandy, or silks. But Jack shook his head, as if he were disgusted by the memory of it even now. "It was rocks, Lizzie. Black rocks! Brandy I could understand, silks we could fence—but rocks! What is the sense in that?"

"I knew it!" Lizzie turned to the Dashwoods triumphantly. "Mr. Hughes is connected!

Beside the sisters, Darcy had gone pale. "Lizzie, we have to hurry."

"We ought to call the Runners," she agreed. "They'll want to apprehend him, and I'm sure the Crown will have something to say about his smuggling. Perhaps they suspected all along and just didn't have sufficient—"

"No, Lizzie—we have to go."

"Why?"

"Because Josette is marrying Mr. Hughes at dawn."

NINETEEN

In Which a Darkened Carriage Incites
an Illuminating Conversation

THIS TIME, DARCY BROUGHT his carriage.

"I don't want this to go to your head, because it's ostentatious, generally inconvenient, and it deprives one of the joys of a good walk," Lizzie said as they climbed in, "but I am glad you brought this rig."

"How magnanimous of you to admit it," Darcy said, settling into the seat across from her. "Are you all right, truly?"

"A bit sore," she admitted. It was too dark for her to see him, the only light coming from the lantern from the driver's perch. But she sensed his tension, so naturally she decided to tease him further. "But very pleased to see you."

"I'm glad you appreciate the convenience of the carriage," he said. "I went all the way home for it when I heard that you planned to come here. I thought it would be more convenient. Then, of course, I couldn't find you at Longbourn and so I went to the Dashwoods' shop, only to discover Farrows and Brandon, about to come out of their skin with worry."

"Is that your way of telling me that you were scared for my safety?"

"No, I'll simply admit it—I was deathly afraid for you."

"Oh," she said. He sounded angry.

"We all were terrified," Darcy continued. "At first, we all wanted to go to your respective homes and stop you from sneaking out, but then Brandon pointed out that Marianne would never forgive him."

"Probably true," Lizzie said.

"And that got me thinking that if I went to your home and told your father what you were planning on doing, you'd be furious with me."

He seemed to pause, waiting for a reaction. "True," she acknowledged.

"And when I really thought about it, I realized it wasn't just that I didn't want you to be furious with me—although you are very scary when you're mad—but I didn't want to stand in your way."

Now he sounded less mad, and more helpless.

"But?" Lizzie asked. "I'm sensing there is a but somewhere in here."

He sighed heavily. "But . . . you didn't wait for me. And I understand why, but . . . Lizzie, if you're going to break the law, which I greatly disapprove of, by the way . . . well, at the very least I'd like to be your accomplice."

Oh.

Lizzie wished now she could see his face, but since that wasn't possible, she pushed herself to her feet, swaying a bit. "Move over," she said, squeezing in next to him.

Darcy's arms came around her and she melted into his touch, even as the carriage jostled all her bruises. Darcy's lips brushed her temple, and she wanted nothing more than to close her eyes and sink into his embrace.

"I didn't wait," she acknowledged. "But it's not because I don't trust you or didn't want you with me."

"The case is important," Darcy murmured.

"Yes. The case. And . . . I didn't go alone. I wouldn't have gone alone. I had the Dashwoods."

"I know. But there are so many dangers in the world, even for three very capable young ladies such as yourselves."

Lizzie sighed. She was so used to arguing that she was more than able to handle herself, she was loath to admit when there were situations she might not be able to wiggle out of. And yet, the beating she'd taken tonight was proof that her modes of persuasion were not infallible. Sometimes, men chose violence. When she closed her eyes, she saw flashes of the dead women she'd encountered over the course of her work—Abigail, Leticia. She might have been one of them, if not for Marianne and Elinor Dashwood.

"I know," she whispered.

They rode in silence, and Lizzie was grateful. She didn't want to argue with Darcy—she just wanted to stay in his arms, feel the beat of her own heart, and give thanks that she was alive.

"I won't ever stop you, you know."

"Hmm?"

"I won't stop you," he said, his voice low but strong in her ear. "I want you to know that whatever you decide to do, wherever you decide to go, I won't ever try to stop you."

Her breath caught. "Oh? And if I decide to sail to the farthest edges of the world on a whim?"

"I wouldn't stop you," he repeated. "I might inquire as to your plans, to ensure you're well taken care of. But I'd never stand in your way."

Tears sprang to her eyes unexpectedly, and she blinked them back. She tried to keep her voice light. "But would you come with me?"

"Lizzie." He exhaled her name like an oath. "I'll follow you to the ends of the earth, if you'll let me."

Now the tears fell, but they were tears of relief. "I think I know this. But I'm still afraid, because you *could* stop me."

"I'd never."

"But you could. And I don't even think that I believe you would. Even before you said it. But . . . Darcy, I need some time. To reckon with what this means."

He kissed her forehead. "Of course. But . . . just to be clear, we aren't speaking of you taking a long sea trip?"

She laughed. "No, I think it's quite obvious that now we are speaking about the future."

Even now, she couldn't quite bring herself to say the word

marriage. But she felt an immense relief as her fears were named and Darcy tightened his arms around her. "I'm sorry I've been rather trying lately," she said. "It's not that I don't want you to call or come to dinner."

"I know," he said.

"You know? What do you know?" She turned to look at him. The light was still dim, but she thought she could see the outline of his mouth, smiling.

"I know what your mother wants," Darcy said. "And I have been a bit nervous that your father is going to corner me and ask me to declare my intentions. And, Lizzie, to be clear—my intention is to continue helping you however you'd like, in whatever capacity you prefer. But it's been rather nerve-racking feeling like I have to dodge them constantly."

"That's my fault," Lizzie admitted. "I've been contriving reasons to keep you away because . . . well, you know what my mother is like! I don't want her to badger you into a proposal if you're not ready!"

"Have a little faith, love. I can withstand your mother."

Lizzie's heart fluttered at the term of endearment, even as she laughed. "Oh, thank goodness. Perhaps we ought to sit in darkened, enclosed spaces more often. It seems to be where we have our most honest conversations."

"I would prefer we leave out the enclosed bit," Darcy said, but she could feel the laughter in his chest. "Speaking of your mother badgering me into a proposal, how did Bingley fare last night?"

"Well, he didn't propose, if that's what you're asking. I'm afraid our case spoiled the mood."

"Oh no," Darcy said, but he didn't sound surprised. "How's Jane taking it?"

"Disappointed but hiding it well. Mama is devastated and hiding it not at all." Lizzie waited for Darcy to say something, but when he didn't she turned to face him. "Darcy. Do you have knowledge of Bingley's intentions?"

"Let's just say that Bingley, while not immune to your mother's pressure, has something a bit more romantic in mind than proposing while your mother's ear is at the drawing room door."

Lizzie playfully whacked his shoulder. "You should have said! Jane will be so relieved."

"It won't be long now," Darcy assured her. "Make sure she acts surprised."

"Oh, she'll be thrilled," Lizzie said, nestling herself back into Darcy's arms. Their conversation had brought a brief respite, but talk of marriage had her thoughts returning to the case, to the marriage they intended to stop now. A hazy gray light was slowly seeping into the carriage. Dawn wasn't far off.

"We have to get a confession," Lizzie whispered. "We didn't find a trace of graphite in the storehouse. All we have is circumstantial evidence and the testimony of a street child and a smuggler. If Hughes wiggles out of this one, he'll flee."

"We won't let him escape," Darcy said confidently. "In a few hours' time, he'll be arrested and you'll see him charged."

She hoped it was true. But there was one thing that was

bothering her: The woman that Tomlinson had spoken of at the storehouse. He said that *she* had been watching. And he had made mention of kidnapping Lizzie.

But before she could voice her questions, the carriage began to slow and Darcy sat up. They hadn't even stopped in front of Cavendish House before Darcy flung open the door and stepped down. He held up a hand for Lizzie, who followed stiffly, and then they were racing to the front door. Darcy pulled the bell, and then began knocking frantically.

"She's not going to want to believe me, but let me try to convince her," he said amid his barrage of knocking. "I have the letter from her grandmother, and maybe—"

The door opened suddenly, and Darcy nearly fell into Mr. Dupont, who stood perfectly poised, although wearing a disapproving expression.

"Josette—Miss Beaufort," Darcy said. "I need to speak with her at once."

"You cannot," the butler began to say, but Darcy cut him off.

"I know that I upset her yesterday, but this is a serious matter!"

"Be that as it may, sir—"

Darcy fumbled for something within his jacket pocket and produced a rather rumpled letter. "I know about Leticia," he said. "I found the letter!"

Lizzie watched the butler's gaze flick from Darcy's face to the letter clenched in his hand. He seemed to be at war with himself, but the sight of the letter was shifting the tides to their side.

"Please, Mr. Dupont," Lizzie said. "We are fearful for Josette."

"She's perfectly safe," Mr. Dupont said, but he didn't sound as though he believed it.

"The day Leticia was killed, Darcy came to inform Josette," Lizzie said. "Mr. Hughes was already here. When did he arrive?"

"Please," Darcy said. "I know what I said two years ago hurt her, and I've been very sorry ever since. But I think she might be in danger."

Mr. Dupont looked between the two of them with understanding. "Twenty minutes, maybe," he said. "Not long."

Darcy let out a soft "oof" and his shoulders slumped. "We must see Josette, now!"

"She's not here," Mr. Dupont said. "She's left already for the church."

"Where?" Darcy demanded.

"Saint George's," Dupont said, "but—"

They didn't waste any time. Back in the carriage they went, with Darcy calling out the address to his driver. Now that it was light, the carriage could travel much faster than it had on the journey across town, and Lizzie and Darcy spent the trip in tense silence, gripping each other's hands. As they pulled into Hanover Square, the sound of church bells filled the morning air.

"No," Lizzie whispered, and Darcy looked ill. The carriage drew up before the church but they were jumping down before it had fully stopped. Without speaking, they ran hand in hand toward the church doors. The steps were deserted, as there were very few people out and about so early. Almost as if Mr. Hughes wanted no audience, no one to stop his marriage.

The great doors opened with a creak, and the interior of the church was dimly lit—so dim at first that Lizzie thought perhaps they'd gotten it wrong and no one was there. But her eyes adjusted as she Darcy ran toward the front of the church, coming upon the sight they were hoping and dreading at the same time.

Josette stood facing Mr. Hughes. A clergyman stood between them, holding the Book of Common Prayer. Josette lifted her hands to take Mr. Hughes', and . . .

"Stop!"

TWENTY

In Which Lizzie and Darcy Object to a Wedding

THE JOINT FORCE OF Lizzie's and Darcy's voices echoed in the church, causing all five people at the front to start in alarm.

Josette and Mr. Hughes looked back at Lizzie and Darcy as they ran down the center aisle, and the clergyman looked up from his reading in bewilderment. In the front pews on either side of the aisle the witnesses, a plainly dressed man and woman, who appeared to be a valet and a maid, twisted around in shock.

Mr. Hughes got over his surprise first. "What is the meaning of this? How dare you? This is a private ceremony!" He took a menacing step toward them, even as Josette attempted to hold him back.

"I'm sorry," Darcy said to Josette. "But I—we—cannot let you do this."

"There is no letting me do anything," Josette informed him in an icy tone. "You have no say in the matter."

"True," Lizzie said, panting and holding her side where running had exacerbated her larger bruises. "What I think Darcy means is that we are in possession of some information you might find relevant about your future husband."

"This is preposterous! What information? I want these two gone!" Mr. Hughes made the demand, looking about the church as if he expected armed guards to arrive and escort Lizzie and Darcy from the premises.

"Oh dear," said the clergyman. "Are you certain it cannot wait? I was just about to—"

"No." Darcy pulled the letter from his jacket and thrust it toward Josette. "Before you take any vows, you must read this."

Josette glanced disdainfully at the letter. "I will do no such thing!"

"Your grandmother wrote it," Darcy said.

Josette stilled—as did Hughes. Lizzie watched him carefully. He looked upon the letter with hungry eyes, and for a moment she was afraid he'd make a grab for it.

"How are you in possession of a letter from my grandmother, Darcy?"

"It's the letter she wrote me before she died. I regret to inform you it only reached me yesterday, after I left your residence."

"Really, my dove—" Mr. Hughes started to say, but Josette held up a finger to silence him. She plucked it from Darcy's grasp and unfolded it.

Lizzie watched Mr. Hughes while Josette read. He shifted back and forth, glaring at them, while waiting. Lizzie didn't think that his squirming was due to wedding jitters—he knew what Josette would find.

Finally, Josette looked up. "So?" she asked.

"That letter was waylaid," Darcy told her, "by a man I believe to be working with your fiancé. I had no idea that your grandmother had died before this week, and I didn't have any inkling she'd written me before you implied as such yesterday."

"Well done," Josette said. "Is that what you want me to say? I am glad that you've finally received her letter, many months later. But does it warrant an interruption to my wedding?"

Lizzie grew impatient. "Did your cousin tell you who was courting her?"

Josette scowled at them both, but there was pain in her expression. "Leticia spoke of many men. She was very charming."

"But she never spoke of having a particular suitor?" Darcy asked.

"No!"

Lizzie plunged her hand into her pocket and produced Leticia's necklace. She held it up, and the gold shone in the candlelight. "She never said anything about who gave her this necklace?"

Josette's eyes widened when she saw the necklace. "Where did you get that?" She stepped forward and tore it from Lizzie's grasp.

"I found it near her body in the park."

The clergyman gasped, looking at Lizzie with something like fascinated horror. Mr. Hughes focused the intensity of his gaze on her, and she returned it. "Whoever killed her tried to take it from her but dropped it."

"It's not worth much," Josette said. "It's gilt and paste."

"I have to disagree with you. I found the jeweler who made it, and I can assure you he deals with gold and gemstones, not gilt and paste. And it's no mere necklace—it's a locket. He showed me how to open it."

"Stop!" Mr. Hughes ripped Mrs. Cavendish's letter from Josette's grasp. "Leticia is dead. I demand that you leave right this instant! You're not welcome here!"

"All are welcome in the house of God—" the clergyman began.

"Oh, do shut up!" Mr. Hughes snapped.

"Richard?" Josette asked. Her voice was small, confused.

"If you push gently on the filigree and press down on the topaz, it opens," Lizzie said. Her heart was pounding as she waited to see if Josette would do so.

"Enough!" Mr. Hughes took Josette by the shoulders. "I don't know why they're interrupting our day, but we have wedding vows to exchange —"

Darcy made to grab Mr. Hughes. "Don't lay your hands on her!"

"Stop!" Josette screamed. Her voice echoed in the empty church. "All of you, stop it this instant!"

They all stilled, unsure of what to do next. Lizzie could feel the angry energy exuding off Mr. Hughes in waves.

"Open the locket," Lizzie urged her. "It'll all make sense once you open it."

Josette looked down at the necklace. She had to feel the

smooth weight of the gold in her hand. She had to realize this was no trifling trinket. Slowly, Josette pushed on the filigree, and with a small click the necklace opened.

Mr. Hughes lunged to take it from her, but Darcy held him back. "'To L.B., with all my love and adoration. R.H.,'" Josette read in a small voice. "R.H. You."

"Josette, it's not what you think—"

"The jeweler named your fiancé as the man who commissioned it," Lizzie told her, knowing that her words were likely breaking Josette's heart. "A year ago."

"A year!" Josette snapped the locket closed. "Explain yourself, sir!"

"She meant nothing to me! It's you, Josette, you're the one—"

Josette drew back her hand and slapped him.

The clergyman cried out in surprise and everyone gasped. The force of Josette's blow sent Mr. Hughes stumbling back a couple of steps. Josette was breathing heavily as she glared at her fiancé. "You! She wouldn't tell me who, but I knew someone had broken her heart!"

"There's more," Darcy said urgently. "Mr. Hughes has been involved in a smuggling scheme. We believe he's been selling his graphite to French smugglers in exchange for French goods. Just this past night we found the French contraband and apprehended those involved, including a man who worked at my father's firm. They can all testify that Hughes was involved—"

"This is ludicrous! Are you going to believe them?"

"Your case," Josette said. "The fire . . ."

"We think that Leticia found out," Lizzie explained. "She didn't set the fire, but she was there when it started. She was angry when she saw what was going on—she broke some bottles of brandy, and when a lamp was knocked over . . ."

"But why would Leticia do that? Why . . . why would . . . ?"

"She must have grown suspicious of Mr. Hughes," Lizzie said, staring the man down. "Isn't that right? She knew you were shifty, to form a secret attachment to her, only to throw her over in favor of her cousin. But, Josette, you didn't know he was so unscrupulous, did you? And so Leticia went looking for proof that he was untrustworthy."

"And when the fire happened, when Simon Mullins was killed, his brother blamed Leticia," Darcy continued. "And in a way you were right, Josette. We did cause her death because Jack Mullins hired Lizzie and we followed the investigation right to your door. Leticia knew what was going on. She told us about Mr. Hughes's graphite mines, and she was going to meet us. She had information she wanted to pass to us."

"She told us to meet her in Hyde Park," Lizzie continued. "But someone got to her first."

Lizzie looked at Mr. Hughes, who protested, "I didn't kill her! You're mad! Both of you! Josette, you can't believe this!"

"You knew she would be in the park," Josette said. "I told you of her plans that evening! But you . . ."

She didn't finish her sentence, and Lizzie decided now was the time to share what Mr. Dupont had told them. "You arrived at Cavendish House only twenty minutes or so before Darcy.

How long is the ride from Hyde Park to Josette's house, Darcy? Short enough to kill Leticia and then pop in on Josette for a quick call?"

"You shut up! How dare you ruin our wedding day with such a cruel accusation!"

Josette began to shake. "No, Richard, you shut up!"

"Be reasonable, darling," Mr. Hughes implored. "It won't do if you start acting hysterical now!"

"Oh, I assure you sir, I am far from hysterical!" Josette shouted. "But if you like, I will show you hysteria! Is it true?"

"Of course not, none of this is true!"

"How dare you!" Josette hissed. "How dare you treat Leticia as though she could be cast aside for anything better! How dare you treat both of us that way!"

Lizzie stepped forward and gently took Josette's arm. "Josette, I'm so sorry—"

Josette was breathing heavily, and Lizzie relaxed her grip. It turned out to be a mistake, for suddenly Josette let out a strangled cry and launched herself at Hughes, shocking them all by knocking him down. She began to hit him—mostly slaps and a few weak, ineffectual punches to his face and chest that, once he got over his surprise, he was able to fend off rather easily.

Lizzie and Darcy rushed forward to pry Josette off Mr. Hughes, although Lizzie was a bit slower about it than Darcy, and she did not begrudge the other lady a swift parting kick as they lifted her away. Josette's maid hovered behind them, likely aware that she ought to offer comfort of some kind but seeming

312

uncertain as to how to go about doing it.

"I'm sorry," Darcy told Josette, his voice soft and tender. "I'm truly sorry. We won't let him get away with it."

"You bastard!" Hughes snarled as he lurched to his feet, blood gushing from his nose.

"Oh my, you landed a rather good hit," Lizzie told Josette. "Well done—"

Click.

Lizzie went utterly still.

The pistol was pointed at her face, and it hovered a mere breath from her right cheek.

"Dear God!" proclaimed the clergyman, and it wasn't entirely clear if he intended to take the Lord's name in vain or was invoking prayer.

"Thank you, Winston," Mr. Hughes said, his voice sounding quite nasal.

In all the commotion, they'd clearly forgotten about the valet. Now he held a pistol to Lizzie's temple, and she released her grasp on Josette and held her hands up in what she hoped was a placating manner. "Don't shoot."

Beside her, Darcy had gone still, but she could feel the tension in his body as if it were her own.

"Stand back," Hughes ordered Darcy. "At least five paces or I tell Winston here to shoot. And he never misses."

"Come now," Lizzie said. "Surely you won't shoot me in a place of worship? Reverend, how much penance might one expect for murdering a lady in cold blood in a church?"

Unfortunately for her, the clergyman was quite overcome by shock and merely shook his head in disbelief at the turn of events.

"With me, Josette," Mr. Hughes said. "Come along, don't dawdle."

"What are you doing?" she asked around choked tears.

"I'm saving our lives," he said. "Honestly, this whole ordeal might have been dropped if Mullins hadn't insisted upon an investigation."

"How do you . . . but . . ."

Poor Josette had had her entire life upended in the space of a quarter hour, on what she thought was to be her wedding day. Lizzie didn't blame her for being confused. "He's in far too deep to back out now, Josette. Whoever is at the head of this smuggling operation won't let him stop."

"Full marks, Miss Bennet," Hughes said sarcastically. "Would you like a pat on the back?"

"No, but I'll settle for having your man point his weapon elsewhere."

"Lizzie," Darcy whispered in warning, and suddenly Lizzie got her wish—the pistol swung from her to Darcy, who'd been attempting to subtly sidle closer to her. He stilled, and Lizzie's heart leapt in her chest.

"No," she whispered.

"We are leaving," Mr. Hughes told Josette. "We sail for France this evening."

"No!" Josette seemed horrified at the prospect. "I'll not go back there!"

"Too bad," he said. "I can't speak French, so you'll have to come along."

Josette struggled to pull out of Mr. Hughes's grasp, and Lizzie felt torn between rushing after her and running to Darcy. "Will that be far enough?" Lizzie called out, remembering Tomlinson's words in the storehouse. *You'll have far bigger worries if you displease her yet again.* Perhaps whoever this woman was, reminding Hughes of her would stop him. "Or will the lady that Tomlinson reports to come after you, even in France?"

Hughes stopped dragging Josette toward a side door long enough to look back at Lizzie. He wore a mocking smile. "Don't worry, Miss Bennet—I think that she will be far more interested in *you* than in me. Lady Catherine de Bourgh doesn't forget those who cross her, and this will be your second time, won't it?"

Lizzie could do nothing but stand in numb shock.

Lady Catherine de Bourgh.

Lady Catherine de Bourgh was the head of Tomlinson's smuggling operation?

So great was her astonishment that she didn't realize that Josette was shouting, that Darcy was speaking urgently, that the clergyman was trying to intercede, or that Josette's maid was weeping in terror. She didn't hear a thing, until Hughes said, "Shoot them as soon as we're gone."

Josette's cries escalated in a crescendo, and Lizzie knew that she ought to be horrified to hear their deaths ordered so casually. She ought to be putting her mind to work, strategizing her way out of this. Trying to reason with Winston, at the very least.

315

Instead, she looked to Darcy and Darcy looked at her, and she had the most insane thought that if this was how she was to die, then at least Darcy was by her side.

And then she decided that she would rather like to live.

Without allowing herself time to think, she slammed her body into Winston, striking his arm holding the pistol so that it jolted up, and then she was falling right on top of him. The pistol went off with a tremendous bang, and gunpowder filled her nose, making her cough and her eyes water. The sound was so much louder than the shot back at the storehouse had been, and louder than the shot that had killed Wickham. Those pistols had been fired from a distance, and this one had discharged right above her right ear. For a moment, she couldn't make sense of what followed because of the ringing in her ears and stinging in her eyes. But Winston was scrambling to get out from under her, and she elbowed him hard in the gut. He groaned, and then there seemed to be shouts all around, from every corner of the church. Or perhaps that was just the echo?

Lizzie decided she was most certainly dazed.

Then, through the gun smoke and commotion, there was Darcy leaning over her, wild with worry. His hands pressed against her cheeks and hair, and then they made their way across her body checking for injury. She groaned.

"Lizzie, oh God, Lizzie. What a bloody foolish thing to do, you lovely, stubborn, headstrong girl!"

She smiled through the pain. "I think you forgot obstinate."

"I was working my way up to it," he said.

He helped her sit up, and Lizzie was rather alarmed to see that the church, which had been mostly empty mere moments ago, was now swarming with men. Men in dark jackets and laborer's caps, all wielding pistols. Fear hammered in her throat once more, but it didn't seem as though they were interested in Lizzie and Darcy. Instead, the closest man had restrained Winston, and beyond that, as the ringing in her ears dulled, she could hear Hughes strenuously objecting to being detained.

"Josette?" Lizzie asked.

"Fine, I think," Darcy said, allowing only a quick glance in the direction of the rectory.

"Darcy, I know that I have been through quite a lot and suffered a number of injuries, but I didn't think any were quite so serious as to incite hallucinations."

"Are you seeing things?" he asked. "Someone call a doctor!"

"Are all these men real?" she whispered, looking around. "They're not a delusion?"

"They are real," Darcy confirmed. He slumped with relief. "Good heavens, Lizzie, you scared me."

"And did Mr. Hughes say that Lady Catherine was responsible for the smuggling?"

"He did."

She sank back into his arms. "How? I thought the navy caught her."

"I don't know. But one problem at a time, love. Can you stand?"

Not if he didn't stop calling her love—Darcy's pet name

for her was making her weak at the knees. Darcy helped her to her feet and kept his arm around her as she took in the scene. There were at least twenty men milling about the church. Three alone were restraining Mr. Hughes while another held a weeping Josette. Another man was seeing to her maid, and two more were speaking with the clergyman.

"Splendid!" came a jovial shout that cut through the church and the chatter.

Lizzie and Darcy turned to see a man who appeared neither young nor old, with hair that was neither blond nor brown, striding down the center aisle toward them. Unlike the rest of the men, who were clothed in dark colors, he wore the red jacket of an officer.

And it was because he was wearing that jacket that Lizzie realized she'd seen him before.

"You," Lizzie and Darcy said at the same time.

"Yes, me," he agreed, smiling with true delight. "I suppose it's time we're properly acquainted now, isn't it?"

TWENTY-ONE

*In Which Lizzie and Darcy Uncover
Leticia Beaufort's Final Secret*

"YOU GAVE US DIRECTIONS," Lizzie said.

"And you were at the club when I tracked down the magistrate!" Darcy added.

The man smiled and nodded, as though they were answering questions correctly. "Yes, and a few other places here and there, not that you—"

"The park, too," Lizzie interrupted. "You were in the crowd of onlookers after Leticia's body was discovered!"

"I've had the most peculiar feeling we've been watched," Darcy added. "Like an itch you can't quite scratch."

"Yes, yes," he said now, his genial expression never slipping. "I've been following you since you asked for directions to the Mullins Brothers storehouse."

"But why?" Lizzie's question came out sharper than she intended, but her long night of no sleep was catching up with her. "Who are you?"

"The name is Graves," he said, purposely omitting any sort of rank or title. "Shall we sit?"

Lizzie glanced at Darcy, who tilted his head in a gesture that she read as, *Let's hear him out.*

She plopped down in the hard pew, her muscles and limbs crying out in relief. Darcy sat next to her and took her hand in his. "All right," he said, studying Graves with suspicion. "Explain."

"Right, well—first of all, apologies about the tail. But I had to know whether or not you were in on the Mullins brothers' smuggling ring. You understand, Miss Bennet—you are Mr. Mullins's legal representation. Lesser men might have helped him avoid being charged in exchange for a share of the profit, or a few bolts of silks . . ."

Any other time, Lizzie might have been indignant to find her integrity questioned. But now she simply nodded. "But I am no man, sir. And you already knew about the smuggling ring. You were already watching the storehouse."

"Yes," Graves confirmed.

"And did you know that the woman at its head is none other than Lady Catherine de Bourgh?"

Graves winced. "Yes."

"You were supposed to have her in custody!" Darcy shouted, jumping to his feet. "I spoke with the admiral a year ago, and he assured me that she would be arrested before the week was out!"

"Yes, well, it turns out she's a wily one. Mr. Darcy, sit, please. I'll answer your questions, but I don't want to have to restrain you."

Lizzie tugged on Darcy's arm. Darcy exhaled, then sat. "All right. Tell us what happened."

"Her ship was intercepted before your information could be shared with the fleet," he said pleasantly, as if they were gossiping over tea. "And that woman—she's a smart one. She convinced the captain that she'd been kidnapped by the crew! They didn't even suspect her, and when they arrived at Portsmouth, she escaped."

Lizzie was almost impressed by Lady Catherine's gall. "And no one sought to inform us?"

"She tried to kill Lizzie!" Darcy added.

"Please don't take offense, Miss Bennet, but we believed Lady Catherine to be engaged in more pressing matters than exacting revenge on you."

"But she might come after me now!" Lizzie protested. "And Marianne and Elinor! They're at the Mullins Brothers storehouse with Jack Mullins and Tomlinson—"

Graves waved a hand. "Not to worry, Miss Bennet. My men will have already secured the storehouse, and the Misses Dashwood and their gentlemen friends will not be implicated."

"You followed us there this evening? And then followed Lizzie and me to this church?" Darcy asked.

"To be frank, there are very few movements of the past week that we haven't been following," Graves told them. "I was rather surprised to find that Mullins had hired you, of course, so I kept an eye out. If Lady Catherine had made a move, we would have stepped in. But she's kept herself carefully hidden."

"How dare you, sir?" Darcy exclaimed. "Leticia Cavendish

was killed! Lizzie was beaten! Someone threatened her family! And all the while you've been skulking in the shadows, standing by as innocent people were hurt—"

"I know," Graves said, his smile slipping for the first time since he'd entered the church. "You're absolutely right, Mr. Darcy."

Darcy was breathing heavily, and Lizzie knew he was trying to keep his temper in check. She needed a distraction. "Tell us why you didn't intervene sooner. You knew about the smuggling ring, and you knew Hughes was involved. You knew Lady Catherine was at the head. Why let us waltz in?"

"Smuggling is a serious offense, Miss Bennet, but my men could spend all the hours in the day quashing smuggling rings and still the British people will find ways to enjoy their goods from the Continent. It is, to a certain extent, a futile fight. One we must fight nonetheless, but we must be strategic about these things."

"But this one was different, because Mr. Hughes was selling his graphite to the French?" Lizzie asked.

"Precisely. And such operations needed to be stopped completely. The war depends upon it. If we had simply raided the Mullins Brothers storehouse, Mr. Hughes could have found a new route. We needed to stop Mr. Hughes, but more than that, we need to find Lady Catherine."

"And now? Can you stop it? Can you find her?"

"Well . . . Mr. Hughes will be tried for treason, I imagine. And murder. And thanks to you, Miss Bennet, we have Mr.

Tomlinson. That is good work—we figured Lady Catherine had probably recruited another London solicitor to do her bidding in the city but we hadn't yet implicated him. As for her whereabouts . . ."

He held up both hands and tilted his head to the side.

"You have no idea where she is," Lizzie said.

"I'm sorry, Miss Bennet."

Lady Catherine was still at large. Now that Lizzie knew this, she felt a bit silly for assuming that the authorities would have simply taken care of her all those months ago. Lady Catherine had been free this entire time! But just as quickly as the shock came, so did the feeling of foolishness. Lizzie hadn't heard even the faintest whisper of a lady being arrested for crimes against the Crown. If she'd been paying any attention whatsoever, she'd might have suspected that the authorities hadn't caught her.

Still at large, and still at her criminal schemes! From piracy to smuggling in less than a year—she clearly didn't waste any time. And the whole time that Lizzie and Darcy had been investigating, Graves had been watching with the answers. While they were snooping around the storehouse and making calls to Cavendish House . . .

"Leticia," she said suddenly. "She had information. She was going to meet us. Why . . . Oh."

Graves watched her, and there was a spark in his eye that told her she was right.

"What?" Darcy asked.

"Leticia was a spy," Lizzie said.

It was the only thing that made sense—Lizzie couldn't quite believe that Leticia would be content to allow her cousin to marry a man she must have suspected of being foul. And the cousins had seemed close enough that Leticia would have warned Josette of Mr. Hughes's duplicitous nature . . . unless she had a very good reason not to.

"Yes," Graves said, and a shadow seemed to pass over his face. "She was a brilliant young lady. Her death never should have happened. I should have . . ."

He looked away, and Lizzie realized he was trying to collect himself.

"Hughes killed her," Lizzie said. "He realized that if Jack was accusing her, it wouldn't be long before someone connected them."

"She knew that was a risk, of course," Graves said. "We approached her months ago, before Mrs. Cavendish's death. My men had been surveilling Mr. Hughes for some time, suspicious of his claims that his graphite production was failing. We knew that he was hunting for a wealthy wife—and we knew that he was seeing Leticia quietly. We suspected he was hoping that her French connections would prove advantageous, and we figured we'd try to convince her to see things our way. Leticia had no wish to get caught up in international affairs."

"You blackmailed her," Lizzie said.

"She was quite happy to help us."

"Because she wanted to stay in London, with her cousin."

"She was quite happy to help us, Miss Bennet, because she

has no love for the war that took away her home and her family. It was her choice. But to your point . . . no, we could not pass up recruiting her—it's not often that one comes across a French-born British citizen who has access to the upper class."

"You took advantage of her, sir!" Lizzie accused.

"Of course I did, Miss Bennet. We are at war."

Lizzie bit her tongue. She supposed she couldn't argue that, although she felt in her heart that it was still wrong. Unbidden, Lady Catherine came to mind. What was it that she had said once? A lady's only choice is in her refusal. Well, Leticia hadn't even had that, if refusing Graves meant, at best, being deported and, at worst, being implicated as a French spy.

"Does Josette know?" Darcy asked.

"No," he said. "That was Leticia's choice. When Hughes discovered that she didn't have nearly as much money as he assumed and he broke things off with her, Leticia realized he could slither away, and she'd have no influence over him. She encouraged Josette to consider him, so she could keep an eye on him and discover where he was funneling goods. She gave us the Mullins brothers. She did very good work. She didn't deserve what she got."

He cleared his throat, and Lizzie caught a flash of emotion that Graves was trying to bury. Lizzie sighed. "And the day of the fire? What was she doing there?"

"That was just supposed to be a reconnaissance mission," Graves said. "But . . . I regret letting her go. I had just told her we didn't have enough evidence yet, and she needed to keep looking.

She was growing desperate. She and Josette were drawing near to the end of their mourning period, and Hughes was pushing for the marriage. She didn't want to compromise her position, but she didn't want her cousin to marry a traitor to the Crown."

And so she had gone looking for proof and gotten caught. Lizzie could imagine the scene that Jack had described, but now from Leticia's perspective. Backed in the corner, running out of time, furiously flinging bottles of brandy as she looked for escape.

And now she was dead.

"You must tell Josette," Darcy insisted. "She thinks that her cousin betrayed her. She deserves to know the truth."

"I can't do that," Graves said, shaking his head. "Official Crown business—"

"She deserves to know that her cousin didn't betray her," Lizzie insisted. "It's the least you owe Josette, considering your meddling cost Leticia her life."

Graves narrowed his eyes. It appeared he did not appreciate Lizzie reducing his clandestine operations to meddling, but he at least considered it.

"Tell her the truth or I will," Darcy threatened.

"If you do, I will have to arrest you." Graves delivered this threat in a matter-of-fact tone.

"How dare—"

Lizzie rested her hand on Darcy's shoulder and stood. "And if you arrest him, you'll be seeing me in court. I'm told I can be quite vexing."

"It would not be a fight you could win," he told her.

"But even so, wouldn't it be better if we settled this matter here? Amongst ourselves? It would save us all a bit of trouble, and after all the trouble we went through in the last week, it's only fair." Lizzie sweetened her words with a smile and watched with pleasure as Graves sighed. She had him.

"Fine. I'll tell her just enough so she understands that her cousin was loyal to her. But if whispers of our conversation make their way back to me, you'll both be hearing from me. And then court cases will be the least of your troubles, understand?"

"Perfectly," Lizzie told him with a genuine smile.

"Very well," Graves said, looking beyond them to the entrance of the church. "I'll go speak with Miss Beaufort now, and then I'll take my leave. I trust we shan't see any more of each other."

"Wait!" Lizzie said. "Lady Catherine."

"I'm sorry, Miss Bennet—she's hidden herself very well. I'm not concealing her location from you."

That was what she had feared. "You didn't tell us that you hadn't caught her. But you didn't believe that she would simply leave me alone, did you?"

Graves smiled enigmatically. "We've been watching, Miss Bennet. We have eyes everywhere."

"But you think she's a threat to Lizzie?" Darcy said, anger making his words come out clipped. "You think that there's a chance she'll come after her again?"

"More than a chance, I'm afraid," Graves said. "In fact, I think you can count on it."

TWENTY-TWO

*In Which Darcy Details a Rather
Embarrassing Proposal*

THE CHURCH HAD EMPTIED completely—even the clergyman was nowhere to be seen. A sudden weariness overtook Lizzie, and she was in desperate need of a cup of tea and a very long nap. "I suppose we solved it," she said as Darcy slowly steered her toward the church door.

"Indeed," he agreed. "But we cannot tell anyone that we solved it. And there are no charges to be brought before a court."

"Even worse, I doubt Jack Mullins will ever pay his bill from Newgate. You don't suppose I can bill that Graves fellow for all our trouble?"

"I wouldn't be surprised if Graves is a fake name, Lizzie."

"Ah, well. My father did tell me there's no money in criminal cases."

For some reason, this set Lizzie off giggling, and once she'd started she couldn't stop. It took Darcy longer, but a smile grew on his serious face, and then he was chuckling, too.

They were laughing when they exited the church into the bright morning. For the first time in weeks, the cloud cover had broken and glorious blue sky greeted them. And despite her exhaustion and aches and pains and the headache she would surely have at having to explain to her mother why she had sneaked out in the dark of night, Darcy was by her side, and she wasn't immediately worried about what the future might hold.

As they stood on the church steps, laughter subsiding, something occurred to Lizzie. "Darcy," she said, "do you suppose it was Hughes who threw that brick through my window?"

"Why?" he asked. "Do you want to sue him?"

She waved a hand at that thought. "No, although he'd deserve it. It just occurred to me I don't know who did. Leticia was dead. Jack might have done it, but why? He'd already dismissed me from the case. It might have been Tomlinson, but he doesn't seem the type to do his own dirty work. And so that leaves Hughes. He had the graphite, after all."

Darcy had sobered at this point, and she realized that he wasn't looking at her—he was looking beyond her. Lizzie turned and saw the figure of a small boy in a green jacket lingering behind a tree across the square.

"Henry!" she said, but not loudly enough for him to hear her. "I told him to stay far away from all of this."

"That's just it," Darcy said. "I don't think he's been very far away from any of this."

Lizzie gasped. "You don't think he's responsible, do you?"

Darcy shrugged. "You could ask him, but I think if you did, he'd run and you'd never see him again. But he has been around every corner of this case, and he has no love for Hughes or the men in charge of the smuggling ring. Perhaps he decided that you were the just what this case needed to expose the truth and wanted to ensure that you didn't give up."

"As if I would," Lizzie said with a huff. But she thought back to the first time she'd seen him, and his nest near the storehouse. There had been building materials and . . . bricks. She recalled slipping her card beneath one and wiping away the grime that had gotten on her gloves. "He's quite clever, you know. I think there's more to him than meets the eye."

"I agree," Darcy said, and he waved toward the boy. "I think we should help him, if we can."

"Really?" Lizzie asked eagerly. "I think that would be lovely, if he ever gets close enough to let us speak with him again."

But to her surprise, Henry lifted a tentative hand and returned Darcy's wave. And then he turned and took off down an alley.

"I have a good feeling about him," Darcy told her, and then surprised her by placing an arm around her shoulders and steering her toward his waiting carriage.

They'd almost reached it when a nearby carriage door opened and Josette Beaufort leaned out. "Mr. Darcy! Miss Bennet!"

They approached the carriage and found Josette, looking quite disheveled and teary, but otherwise unharmed. "Are you all right, Miss Beaufort? Do you need us to accompany you home?" Lizzie asked.

"No, no," she said, wiping her eyes with an embroidered handkerchief. "I just wanted to thank you. I had a very enlightening conversation with a gentleman . . . actually, I didn't get his name. But he told me that Leticia was trying to expose Richard, and that you put all the pieces together. Thank you."

"You're welcome," Darcy said.

"I'm sorry it wasn't more," Lizzie added.

Josette shook her head and gave them a small smile. "Leticia was headstrong, and if she put her mind to something, there was no talking her out of it. She was trying to help, I know. I just wish she'd told me."

An awkward pause ensued, and Lizzie was at a loss for what to say. But then Josette smiled, and said, "Take care of yourselves, Mr. Darcy and Miss Bennet. Please do not take offense, but I hope we shall not run into each other again."

"No offense taken," Lizzie assured her.

"I am sorry, Josette," Darcy said. "Not just for Leticia, but for . . . everything."

"I know," she said. "You've changed, Darcy." Lizzie waited for her to say something more, but instead she closed the carriage door and leaned back in her seat. A moment later, her driver pulled away and she disappeared from sight when the carriage turned a corner.

Lizzie looked up Darcy expectantly, but he remained quiet.

Finally, she couldn't stand it anymore. "What did she mean?"

"What?" Darcy asked, as if he hadn't been present mere moments earlier.

"Don't pretend you don't know what I'm talking about," she teased, but she was half serious. "You've never told me what transpired between you and Josette. Not precisely."

Darcy looked supremely uncomfortable. "I told you—we courted, but after a short time we parted ways. She wanted different things, and I . . ."

"You apologized for everything," Lizzie argued. "Tell me what *everything* means."

Darcy looked at the ground and sighed. "It's not that I want to keep it a secret. But I'm afraid you won't like me very much after I tell you."

"Impossible," Lizzie promised. "Now, out with it."

Darcy sighed. "It's embarrassing, Lizzie."

"Because she turned you down?"

"No. I mean, a little, but . . . that's not all. Or not it, entirely." He seemed desperate to look anywhere but at her. "As you may be aware, I am not always the most sociable person."

"I *am* aware," Lizzie said with an indulgent smile. "Was she?"

"She knew that I didn't relish fanciful social interactions. It was what drew us together initially. I grew to like her, despite what I viewed at the time as certain . . . disadvantages."

"What disadvantages?" Lizzie asked.

332

"This is the part where I don't come off so nicely," he told her, finally looking her in the eye. "I told her she wasn't always accepted in society circles, although she was liked well enough. But some people choose to hold her parentage against her, and it makes certain social situations awkward. I knew that anyone she married would share that burden, and I truly didn't mind, but . . ."

Lizzie knew Darcy well enough by now to predict where this was going. "Darcy. Tell me you were not so frank with her about this matter when you proposed marriage!"

"Well, I didn't use those exact words!"

Lizzie turned her gaze up to the sky. "What *did* you say?"

"I believe what I said was . . . I understood that our family circumstances made a union between us unlikely, but I admired her and, despite the fact that it went against the wishes of my family, I would gladly ask for her hand in marriage."

Lizzie merely stared at him. She could not imagine a more atrocious proposal.

"It was awful of me," he rushed to add. "And it should comfort you to know that she told me so. She would have been within her rights to turn me out at that instant, but somehow she managed to refuse me and make me understand that we were fundamentally ill-suited. Which was kinder than I deserved."

Lizzie finally laughed. "I would have slapped you!"

Darcy raked a hand through his hair. "I was striving for *honesty*. I thought ladies appreciated that quality."

"Honesty is all well and good," Lizzie agreed. "But I am not sure you needed to be *that* honest when proposing marriage. You might want to work on improving your technique if you ever want to be successful."

An instant later, Lizzie realized the implication of her words and she felt heat rush throughout her body. She opened her mouth to take back what she said, explain that she was merely teasing Darcy. But no words came out. Because . . . perhaps she didn't want to take it back. She wanted Darcy to propose to her. Not now, and not next week or next month. But someday. Someday, she thought that she might like to hear whatever pretty words Darcy could muster. And even if they weren't perfectly romantic—this was Darcy, after all—they would be heartfelt and honest, and they would be from *Darcy*. And she'd be ready to hear them, and she would say yes when he was done. Because Lizzie knew that Darcy wanted her to say yes, and have it be her choice, not influenced by her mother or society.

Darcy watched her carefully, and it was as though he could read her like an open book. He smiled slowly, and said, "Duly noted, Miss Bennet."

She grinned then, but because she was herself, she couldn't help but add, "I suppose from now on we ought to watch our backs. How long do you think it will take before Lady Catherine hears of what happened and our part in it?"

"I don't know," Darcy said. "Not long, probably. But right now I'm far more worried about what your mother is going to do to the both of us when I escort you home."

334

"Are you sure you want to come to the door? You could drop me off at the top of the street once more, for old time's sake."

"Not a chance."

Lizzie laughed. "Are you prepared for what will follow?"

She meant it in jest, but Darcy met her gaze with a quiet intensity that took her breath away. He offered her his hand. "I am. Are you?"

"You know," she said as she took it, "I do believe I am."

ACKNOWLEDGMENTS

When I first wrote *Pride and Premeditation*, I didn't expect that I would ever write a sequel starring Lizzie and Darcy. In fact, I was almost a little too eager to leave them behind so I could write about the Dashwood sisters and Fanny Price solving their own crimes. But when the book released, so many readers wrote to me with the expectation that *of course* there would be a sequel, and I was genuinely surprised by the outpouring of love for these characters. So first, thank you to all the readers who picked up *Pride and Premeditation*, and for showing me there were more cases to be investigated. My second massive thank-you is to Claudia Gabel, who made this book possible and who loves this version of Lizzie and Darcy as much as I do. I'm so glad we got to go on this journey together.

Thank you also to Sophie Schmidt, who cheered on this series from the start, and thank you to Sarah Homer and Tara Weikum for ushering this book into the world with enthusiasm. I have so much appreciation and respect for everyone at HarperTeen for all of the work they put into bringing my books into the world: Anna Bernard, Taylan Salvati, Jessica Berg, Martha Schwartz, Corina Lupp, Meghan Pettit, Shannon Cox, and the many people behind the scenes that I don't interact with.

Thank you also to Emma Congdon for creating such a gorgeous cover that made me gasp from the moment I saw a preliminary sketch.

To my agent, Taylor Martindale Kean, thank you for being such a great cheerleader of my work and such a great partner on this journey. I appreciate you and everyone at Full Circle Literary.

Books would be nothing without readers, and so I want to thank the many booksellers, librarians, teachers, bloggers, and BookTok and Bookstagram readers who've shared and recommended my books over the years. This book is a direct result of your generosity and enthusiasm, and I am grateful.

I have to thank my friends Monica Roe, Anna Drury Secino, Annika Barranti Klein, Emily Martin, Melissa Baumgart, Tegan Beese, Chris Vonder Haar, Joey Crundwell, Jaclyn Swiderski, and Paul Grosskopf for being so wonderful and funny and encouraging, and for always being supportive.

I am always thankful for my amazing family, particularly my parents who instilled a love of reading in me at a young age and who also gave me a place to land as I worked on revisions for this novel. And thank you to my partner, Tab, for your unfailing faith and for making me laugh even when I think everything I write is garbage. You're the best.